THE FLYING Z

Also by Leo W. Banks
Double Wide
Champagne Cowboys
.45-Caliber Perfume

THE FLYING Z

LEO W. BANKS

ISBN-13: 978-1-954841-62-8

Published by
Brash Books, LLC
PO Box 8212
Calabasas, CA 91372
www.brash-books.com

CHAPTER ONE

The rider picked through the tangle of mesquites, ducking and twisting to avoid the thorny branches. When he emerged from the thicket, he stopped on the dirt of Morales Road and studied the rock ridge to the south. By his calculation, the smugglers were ten minutes away, surely less if they hurried.

He looked west along the road at the woman walking toward him. He'd seen her earlier while scanning the hills with binoculars and rode hard to get closer, all the while thinking she'd recover her senses and turn back.

But she hadn't, and he felt certain alarm.

Watching her, his breath quick in the high-desert cold, he said, "Whoever you are, ma'am, you have no idea what you're walking into."

The rider sat his horse and waited. He had big hands and a handsome face, although his jaw, slightly off-center and marred by a scar, brought the matter into dispute. It had clearly been broken. The skin around his eyes showed fine wrinkles from time spent in the sun horseback. He had three days of whiskers, and his eyes, a striking black, were often remarked upon for their intensity.

He had on a red snap-button shirt, a canvas range jacket with the collar up, and black Ramírez boots that had walked through mud and worse. His shaggy black hair hung beneath the brim of his beat-to-hell hat.

At that distance, only the woman's cowboy boots stood out. The sun hit them and sparkled from some silver ornamentation. From that alone he knew she was not from the Arizona borderlands, for no woman born of that place would wear such boots.

He had seen women wearing similar varieties on his infrequent visits to the city, guessed them to be in style, and like most things of current fashion, considered them unworthy of his time. He knew, too, that no woman aware of the trouble that had come to that country would risk walking alone.

The land had always been home to rattlesnakes, but in recent years it had filled with men who acted like them.

Listening hard, the rider heard nothing and wasn't surprised. The ridge would block the smugglers' sounds even as they moved closer.

Morales Road went up and down, hid for a stretch, reemerged, tilted with the ground, and hid again. Beyond the road and for miles around, the tan hills rolled out, covered with brush and pancake cactus, one hill after another separated by deep draws that swallowed the ground, all the country looking hard and forbidding under the November sky.

The woman came into view again. Certain now that she wasn't going to turn back, the rider could wait no more, and he couldn't leave her. The Mexican border was two miles south. Having jumped the line, those mules were free. No churches or mothers in sight. Nothing to hold them back in a dangerous no-man's-land.

The rider blew into his hands and spurred Lobo closer.

Now aware of the approaching *clop-clop-clop*, the woman hopped on her toes and waved. "I broke down!" she called and skipped to a trot. "Thank God you came along. My car's stuck back there. Can you give me a push or something?"

"Right now we need to get you out of here and fast," the rider said.

She pulled up short and gave him a confused look. "Excuse me?"

He reined his horse around and found her a most pleasing sight. She had a model's face, fresh and shining with youthful good health. Her eyes were a rich green, the skin smooth with rose circles on the cheeks.

Her long hair was a shiny chestnut color, an uncommon shade in that region. Her mouth was wide and full, her lips curling up at the corners. She wore a gray bolero jacket over a simple white shirt. She carried a shoulder bag with the image of Ralph Lauren's polo player embossed on the side.

"There's some men going to be topping that ridge any minute," the rider said and pointed. "Best for us to be gone when they get here."

"What men? What're you talking about?"

"Ten of them in camos backpacking loads. Their boss has a rifle and wants more than anything to get his shipment through."

"Rifle? Oh, you mean hunters."

"Mules. Drug smugglers."

"Drug—what? Like in the movies?"

"Like right here. No previews, no popcorn."

She gazed up at the ridge with worried eyes.

He reached down. "Grab hold and jump on back."

Her mouth took a stubborn bend. The rider noticed her boots. They were worse than he thought, a pale red, snakeskin, and he was right about the silver decoration. The sequin inlay began at the toes and wrapped around the sides. They probably cost $1,500 at a store in Santa Fe with "coyote" in the name.

Good for crossing the street to the next nightclub, not much for working stock. Even with the boots, she wasn't taller than five foot three.

The rider said, "I don't recommend standing here talking things over." He leaned down and wiggled his fingers. "Let's go."

"Let's go? With you?" The look on her face said she'd scarcely encountered an idea so disagreeable.

"Ma'am, it's best you do what I say."

"Ha! I don't think so, mister."

She stomped the dirt in protest and accompanied her performance with the last words in her vocabulary. Nothing the rider hadn't heard before or barked out himself several times before breakfast. But he didn't often run into women with such skill for the spoken word.

"Do you always cuss that way?"

She stared up at him. "Only when I need to."

From the top of the ridge came a man's voice, followed by others in quick succession, all in Spanish and in tones that spoke of serious business. The woman stiffened and threw her arms out in frustration.

"I don't even know you. Where are we going?"

"My ranch is down the road." He reached closer. "I'll ride you clear of those men."

The words soothed her, even though she balked at the idea of needing anyone's protection. The voices on the ridge grew louder. She huffed in frustration as her mind raced through her options, which were exactly none.

"Dammit all." She stuck her foot in the rider's stirrup and grabbed his wrist. She had a strong grip, and even with that bag on her shoulder she looped her leg over Lobo's back with ease. She sat as far back as she could without sliding off the hind end.

"Scooch up and put your arms around my waist," the rider said.

"I will not."

"Do it or you'll fall off."

"For the love of God."

She muttered foul oaths as she wrapped her arms around his middle. The rider spurred and Lobo lurched, and together they galloped down Morales Road.

CHAPTER TWO

The rider kept Lobo running hard until they were clear of the smugglers. Slowing to a trot, he leaned over and spat out a mouthful of getaway dust.

"Lovely," she said in his ear. After a long pause and finding the silence hard to withstand: "I'm assuming you have a name."

He reached his hand over his shoulder. "I'm William Juan Zachary. Nobody calls me anything but Will."

She gave him a three-fingered handshake, the most she was comfortable sharing. His rough skin felt like rotting wood. "I'm Merry."

"Merry. You mean like happy?"

"Most of the time. I'm afraid today's an exception."

"Do you have a last name or is that a government secret?"

"O'Hara. And you don't have to be so smart."

"Can't help it, Merry O'Hara. How'd you wind up out here?"

Not eager to recount her embarrassment, Merry waited a beat to begin. She told a winding tale that started with her acceptance at Harvard, continued through four years of study, and ended with her recent graduation and her parents' gift of a refurbished 1966 blue Ford Mustang convertible.

She'd accepted a fellowship to study for her PhD in English at Stanford and was driving across the country to Palo Alto.

After listening to talk meant to sanitize her blunder, Will said, "Harvard, eh? Guess they don't teach you how to make up good stories."

"I beg your pardon?"

"You didn't break down. You drove off a road you shouldn't have been on in the first place, and your car's still back there, high centered and going nowhere."

"You're not going to spare me any embarrassment, are you?"

"That wouldn't be any fun."

"I hope I don't sound cross."

"We'll unravel this predicament before you know it."

"I'm usually more agreeable when I careen into a ditch."

"Lucy Garcia should be along soon," Will said. "She cowboys for me and runs the tow truck and junkyard in town. What I can't figure, you didn't find this road on anybody's map."

"I've never seen a border town and was trying to get to Nogales. Well, eventually. This was a detour." Merry had a husky voice and some kind of accent too faint to identify. "I wanted to see the country. I've never been to the far West."

"I'll pretend I'm surprised."

"It looked interesting. You know, the road not taken? Robert Frost?"

"This country's made for poets all right. But the stupid ones don't live long."

Merry passed over the insult. She fished through the shoulder bag to retrieve her cell phone. She held it over her head, turned to hold it behind her and to all the compass points. No signal anywhere.

"The worst day in human history continues." In desperation, Merry shook the phone, as if that would help, and looked at the screen again. "Really? No bars? Go ahead and remove a limb, why don't you."

"You might get lucky on the rise behind my barn. It's a hike to get up there."

"I'll just use your landline, if you don't mind."

"Don't have one," Will said.

"Does your cell work around here?"

"Had one of them once but folks kept calling. Check between the cushions."

"Good Lord. Where the hell am I?"

"Paradise."

Merry harrumphed. "Looks like nowhere to me."

To her, it must've seemed the very picture of nowhere, for his ranch was set in the deepest part of southern Arizona, a lost place called Cabezas Canyon. They rode at an easy canter up through roadside chaparral and scrub oak. Lobo struggled up the incline, snorting and high-stepping on the hard-packed ground.

Will felt Merry sliding away behind him. "Get close or you'll land on your rump."

"You can forget what I might land on."

"Have it your way, ma'am."

"Why do you keep calling me ma'am? I told you my name."

"Manners, a bad habit of mine. Been working on it."

"There's nothing to hold on to. Anyway, I'm plenty close now, Will. If I can call you Will?"

He couldn't resist the mischief and said, "I prefer Mr. Zachary."

That made Merry mad. "Well, *Will*, I'd be fine sitting close, but you're covered in dust like I've never seen. Where do you live anyway?"

"Right here." He pulled back on the reins and pointed.

Merry peered over his shoulder into the depths of Cabezas Canyon.

"That's it? Way down there?"

Will's house was a 150-year-old adobe set in a clearing of Mexican oaks, the branches bare with the coming of winter. It was faded white and needed a paint job. Smoke curled from the roof pipe. The tin porch slanted over rough-hewn mesquite poles.

In spite of rebuilds and three fires, the house still had visible bullet holes where patches in the original adobe had worn off. The walls were eighteen inches thick and had rifle ports from the days of the Apache depredations.

Beside it on one side stood a water tower, and on the other a corral made of salvaged railroad ties. Behind the corral was the barn, its roof consisting of mismatched metal sheets held down with old truck tires.

Merry felt better. She'd arrived at an actual settlement, and however rudimentary, it put her that much closer to getting back to civilization.

Morales Road circled Cabezas Canyon and a narrow spur curled to the bottom from there. With no risk of breaking any bones, she gripped Will's shoulders as Lobo stepped slowly down.

At the ranch entrance stood a carved-wood sign: ¡Bienvenidos! A second sign of welded black iron formed an arch over the cattle guard: *The Flying Z.*

As Will tied Lobo at the corral, he heard the racket of Lucy's tow truck on the canyon rim. "Looks like we're in luck. She's heading home already."

Lucy Garcia drove a cream-colored rust wagon of a truck with *Lucy's Tow and Junk* hand-painted on the side. Tow chains rattled all the way down the spur. Lucy poked her head out the driver's window. She had long hair gone prematurely white, and a face of paper-thin skin and hollow cheeks.

"I take it you're the one called Meredith Breck O'Hara?"

Merry startled. "How'd you know that?"

"I checked the registration on that silly rig you left back there."

"It's a vintage Mustang. Hold it, you went through my car?"

Lucy opened the driver's door and sat sideways on the seat. She wore a long-sleeved white thermal undershirt, a red lumberjack shirt over it, and orange construction boots. The bottoms of her jeans were rolled up, showing three inches of chalk-white legs not much wider than a garden hose.

She tapped some tobacco into a rolling paper and smoothed it with a greasy finger. "The one you was driving on that blasted road, I sure did."

"We've already been through my unfortunate episode."

Licking the paper, Lucy said, "You must be slow."

Merry looked at Will in astonishment, and back at Lucy. "I think we've established my mistake. Now, if you could pull me out of that hole, I'll be on my way."

"You ain't going nowhere with a busted axle and a busted radiator."

"Great. You checked it already?"

"That's only half of it." Lucy stuck the burning cigarette in her mouth. The rising smoke didn't hide her satisfied smile. Her teeth were a here-and-there proposition. "It's a for-sure mess. I won't know what else is wrong until I get it up on my lift, which I can do afore dark if we hurry along. Ain't much light left in that old sky."

Merry made a face. "What luck, you're a mechanic, too."

"Only one between here and Tucson that does work such as this, and it won't be cheap." Lucy held up her hands to head off further discussion. "But I don't handle money, any economic, er "–Lucy struggled to find the word. "What do you call 'em, Will?"

"Transactions. Told you a hundred times."

"Yeah, transactions. Now, it'll take a while to get the parts shipped in and probably a few days to do the work and like that. But we got a motel in town that Roger just painted and cleaned up nice. If you don't talk too much, I'll go ahead and drive you there, and we'll hook up your rig on the way."

"Well, if Roger cleaned," Merry said, but didn't budge.

She wasn't interested in Lucy Garcia's offer. Will had an extra bedroom and told Merry she was welcome to it. She knew right away she'd accept his offer, but for propriety's sake, she didn't jump at it. After pretending to think it over and letting a proper amount of time pass, she agreed and thanked him for his generosity.

"If you could just take me back to the Mustang to get my bags," Merry said.

"They're in the truck." Lucy pointed with her black thumb.

"You took my bags?"

"Figured you didn't want no undesirables messing with your stuff."

"Nope, I certainly would not want that."

Will broke in and said to Lucy, "See any tourists on the Canyon Trail? I tracked a group all morning."

"Seen 'em," Lucy said. "Jazzy was leading 'em again, armed as usual. He's been making that run for a month now." She started the truck and gave Merry an impatient look. "Don't wait for me, dearie. I ain't no porter."

With a hard grinding of the gears and the engine sputtering, Lucy let the truck roll forward. Merry snatched her bags out of the flatbed just in time, and with a suitcase in each hand, she watched Lucy's truck roll over the cattle guard coughing black smoke.

"She's a sweetheart," Merry said.

"Best cowhand ever rode this ground," Will said. "Come in, I'll get you settled."

CHAPTER THREE

The two porch bloodhounds sat up and let out half-hearted *woofs* in greeting. With their droopy faces raised, they stared and sniffed and decided there was no trouble worth getting up for and went back to sleep.

The kitchen had a butcher-block table and four red vinyl chairs. The floor was red-painted cement that bulged and bowed, making it tricky to walk. The cracked white Formica counters looked as if they'd been installed when television was new.

Merry saw no sign of a woman's hand in the sparseness of it, the lack of warmth or livening color, and tried not to show her surprise at how run-down it was. The only Western ranches she'd seen were on television, and they were usually grand and opulent.

Will put Merry's bags in the corner and invited her to sit. He retrieved plastic food bins from the refrigerator. "You must be hungry. How about I heat up Uncle Buck's leftover biscuits and stew?"

"I don't want you to go to any trouble. But I could eat."

Merry took in the room. She sat erect, the way guests do. Will poured the stew into a pan on the stove. He put soup bowls on the table and poured lemonade into big glasses and handed her one.

"You being a scholar and all, I should show you Buck's book collection," Will said. "He's got the best book collection around."

She sipped her lemonade. "Your uncle's a reader?"

"All his life, yes, ma'am. I picked up the habit, too."

"That's interesting. I'd love to see it." The literary connection interested Merry and made her feel more at ease.

As he worked, Will talked about Buck's favorite books, by authors like Will Barnes, Owen Wister, Charles Portis, Larry McMurtry, J.P.S. Brown, and Max Evans. He told her that his bloodhounds, JB and Bond, were named after J.B. Books and Bond Rogers, the main characters in *The Shootist*, by Glendon Swarthout.

The names and the book meant nothing to Merry.

"John Wayne and Lauren Bacall were in the movie," Will said. "Wayne played a dying gunfighter in 1901. I'm sure you know of it."

Merry had no clue.

"Well then," he pushed on, "what about Rooster Cogburn?" Again, she sat stone-faced and Will added another: "You must've read *Shane*? Jack Schaefer? Wrote *Shane*?"

"Heard that name," Merry said. "Wasn't that a movie, too?"

"That's peculiar."

Merry smiled politely. "What is?"

"Can't imagine what they're teaching at school these days. Jack Schaefer lived over in New Mexico. He and Buck were good friends. Buck's got himself a *Shane* first edition, signed by Mr. Jack Schaefer himself."

"My tastes run toward *One Hundred Years of Solitude*."

"Sorry, don't know it."

"Oh, my God." She pressed her hand to her chest in devotion. "It's a wonderful book, my all-time favorite."

"What's it about?"

"A family in this isolated town in Colombia called Macondo. There's so many cool characters. My favorite is Melquíades. He's a gypsy who introduces all sorts of new things into Macondo, like ice."

"Ice? Doesn't sound action-packed, exactly."

"It's hard to explain. You fall into it completely and really feel the loss at the end when Macondo disappears. A terrible wind takes it away."

"I've always been partial to happy endings."

"You'd love this. I carry a copy wherever I go."

"I like going to bed at night knowing the world's just about okay. What was that title again?"

"*One Hundred Years of Solitude.*"

"We get all the lonely we need around here."

In between the conversation and routine kitchen noises came a troubled voice from down the hall. "That's my uncle," Will said. "Only man I know who makes more noise asleep than awake."

Buck's gibberish became louder and more agitated.

"Those don't sound like sweet dreams," Merry said.

"He's feeling poorly lately." Will spooned the stew into the bowls. Merry put her napkin in her lap. Will sat opposite her and did the same. Her nails were nicely kept and painted red. He thought them a frivolous use of time. A day cleaning out waters on the Flying Z and they'd never look that way again.

The day's last light showed at the kitchen window and they ate through its fading. The stew was a unique concoction that Buck had picked up while working at cow camps in Mexico. In Spanish they called it *molcajete con chorizo con chili verde*, and it had a list of ingredients found nowhere else.

But the chilis were delayed in their impact, and diabolical, and when they hit bottom, Merry's face flamed up. She squirmed and squeaked in her chair, fanning herself vigorously with her napkin.

"The chilis are the key," Will said. "Wonderful, aren't they?"

"Awful, actually. Completely awful." Merry gagged and wiped away tears. "Why didn't you warn me?"

"I wanted you to have a proper Arizona welcome."

Will laughed as he poured her a glass of milk to put out the fire. By then, Merry had given in and was laughing, too, and they talked pleasantly until Buck appeared in the kitchen looking angry and holding a Winchester rifle.

"Them drug men know better than to attack the Flying Z," he said.

"What're you talking about, Uncle Buck?" Will said. "Nobody's out there and nobody's attacking us."

"I seen 'em. They's sneaking down the canyon on us."

Buck was a big-chested man with a fleshy face normally full of good cheer. But now it was twisted with rage. Will yanked the weapon out of his hand. "You can't be waving that rifle around all the time. Somebody might get hurt. Told you that before."

"Who says I can't? Give it here." Buck lunged for the gun.

Will pressed his powerful hand against Buck's chest to hold him back. "You're acting like a fool and worst of all you're not being polite. You haven't even said hello to our guest."

"What guest?" Buck drew back as his vacant eyes roamed the room. He saw Merry standing past Will's shoulder. After a moment, his confusion lifted and he realized someone new was in his house, and she'd seen everything. He shrank back in embarrassment.

"I done something bad, didn't I, Will?"

"You can't go around scaring people that way."

"I didn't mean to." His voice was raspy and regretful. "But I see things. The doctor said I got a condition. You know I got a condition, Will."

"Let's get you back to bed."

15

Will took him by the hand and led him down the hall. Buck stopped in mid-step. "Say, what about Emma? When can I go visit my Emma?"

"All the way to Zaragoza? Riding that far takes a lot out of you."

"That's what you always say. I still get around lively, Will. You know that's true."

"Don't forget we have to get Durango and Petey shod and the windmill needs work. And Hector could use help finding that lost calf."

Looking exhausted, Buck took a few more stoop-shouldered steps, seeming to surrender to Will's wishes. Then he stopped again and spun on Will in anger. "You don't think I can ride no more, ain't that right?"

"We'll go one of these days. I promise. Let me get you back to bed."

"The hell you will!"

"Don't be that way, Buck. It's late and you're tired."

But Buck wouldn't stop. A fuse had been lit.

"I can't ride, can't go see my Emma. Now you don't think I know how to go to sleep. The hell you'll show me. I know how to go to sleep. Been going to sleep a lot longer than you."

After taking care of him for so long, Will knew that Buck needed time to emerge from the dungeon of his mind. He placed a gentle hand on his uncle's shoulder and waited, until the light returned to Buck's eyes and he relented.

Will got him into bed, gave him his medicine, and fussed with the covers to tuck him in against the night chill. In the kitchen, he found Merry in the same place at the table, only now with the color gone from her cheeks.

"Suppose you could've done without that bit of excitement," he said.

"Don't be silly." Merry gave a jaunty wave, as if it were nothing. "I had guns pointed at me lots of times in my comparative lit seminar."

Will apologized and freshened her stew. "Buck's my father's uncle. He's eighty-two now and his body's good as new. But he's gone lame in the head."

"I'm sorry. Dementia's an awful thing."

"Strong and sure all his life, and now he's flat crazy half the time."

"You mentioned Zaragoza. Is that a town?"

"My biggest pasture. It's under the mountains out east where our people homesteaded." Will blew on his stew. "Emma's buried there in the ranch cemetery."

"Sounds recent."

"Six months. Sixty-six years they were together."

"That's so hard. He must be having a terrible time."

"Every night he asks if he can ride to her grave and I have to tell him no. He's hard to manage after going out there." Will was surprised he'd said so much, and even more surprised that he wanted to talk more. "I'm gonna say something I never told anybody. It's strange, I'm afraid."

"Of course, please."

"Buck's mind was fine the whole time she was sick. But when Emma died, he lost it. Literally lost his mind."

"That's not strange at all. He was holding on for her."

"That's what I think." Will was glad that she shared his belief. "Buck willed it that way so he could take care of her. Now it's his turn and he's got nobody in the world but me."

"I'll tell you a story of my own," Merry said. "My grandpa Cornelius had dementia, too. I found out he'd died as I was driving out here. It was so hard to leave Boston knowing his condition, but my mother promised to be with him."

"At least he had somebody there to see him off."

"Grandpa Corny we called him. I felt guilty leaving him and feel it even more now."

After supper, Will put more logs in the living room fireplace and led Merry into the third bedroom. No one had used it in a while and it smelled of dust and gun oil. There was a bare mattress and boxes full of books stacked in the corner, three rifles laid across them.

Will got out linens and blankets, and Merry jumped in to help make the bed. It gave them something physical to do, easing the awkwardness of the bedroom. Three DeGrazia paintings hung on the walls.

The black-dot eyes of his Indian children stared at them as they worked.

When they were done with the sheets, Merry put her hands on her hips in inspection, and Will noticed her fingernails again. This time he didn't find them frivolous at all. He liked the way they looked, and the way she looked. He didn't want to make her uncomfortable by staring.

But he could've stared for a week and another week after that.

"About tomorrow," Merry said. She was holding a pillow under her chin to fit a pillowcase over it. "I don't want to get in your way. Go about your business and don't worry about me."

"You're not getting off that easy," Will said.

That was what she'd wanted to hear. "I'm not? Oh, dear."

"Come riding with me. You can help with chores."

"That's a word I haven't heard in ages. Chores."

"We'll ride fence."

"Count me in." A thought intruded: "What about those men on the road today, the, ah, tourists. Won't they be a problem?"

Will's expression darkened, and with absolute confidence he said, "I don't hide from anybody on my own land." He smoothed the sheets a final time before starting out the door.

"Not to get dramatic or anything," Merry said, "but you rescued me from something pretty bad on that road today, right?"

Will didn't want to say what she had escaped and tried to think of a way of saying nothing at all. Merry broke in before he could speak.

"I need to thank you."

"You just did."

"Okay, then. Well. Good night, Mr. Zachary."

"Good night, Miss O'Hara."

CHAPTER FOUR

Will stepped onto the porch before dawn. JB and Bond climbed out of their beds and stretched and circled Will's legs in greeting. There was always a competition between the two to see who could be the first to win his attention. JB usually got there first, while Bond was polite and willing to wait her turn.

He gave them good-morning scratches and went to the barn, got his saddle from the tack room, and threw it over the top railing of the corral. He brought Lobo over and saddled him.

Long-legged and light gray, Lobo had patches of white on his chest and a white blaze on his forehead. Will tethered him to the porch and brought another horse around and tied this one beside Lobo.

"Merry! Merry O'Hara! You gonna sleep all day!"

At that early hour, the house and the corrals were in darkness. The sun would need more time to chase the night out of Cabezas Canyon. Only the top of the spur had caught the early light, turning it a beautiful rose color. But it was cold all over, and a breeze made it colder still.

Merry stepped outside in her stocking feet. Lively, smiling, full of the morning.

"Put your shoes on," Will said. "Got something to show you."

Merry pointed at the second horse. "Is that one mine?"

It was a bushy-tailed bay with short, stout legs.

"Sometimes she gets broncy, but she knows how to carry a rider," Will said. "She's got mustang in her so she's iron-footed in rocky country. Name's Candy."

"What do you know, I like candy."

"She doesn't like to run too much and shouldn't give you any trouble. Grab a jacket off the hook behind the door."

"I haven't even run a comb through my hair yet."

"No time for that. The day's starting to wonder where we're at."

Merry found a canvas jacket, tan with a high white fur collar. She was lost inside it, only her fingertips showing past the sleeves. She came outside carrying her Santa Fe boots. She plopped down on the porch steps to pull them on and Will handed her Candy's reins.

"Best follow my lead," he said. "We'll take it slow to get started."

Merry adjusted the stirrups and climbed into the saddle. She gave Will a challenging look. "Slow? And let the day start without us?"

Before he could object, Merry kicked Candy and galloped up the spur to Morales Road, and from there, she rode south over the hills. Will stayed at Candy's tail as they plunged into a dry wash and followed its zigzagging path.

At a narrow cut in the embankment, they climbed out through creosote and whitethorn bush to a broad flat on the opposite side. Merry reined up and Will pulled alongside.

"We don't like to run a horse unless we really need to," he said.

"I know but I really needed to."

"Don't want you getting thrown either."

"Are you worried about me, Will?"

"I have a lot of work to get done next few days."

"So you're not worried about me?"

"No time. You land on a cactus, I'll be pulling needles out of your hide for days."

"We'd get to know each other."

"No doubt."

Merry looked out at the land. In a bad drought, the brush turns blue, a washed-out blue, like old eyes. She breathed deeply. "I like taking chances. What about you, Will? Do you like taking chances?"

"I cowboy on this border, Merry. Las Vegas gives a man better odds."

"So why do you do it?"

He shrugged. "Born here."

"That's all?"

"That's the whole story, beginning to end."

She wanted more, but he was silent. She waited, figuring a way to draw him out. "Past few days I've taken some chances myself." She gave him a sidelong glance that he missed entirely.

Frustrated, she said, "You don't give up much, do you? There's a word for that. They call it 'taciturn.'"

Will wrinkled his brow. "I'll be sure to look that up when I get home."

"You know exactly what it means. You know what I think?"

"Rest assured I do not."

"I think you talk that way because that's how men in your books talk."

"Yes, ma'am."

"See, right there, that's what I'm talking about." Merry saw a change in Will's face, the beginning of a laugh. But he held it back.

She pointed ahead. "I reckon we should ride yonder."

Will fought it but couldn't help himself and laughed aloud. It pleased her to know that she could break through. She leaned forward in the saddle and rubbed Candy's neck.

"Thought you said she doesn't like to run."

"She will if she's got a good rider up top," Will said. "Where'd you learn?"

"Ireland."

"Thought I heard something in your voice. A brogue, right?"

Merry motioned to the black oaks atop the next ridge. "You know what? I'd rather ride than talk."

They went along at an easy pace this time, crossing more hills and coming to the Mogollon pasture, full of grazing cows. Will saw a horse's tracks and followed them along the pasture's edge to a cut in the barbed-wire fence.

The top three strands were down, the fourth still in place. That meant the rider had leaned over and, without getting out of the saddle, cut the three strands and stepped his horse over the bottom one.

Will grabbed his work gloves, fence pliers, and a circle of new barbed wire from the sack on his saddle. He stretched out the strands between the posts, getting the lengths correct before cutting them.

One of the wooden posts wiggled in the ground. Merry saw the problem and without hesitation jumped down to help. She found a rock and dropped it into the hole. On her knees, she wedged it in against the post.

The cows turned their heads to watch. The sun had cleared away the morning haze and the day had become clear and blue. Will gripped the post and leaned back with his arms outstretched, knees bent, and Merry dropped a second rock in, kicked dirt into the hole, and stomped on the rocks to shove them in tight.

"You think that'll hold?" she said, sweeping the hair off her face.

"Not for long. I'll put it on my to-do list."

"I'm guessing your list is long."

"If there's ten things on it when I get up in the morning, there's fifteen by noon and I've worked all morning."

Merry brushed her hands together to clean off the dirt. Will watched her with admiration. "If school doesn't work out, I pay a fair wage."

"I might take you up on that."

Will brooded about the fence cut. He looked across the pasture at the path the mystery rider had taken, his eye following the backward-bent grass until the tracks sloped out of sight.

Two sets of hoofprints for sure, and that meant drugs.

There wasn't enough profit from one horse carrying one load, and it wasn't a cartel scout. He got to his position on foot, not horseback. He worked from hilltops and carried whatever he needed to live for as long as he needed as he kept watch for Border Patrol or anyone else who might threaten the shipment.

The rider could've been a supply man leaving food and water at set points along the trail. But that seemed unlikely, too. One horse could accomplish that.

No, this was definitely a drug runner trailing a pack mule, and that meant he was armed. Some loads aren't protected. They're led by unarmed guides. A pack mule carries a big shipment worth a lot of money. It has to get through and that guarantees an armed escort.

But there wasn't supposed to be any traffic at all across the Mogollon, the Canyon Trail, or anywhere else across the Flying Z except Zaragoza. Will had seen to that.

On foot, leading Lobo by the reins, he followed the tracks until he found a clear hoofprint and bent down to look. Most horses were shod the same way, and the shoes so similar that only a skilled tracker could tell one from another.

But this one was different. Two-inch metal pads had been welded to the bottom of the shoes, one on each heel and a longer one on the toe. This so-called hard-face weld, common in Sonora and known as the abrazo weld, gave the horse better traction in rocky country and made the horseshoe last longer. It also left a distinct print.

Back in the saddle, Will pondered the abrazo rider.

Merry broke in: "You wanted to show me something?"

"Sorry. Lost myself for a minute." He pointed to the mountain ahead. "It's up past that stand of trees on the slope."

They rode on, the ground rising gradually at first, then sharply. Lobo squeezed between two huge boulders that marked the final stretch up the mountain. They couldn't see the peak but knew of its coming by the bright blue ahead and the feeling of a great openness, and when they emerged into it, the view broadened for miles in all directions.

"We call this the Split," Will said. "You're looking across the bottom of Arizona and way down into Sonora."

The elevation had them looking down on juniper-covered ridges in the middle distance, and beyond to desert lowlands baked in sunlight. The Mexican cattle were black marks on the land, and black, too, were the mesquites, black and bare as scarecrows.

A creek meandered below the grass line, invisible but for patches of silver where sunlight fell through the willow trees along its bank.

"This is amazing," Merry said. "It's so huge, so endless."

"That's what makes it special, the open space. Not much of it left anywhere these days. See this mountain right below us here? That's the start of Mexico."

He pointed farther out to a white circle carved into the flatlands.

"That open patch is Rancho Dolores. Way back when, it was part of a Spanish land grant that included where we're standing right now. After we quit being part of Mexico in the 1850s, it broke up and the Flying Z got going after that."

The Dolores ranch house was mostly invisible, but for the green roof and the faint markings of outbuildings and corrals. The valley behind it stretched all the way back to more forested mountains and deep canyons, all of it bathed in a faintly purple light.

Merry said, "You mean that little speck is the house?"

"Yup. That's where Emma grew up, and she met Buck there. When I was a teenager, I spent summers breaking horses at Dolores and at Rancho La Bandera, the next spread east."

Merry stared out at the majestic land. "This was your backyard as a boy. This was where you played. You must know every rock and tree."

"By the time I was seven, yes, ma'am."

"I feel an energy just being out here. Is all this yours?"

"My allotment stretches down to the Mexican line and over toward Nogales."

A wind roared up, the sound of it coming first, followed by the wind itself. But it was gone in an instant, and the silence of the mountain returned.

"Between my Forest Service lease and my patented land, it comes to seventy-one thousand acres, give or take."

"Give or take what, Connecticut?"

"You need room to run your operation right, to stretch out."

"Did you ever leave here to go to school or anything?"

"Drove a truck for a produce company after high school, about two years. Saw what there was to see and came back. Buck needed me."

Yes, Buck needed him, and the same day Will returned to the Flying Z, he saddled Lobo and rode to the Split. The place owned a piece of his heart, for its history, for its view of Rancho Dolores, and because it was one of the remotest spots on the ranch.

If something happened on that mountain, a bad act of nature or man, he was all alone with no way out except by his wits.

As a boy, Will liked to sneak away from the ranch to ride there against Buck's orders, never ride alone being the first. He wanted to feel the pride of getting there and back on his own. Such an unforgiving place was good for what a boy needed.

Once convinced of his bravery and skill, he could go on to learn humility. That was the important one for staying alive in a harsh land that had no interest in whether a boy made it home for supper.

But Will had another reason for going to the Split. In his absence, the smugglers had grown bolder, and the Split had become their preferred crossing point. Will stood at its highest point for three hours his first day back to make sure the cartel scouts saw him.

He wanted them to know that he'd returned and wasn't afraid. He wanted them to know that help had arrived.

Now, standing on the mountaintop, they heard the sound of hooves clapping on rock, a rider coming up the Split Trail. It was Hector, Will's hired man. He was waving a strip of burlap.

The smugglers wrapped their drug bundles in burlap. When the elements or the brush shredded them, they pulled out replacements and the discards blew across the land like tumbleweed.

Out of breath, Hector called out, "He shoot at me, Will!"

"Who shot at you? Where?"

"Zaragoza. I tell him, 'You get out now. I clean this cemetery for Mr. Will Zachary. You get out now.'"

"He was crossing my cemetery?"

"*Sí.* Kicked our fences down." Hector wrinkled his face as if he'd caught a bad smell. "Trash all over, Will. Burlap, too." He pointed to his saddlebags, bulging with burlap.

"Nobody's supposed to cross there."

"I tell him this. I say this. *Sí, sí.*" Hector had a round face and a bushy mustache. His eyes were red-rimmed and bloodshot. He wore an old-style border hat—tan, misshapen, and wide-brimmed with a round, flat crown.

A speckled Australian shepherd from the ranch had trailed him up the mountain. Girl Dog followed Hector wherever he went.

"Big rifle, Will," Hector said. "*Cuerno de chivo.*" Translated, it meant "goat's horn," for the curving magazine on an AK-47. Hector punched his chest in mock defiance, imitating the gunman. "'I control this place.'"

"We need to straighten this fellow out," Will said.

"Come on, Will. Follow me!"

Hector slapped the reins back and forth, wheeled his horse, and hurried down the mountain, and Will and Merry did the same.

CHAPTER FIVE

U p in the saddle, the wind filling their jackets, they rode along a narrow trail cut by ditches and washouts, the horses jumping them without slowing. They climbed a hill overlooking Zaragoza, a broad expanse of rangeland, full of light and sky, broken only by twisted mesquites, its grasses burned to orange from the drought.

Hector stood in his stirrups, excited, pointing: "There! There!"

Will fetched binoculars from his saddlebag and looked.

The mules were laid up inside the cemetery. A few of the graves had stone monuments. Rock piles marked the others, along with wooden crosses painted white, though some were crude, unfinished oak and cottonwood branches held together with rawhide. The waist-high iron fence surrounding the cemetery had been knocked down at the front and back ends.

Will counted nine men dressed head to toe in camouflage clothing and carpet booties to throw off trackers. They had removed their burlap-covered loads and stuffed backpacks and left them beside them as they rested.

The gunman sat leaning against a headstone, his rifle propped up beside him.

"It's an AK, all right." Will lowered the binoculars, wiped his eyes, and looked again. "I don't recognize him. Have you seen this character before?"

"Never. Never before, Will."

"He looks young." Turning to Merry, Will said, "Stay right here. We'll come get you when we're done with business."

Will and Hector rode down the hill. The mules saw them approaching and didn't move, and neither did the gunman. They just stared as Will reined up and inspected the cemetery. The ground between the downed sections of fencing bore the markings of heavy foot traffic.

Rather than take the long way around, the smugglers had kicked the fence over and tromped through the cemetery, and along the way they'd discarded water bottles, tin cans, and paper trash.

The sight fired Will's temper. He held it in check as he stepped out of the saddle, handed Lobo's reins to Hector, and walked in among the mules. He picked up a backpack, unzipped it, reached inside, and took out a cellophane bag containing white crystals and held it up for Hector to see.

"What do you suppose we got here?"

"Meth," Hector said. "For sure, boss."

Will tipped the backpack upside down and shook it. A dozen identical bags spilled out. He did the same with a burlap sack and more bags fell to the ground. He sliced one of them open with his pocketknife and shook out the crystals.

The gunman watched closely. He couldn't have been too long past his teens, too few years for much good and certainly not enough for wisdom. A young man with something to prove could make the worst kind of trouble.

But he made no attempt to go for his rifle. He sat with his hands folded in his lap, chewing a blade of grass. He had a boy's face and a weak goatee. He wore a green sweatshirt and blue jeans that were several sizes too large.

Slowly, calmly, Will walked deeper into the cemetery. He picked up an unopened soda can, held it for a moment, and looked over at the gunman. "You got a name, boy?"

He stared at Will, cocky and disdainful.

"I asked your name."

"I'm Salazar."

Will spun around and whipped the can at him. Salazar ducked as it sailed past his head. The mules jumped to their feet, tense and watching. They were of little concern to Will. He knew they wouldn't move against him. He'd encountered thousands over the years and knew that most weren't in it to fight, and he could recognize the ones who were.

"I need to know something, Salazar," Will said. "Why are you dirtying up my cemetery with your trash? These are my people you're stomping over. This is *campo sagrado*"—sacred ground. "Do you understand that?"

Still sitting, motionless, arms on his knees, Salazar didn't respond.

"Marcelino," Will said. "You know that name, don't you, boy?"

"That's twice," Salazar said. "I'm no boy, mister."

"You can't walk this land without knowing Marcelino. Me and him have an agreement that says none of his people can cross this cemetery, and here you are dropping trash all over the place and shooting at my man."

Hector was still in the saddle. Girl Dog stood in the grass beside him, growling, the hair on her back standing up.

"Here's what's going to happen," Will said. "You and your slaves need to walk back into Mexico just as fast as you can. You need to do it right now. This cargo you escorted, it stays with me."

Salazar jerked the blade of grass out of his mouth and tossed it away. He jumped to his feet, his face pinched and angry. He glanced at the rifle leaning against the headstone beside him, deciding whether to fight.

"Now's not the time to get brave, boy."

Will spoke without any evident fear or concern, but inside he was coiled and ready. He held Salazar's stare for a minute, not blinking, barely breathing, breaking him down with his black eyes, and that ended it. Salazar exhaled and looked at the ground.

He'd made his decision. He wasn't going to fight.

Will picked up the rifle and held it as if in inspection, turning it this way and that. Without a word, his temper cracked and he swung it furiously against a rock, breaking it to pieces. Girl Dog tucked her tail and whined until Hector whistled for her to be still.

The violence of Will's action left a cut on his hand. He took a bandanna from his pocket and wrapped it around the wound. He picked up the shattered stock and handed it to Salazar.

"Souvenir," he said.

Flustered, Salazar took it.

"There's something you need to understand and never forget," Will said. "This cemetery is mine and the folks living underneath it are mine. They're my people and nothing means more to me. If I see your tracks through here again, I'll follow you back to Mexico and it won't be to talk. Now, beat it."

"Not without my property," Salazar said.

"Your property?" Anger again sliced through Will like a sword.

He ordered the mules to bring the burlap sacks and the backpacks to him. They did so, depositing them at Will's feet. Then he ordered them to collect kindling, and they dropped armloads of brush and branches into a pile on the ground.

Will emptied the backpacks and the sacks onto the ground and placed the meth packages atop the kindling. From his vest pocket he drew a stick match and held it up to show Salazar.

"When you bring poison through my family's cemetery, it becomes my property. Go back and tell Marcelino what Will Zachary did here today."

Hector kicked his horse forward. "Will, no. Don't!"

Ignoring Hector, he fired the match with his thumb. The kindling was so dry it flamed up immediately.

"You're welcome to your property," Will said.

The frightened mules hurried back into Mexico, and Salazar, his resistance gone, did the same. Hector stood the fences up as best he could and collected more loose burlap from the cemetery. He swung into the saddle, all the while looking sideways at Will.

"You got something to say, go ahead and say it," Will demanded.

"We're A-OK here, boss."

"I'll handle Marcelino." Will motioned toward Hector's saddlebags. "You just make sure Buck doesn't see that burlap. He doesn't need to know the kind Emma's resting with."

Hector grumbled something through the thicket of his mustache, whistled for Girl Dog, and rode off.

CHAPTER SIX

Will stepped into the cemetery and got down on his heels at a granite marker. It was three feet high, rounded across the top, and carved across its face with Emma's name in indented white letters, and below that, her years.

The simplicity of it fit perfectly for a woman of no pretense or guile, easy in her manner, a tireless worker who couldn't stand to see ranch jobs go undone, always welcoming to travelers and newcomers, a great dancer, and a champion horsewoman in her youth in Mexico.

A cook of great renown, neighbors from miles around came to sample her pies. She was known equally for her intolerance of any no-accounts who wandered into her path. *Las Mofetas*, she called them --- skunks.

As Will smoothed the ground around Emma's monument, he heard her sweet voice rising from the grave: *Keep Buck safe, Will. Protect him, watch over him. That's what I asked of you. Reason with him about this war he's fighting. Is this your idea of reason? This fire?*

The voice was clear and strong, as if she were standing at his side. He listened respectfully and, thinking Emma was done, returned to his landscaping.

But she had more to say: *I thought Buck was the one with the temper. Now you start this fire? You promised to keep Buck safe and stay safe yourself. You and Buck, honestly. Ustedes son tecolotes de la misma sucursal—you are owls of the same branch.*

As Will's mind cleared and his temper cooled, he realized Emma was right. But there was nothing he could do about it now and told her so. He'd filled the sky over Zaragoza with smoke, given his ancestors a good show on a fine afternoon.

He went back to his groundskeeping, eliminating all the footprints the smugglers had made. The work exposed the pistol holstered at the small of his back, and Merry saw it. She'd ignored his command, ridden forward, and overheard everything in his encounter with Salazar.

She held Lobo's reins as he stepped into the saddle.

"You should've stayed back like I told you."

"No chance of that, Will. Did I hear you talking to someone?"

"Emma."

"You have conversations with people who—aren't there? Like, gone?"

"Didn't have a choice. She was in a talkative mood."

"This place gets more interesting all the time."

They rode away from the cemetery.

"I know this is none of my business," Merry said. "But who's this Marcelino?"

"He owns the trails across my ranch and for a good way farther west."

"Owns the trails," she repeated. "How does that work?"

"Somebody on the south side owns all the trails on this border. Around here it's Marcelino. Anybody who uses his trails without paying him or getting his permission, he kills them."

"You made a deal with this guy?"

He stiffened at the judgment in her tone. "You think it's something I wanted? I was trying to save Buck's life."

"Will, you don't have to tell me anything."

But he saw no point holding back. No one knew of his deal with Marcelino except Hector, and now he felt a certain freedom.

Merry was leaving soon, so why not?

With Merry riding by his side, Will explained that folks had been walking north across the border as long as he'd been alive. As a boy he never thought a thing about it. If he or Buck saw candles flickering in one of their outbuildings, Buck would say, "Looks like some Christians are settling in for the night," and they'd go to bed without a worry.

They were farm boys and ranch hands looking for seasonal work, and you couldn't find a bunch with better manners. In the morning they usually left the shack cleaner than before. The dishes were sparkling and stacked up, and maybe there was a note saying thanks for the shelter.

Will had been around them so much he spoke corral Spanish by the time he was four. They taught him to cook tortillas the right way, how to build a cattle guard and shoe horses and never once was there a problem that required calling the law.

But all that had changed. The crossers weren't rural folks anymore, and many of the trails had been taken over by Marcelino's cartel. "It changed when we started getting folks with soft hands," was how Buck explained it.

He meant city men, young and bursting with attitude. They had no respect. The only work they wanted to do was haul the cartel's drugs at $1,000 a run.

The traffic had become relentless, and it was torture for Buck. He despised drugs, hated to see them crossing the Flying Z, hated what they did to people in the interior, to the whole country.

When he saw someone crossing his land, he sprang up like a dog at night and rode at them with a fire in his gut. If they were looking for work, he'd empty his pockets, turn over all the money he had. But if they were drug mules, he'd run them off.

And if mules showed up at his door dehydrated, lost, or injured after faltering in the mountains, Buck wouldn't hand out food or water to keep them alive. He'd push them back across the line with his Winchester, and they moved fast.

Living that way had made Buck bitter, and Emma's death had made matters worse. When she was alive, he stayed close to the ranch to look after her. She needed a caretaker and companion, and he needed her more. Emma's beating heart taught him caution. It gave him something to live for.

After her death, Buck stopped playing by the rules. He'd lost his fear and his good sense. It was hard to know how much of that was Emma being gone and how much was his sickness.

But he saw smugglers everywhere. He became obsessive about defending Zaragoza and Emma's grave. He started making escapes, riding off to set up in the rocks along Zaragoza Trail to waylay the mules as they came through.

Soon, the rumor started that Marcelino wanted Buck dead. The borderlands percolated with rumors, and most were nonsense. But Hector warned that this threat was real, and he had the best trail sense around.

Will sat Buck down and told him his bushwhacking days were over. From then on, Zaragoza was off-limits unless Will rode with him.

Three months later, Buck wanted to visit Emma's sister at Rancho Dolores. There hadn't been an episode in the intervening weeks and the trip was short and on paved, well-traveled roads. Will agreed as long as Artie Avila went with him. Artie and Buck had been friends forever.

As they drove back home at dusk just south of the Arizona line, a sniper put two rounds through the windshield and two more into the engine. Artie and Buck hid in the brush, close enough to hear the voices of the men hunting them, and after dark they scrambled across the border on foot, shaken but safe.

Will had to do something because he knew Marcelino would try again. His only option was a face-to-face meeting to somehow convince Marcelino to stand down. But he had to find him first, and for that he relied on Cuco Muñoz.

He was a local ranch hand who'd grown up in Sonora and knew all the players in the drug trade there. He told Will that Marcelino made his headquarters at the Gran Hermano Hotel in Nogales, Sonora, and agreed to broker a meeting.

Over four consecutive mornings, Will drove to the hotel and waited, and each time Marcelino refused to see him. On the fifth day, the meeting happened, and Will proposed a deal.

He offered Marcelino Zaragoza, all of it, for his *plaza*. It was the best smuggler ground on the ranch, remote, sheltered by mountains on its eastern side, and with a shaded creek bed to follow all the way to drop sites near the highway.

Will promised to tell Border Patrol that Zaragoza was quiet. And he promised to keep Buck away and to end his vigilante rides. In return, Marcelino agreed to let Will and Hector tend the family cemetery unmolested, agreed to keep his mules outside its boundaries, and agreed to no longer use any of the other trails across the remainder of the Flying Z.

There were hundreds of trails, but Marcelino would forgo them all to allow Buck to ride safely through his final days. It was a basic parceling out of territory, this for one, this for the other, and in return Buck Zachary could live.

When Will had finished talking, Merry said, "You went into Mexico to confront a cartel kingpin? Was that, ah, what am I trying to say—smart?"

"Not the word I'd use. But I had to do something."

"That rider across the Mogollon yesterday, he was with Marcelino, too?"

"Every living thing that moves across the Flying Z works for him, even the coyots."

Will and Merry topped the rise overlooking Zaragoza. The wind whined through the brittle grass. Merry twisted in the saddle to look at the smoke filling the horizon.

"You think Marcelino's going to make trouble, Will?"

"Never mess with the loads. That's the one unbreakable rule."

"You sure broke it back there."

Will didn't look back at the smoke. He said, "When you back up and back up, day after day, doing what these drug men want, one day the sun's going to come up and you can't back up anymore, at least if you're a certain kind of man. If I did make a mistake back there, it feels better than anything I've done in a long time."

CHAPTER SEVEN

They arrived home with dusk settling over Cabezas Canyon. Buck heard JB and Bond howling and the fuss and snort of the horses and came out to the porch wearing overalls with red suspenders over a white T-shirt.

He walked on bowed legs, his weight shifting heavily from side to side. He might've had three holdout hairs on his head and they all stood at perfect attention. He and Artie had been cooking, and supper was almost ready. Hector headed toward the barn, using his body to shield the saddlebags filled with burlap.

"What's he got there?" Buck's eyes narrowed. "Did you go to Zaragoza?" Nothing set Buck off quicker than burlap. It was like waving a red cape in front of a bull.

"We rode to the Split," Will said. "Things quiet around here?"

Buck watched Hector until he disappeared into the barn. He turned to face Will. "Fine, fine. Had three Christians come through. I give 'em peanut butter sandwiches and let 'em fill their water bottles. Talked a bit."

"Did they say where they crossed?"

"Juniper Tank. Nice fellows. From Chiapas, believe they said."

"Now I have to ride up there and fix my fences again."

"They don't mean no harm, Will. They's workingmen like us."

"I don't go to Mexico and havoc around down there."

"They'd shoot you, by dern. Them Mexicans would shoot you." Buck laughed heartily, seemingly his old self again. He saw Merry and his face brightened. Showing no memory of their Winchester encounter, he wiped his hands on a kitchen towel, draped it over his shoulder, and looked at Will expecting an introduction.

Merry played along, smiling at Buck and shaking his hand as though for the first time.

"Glad to make your acquaintance," he said.

"Merry's going to spend the night with us," Will said.

"Great news. I'll put out another plate." As he went back into the house, Buck leaned toward Will and whispered, "Too skinny."

Will looked out over the darkening canyon, and as always on returning to the ranch felt great contentment. He felt it more keenly this night because of Merry, and she felt the same.

Now she had a decision to make. About this man, so unlike anyone she'd ever met. Handsome, sure, but not in a catalog way. His face was lived-in, and she liked that. She liked his voice. Even in anger there was calm underneath it, and confidence.

She thought of the gun he carried and it made her shudder. But the excitement was undeniable, too. Yesterday, she'd driven off the pavement onto Morales Road looking for something and didn't know what.

Change my life. Take this dirt road wherever it leads. I wanted to find adventure on my drive west, and here it is. Don't turn away now.

"I need to call about the Mustang," she said. "The hill behind the barn, right?"

When she reached the top of the hill, she told Lucy that she'd changed her mind and there was no hurry to make the repairs.

"I like a job done right," she said. "I'll call you in a few days."

Returning to the house, Merry saw the grin on Will's face and immediately understood what it meant. "You heard me, didn't you? You heard everything."

"Voices carry in this dry air."

She hid her face in her hands. "That is so embarrassing. Am I that much of a bigmouth?"

"That shoe fits good and snug."

"You want me to stay?"

"I do. Just figured there wasn't much chance after Salazar."

"You should've said something."

"Was about to, but you were up that hill before I could get the words out."

From the kitchen came the sounds of supper being readied, the clatter of plates, Buck and Artie talking, and Artie whistling a cheery song. He was a known whistler.

Will and Merry stood on the porch together.

"I'll tell you a secret," she said. "When you and Salazar were talking, I was thinking about bagels."

"You, too?"

She tossed her head and laughed. "Seriously. Every morning at home I stopped at the same Starbucks in Somerville to get a bagel. Eight days ago, when I was leaving Boston, I stopped there for the last time."

"You really were thinking about bagels?"

"Blueberry with cream cheese and a double caramel macchiato."

"The trouble with Salazar didn't scare you?"

"Are you kidding? I was terrified. I was shaking."

"When you're scared you think of bagels?"

"No, when I'm scared I think of home. I was retracing my steps. Haven't you ever done that? From the day I left to right then, wondering how I landed here."

"Same country, different worlds."

"Slightly. I mean, a week ago I was in Cambridge, Harvard Square. Traffic, all kinds of people rushing around, different accents and clothes." Merry spread her arms. "Now I'm in the middle of this—crazy place."

"Good luck, right?"

"Amazing luck."

The feeling that had been small and uncertain in the morning had built throughout the day, and now they'd stepped into the open, agreed to start something together, and it was thrilling. Merry leaned against one of the porch's mesquite posts, hands clasped behind her back.

Night had come. A single hanging bulb threw an orange glow across her face. Will tried to think of the last time he'd seen anything so beautiful. He couldn't remember a time, so he decided the word was never.

"So. What do we do now, Will?"

The question was an invitation, certainly, but it wasn't untoward. It fit the moment perfectly. But Will didn't move, didn't trust the emotion he felt.

His hesitation made Merry waver. "I must look like a wreck after today."

"I wouldn't say that. You hold up better than most."

"Gee, I'm so flattered." Merry looked away and back again, her green eyes shining up at him. "Can I ask you what you're thinking right now?"

The question threw him. Will managed some halting words in response and that was all. Merry curled her lips in pretend confusion. "You have no idea what to do with me, do you?"

Again Will plumbed his mind for something to say, knowing it wasn't words she wanted. But nothing came. Buck saved him. He poked his head out the door.

"Suppertime! You kids hungry or ain't ya? We're eating off the miners' menu tonight."

They had beans, beef brisket, sweetbread, black coffee, and an apple pie from Walmart. They hadn't eaten all day and emptied their plates in a hurry. After supper Buck got busy with the dishes, Artie and Merry helping.

Artie Avila had worked doing shovel labor on a county highway crew for four decades, and still wore the same blue work shirts with his special greeting—*Howdy, I'm Artie!*—stitched into the white patch on the chest.

The three of them laughed and talked at the sink. Merry was enjoying the evening and so was Will. He sat with one leg up on the corner of the table. He sipped from a bottle of Coors and tried to puzzle out his confusion on the porch.

No such thing had ever happened to Will Zachary. In his whole life he'd never been confounded in his own canyon. The notion made him smile, and Merry, secretly watching him, smiled, too.

Buck grabbed another Coors from the fridge and handed it to Will. He raised the bottle in thanks. The action made the wound in his hand throb, and he unwrapped the bandanna to examine the gash.

"You need to have a doctor look at that," Merry said.

"At fourteen miles to town, it'll keep."

"At least let me clean it."

Buck stepped aside and gestured Will to the sink. Artie did the same, giving them space to get better acquainted. The two old men nodded and grinned with satisfaction, a pair of accidental matchmakers watching as Merry gently took Will's hand and held it under the warm water.

CHAPTER EIGHT

The next days passed happily. Merry and Will fixed fences, put out salt, and cleaned out waters. They rode out in the freezing cold of sunrise and worked through the warmth of the afternoon, through the lengthening shadows and the thrilling sunsets.

They saw no outside people. The world shrank, becoming only the two of them, the smell of horses and cows, blue sky, sweat on their backs, physical exhaustion, talking. At night, the work done, they gathered at Buck's table to enjoy his cow-camp specials, and later, they went to the living room to listen to his stories.

"My great-grandfather built this house in 1886. And believe it or not, I came into this world in that back bedroom, same one I sleep in today," Buck said. "A *patrona* come up from one of the big ranches on the Mexican side to help my mother with the birth, and when I grew up, why, I worked for that same ranch and plenty of others around Sonora, the best cattle outfits in old Mexico."

"Tell me about your great-grandfather," Merry said.

"Silas Pearl Zachary was his name. He nearly lost his fanny trying to grow cattle out here." Buck drew from his pocket a gold watch. On the back were the letters *SPJ* in elaborate script. He opened the spring lid to reveal the tiny photo of a bug-eyed, thickly bearded, Old Testament–looking character.

"That's Silas right there."

"He looks tough as heck," Merry said.

"First summer here he near died of thirst," Buck said. "Many's the time he took his water from a hole in the ground and was glad to have it. When that first winter come along, he thought, 'I'll be okay now.' But instead of the heat trying to kill him, it was the cold."

"I can't believe how cold it is here," she said. "I thought this was desert."

"Silas told me one thing real important. Always carry stick matches in winter because if you get throw'd, you'll freeze to death without a fire. Stick matches and this watch for luck. Always got 'em with me."

"It looks like an expensive piece," Merry said.

"Had offers on it, you bet."

"Don't ever sell. It's priceless."

"Carried it every day of my life." He snapped the lid shut and returned it to his pocket. "Silas come over here from Tombstone with nothin' but this watch and his belongin's packed onto a mule named Mercy, and that's the truth."

Even with the closing of his mind, Buck still had times of remarkable clarity and exuberance. When he told a story he threw himself into it, waving his arms and making an assortment of wild faces. Then he'd calm down before starting all over again.

"It's getting to be bedtime, Buck," Will said. "Don't want you overdoing it."

"By dern, Will, why can't I talk?"

"You've been down a rabbit trail all night. It's late."

"All right, I'll tell Merry my stories when you ain't around. Stuff that in your pipe." Buck's booming laugh filled the house.

Truth was, Merry had grown fond of Buck and enjoyed his reminiscing. She understood that he was fighting a deadline and that all that he described would be gone forever the moment his mind gave out for good.

Listening helped her, too. Merry wished she'd been there at the end for her grandpa Cornelius, and Will could see she was shifting that regret to Buck.

He asked repeatedly about going to Zaragoza. But Will kept putting him off and made sure that whenever he and Merry left the ranch, either Hector, Lucy, or Artie stayed behind in case Buck tried another escape.

Will used one of those trips to settle the troubling issue of Merry's boots.

"There's a craftsman in Mexico we need to visit," he said. "Name's Carlos Ramírez."

"Who's Carlos Ramírez?"

"The best bootmaker in all of Sonora. You need cowboy boots."

"I've got cowboy boots," Merry protested.

Will pretended it hurt to look at hers. "Oh, no, you don't."

She turned an ankle to show off her Santa Fe snakeskins. "What do you call these?"

"You don't want to know what I call those," he said.

"Buck?" Her tone begged for agreement. She stood on her heels and pulled up both pant legs. "Don't these look like boots to you?"

Buck might as well have been looking at a rat on his pillow. Shaking his head sadly, he said, "Merry, Merry, Merry."

They drove across the line in Will's ratty old Silverado pickup to the little Sonoran town of Pitiquito. Merry settled on a simple pair of chestnut-brown calf-leather boots with gold stitching and pointed toes.

Outside Ramírez's shop, she did a little dance that started out badly when she fell off the big slant heels. She yelped and

Will caught her, and she performed a silly promenade along the sidewalk.

"I've got the trick of it now," Merry said. "I'm ready for the rodeo."

"You're ready to go to town."

"You mean now that I won't embarrass you with my tender-foot boots?" She wrinkled her brow. "Wait, tenderfeet?"

"You can show them off tonight."

"What's tonight?"

"Only the biggest social event of the year. It's the Thanksgiving dance at Padre Pedro's Saloon."

Patagonia began as a mining town and a ranch town and was still a bit of both. It was as much Mexican as gringo in look and language. The homes were small, frame and adobe, brightly colored and flat-roofed with strings of red chilis hanging on the front doors.

The town's population numbered fewer than a thousand, and downtown encompassed all of four blocks. Between the store-fronts on both sides of Naugle Avenue, the main street, was a grassy park where the railroad once ran.

But the trains hauling ore from the mines were long gone, and on most afternoons the rattle of a passing horse trailer was the only sound loud enough to excite notice.

Sweetie's Feed and the Remuda Bar anchored the north side of the street, and on the south side, along a covered sidewalk, were the Silver Bullet Motel, the Hurdy House Restaurant, and Baja Joe's coffeehouse.

Two vacant lots west of Baja Joe's was Lucy's repair shop and junkyard. Surrounding it stood a razor-wire-topped fence to keep away anyone plotting to make off with the rusty, discarded, and broken items she'd spent years collecting.

She had toasters, microwaves, electric drills, and boxes of kitchen utensils. She had couches and horrid hotel paintings of ducks on placid lakes. She had boxes of old shoes, boxes of personal papers, and family photos bought by the armload at estate sales. She had stand-up racks of shirts and coats for men and women.

Best prices anywhere, promised the crayon sign.

Her Quonset hut garage was green and peeling. She sat under the half-moon entrance on a decrepit couch, the stuffing oozing all around her. She talked on her phone and smoked and peered out at the world beyond her fence.

As Will and Merry approached, she dropped the phone onto her shoulder and called out that she had finished with the Mustang.

"Don't want that silly rig around here," she said. "I need the space."

"It can stay here as well as at the ranch," Will said.

"What happened to California?"

Will didn't respond. He looked at Merry and smiled. She smiled up at him and bumped his shoulder. That told Lucy what she needed to know.

"I feared this here situation," she said. "Don't ask if I'm happy for you two 'cause I ain't."

Merry offered to pay her for the work, which gave Lucy a pained expression. Offering a speedy goodbye, Will tugged Merry away. From the corner of her mouth she said, "Did I say something?"

Will explained that Lucy didn't handle money. It made her emotional. She only did business in cash and it all went to Buck. He was the actual owner of the junkyard and the auto shop, the one who'd set her up in business in the first place.

"If she doesn't do money," Merry asked, "how does she get by?"

"Buck gives her an allowance and puts the rest in the bank for her. She lives in an old bunkhouse up the canyon."

"I wondered why she was going up there."

"Have you heard noises at night, the fridge door opening and closing, things like that?"

"That's Lucy?"

"She comes around to get food and charge her phone. She doesn't sleep and spends most of the night walking around the canyon. I meant to tell you."

"I was afraid you had giant mice. I meant to tell *you*."

As they walked arm in arm from Lucy's shop, Merry said, "I hope you know she's in love with you."

At the post office, Will got arched eyebrows and knowing grins. Out on the sidewalk Merry said, "I feel like I'm getting the eye."

Word had spread like a grass fire that they were keeping domestic.

"Should I be creeped out?" Merry said. "I think I'm creeped out."

"No, it's good. I know these people. They're happy for me."

"I'm happy for you, too. But shouldn't we tell them I'm sleeping in the guest bedroom? Nail a decree to the church door, something like that."

"Won't do any good."

"I'd hate to cause an uprising. Can't they look at someone else?" Merry pointed. "Look, there's another one."

Across the street, a man had stepped out of Sweetie's Feed carrying a sack of grain on each shoulder. He dropped them in the bed of his truck, thumbed his hat back, and stared across the street with his hand on the tailgate.

He held that pose a moment before going back into the store.

"That's Bud Tisdale," Will said. "His people have been here forever. They started out working the mines in the Patagonia Mountains when we were just a territory."

"He should learn not to stare."

"He wanted me to notice his truck. That's a new Dodge Ram."

"You mean he wasn't staring at me? I'm even more insulted."

"He ran a backhoe service for years, digging wells for folks. Had to shut down. Money trouble."

Tisdale stepped out of the store and walked across the street. He was short-legged and broad across the shoulders. He had wide-swinging arms with lots of hair on them and tobacco stains bracketing his mouth.

There was a bulge in his left front pocket. From his teenage years on, Tisdale had carried a palm-sized Ruger .22 pistol wherever he went.

"Nice truck you got there, Bud," Will said.

"Ain't it, though? Shoot." He stared back at it with pride.

"Sorry to hear about your business."

"Save your pennies, Will. That's my advice. How's Buck, anyhow?"

"Time's passing. But he's tough."

"He's a great man, your uncle." Tisdale clucked his tongue in concern for Buck's condition, which was well-known around town. "It's a tough thing. I wish him the best, I really do."

"How about coming out for a visit? I'm sure he'd enjoy seeing you."

"I might do that. Last year I was out your way on a deer tag. Killed me a mulie and jerked the meat. How about I bring some by?"

"I'll be waiting."

Without prompting, Tisdale turned to Merry, took her hand in two of his, shook it rapidly up and down like he was trying to draw water out of a well. He introduced himself and stared too long. "Gets prettier round here all the time," he said.

When he left, Merry said, "Okay, what's the deal with Bud Tisdale?"

"Don't mind him. His wife just took off. Number four."

"Washing his face might've helped."

"They had a huge battle, but he finally got the dog. I could tell you stories."

"Please do."

It surprised Will that Merry cared about such things, but she did. She wanted to hear about all of it, the broken loves, the little wars, the whispers. They were town legend and she was part of it now.

Will was impressed. Here was a young woman of privilege dropped into a place left blessedly alone by time and comfort, all the things she knew, an unforgiving world, and she'd happily grabbed at every part of it.

The question of Stanford had been put away, treated as a distant dream. They allowed only one intrusion on the perfection of their days together, Merry calling her mother, Glenna Hannon, an English professor at Boston University, with word of her car trouble in a lost corner of Arizona.

"Is that a real place?" Hannon wanted to know. "On an honest-to-goodness map?"

CHAPTER NINE

Patagonia buzzed with excitement on dance night. Through the dark mountains the headlights of pickup trucks streamed down on lonely dirt roads, emptying the ranches in the Patagonia Mountains to the south, all the way to the San Rafael Valley on the Mexican border, and north and west into the Santa Ritas.

The folks in that remote country didn't often make it to town. They lived hidden lives, patriotic when it came to their particular canyon and scornful of what lay outside. It took a lot for them to pull on a clean pair of pants, brush off their best hats, and make the bumpy drive out.

The Thanksgiving dance at Padre Pedro's Saloon was it.

Mexican stonemasons built the building in 1903, and little had changed in its exterior since. It had two huge oak doors with full-length crosses carved into them and a bell tower with another cross atop that. The bell worked.

Rudy Montero stood in the first-floor vestibule pulling on the rope. He had a mound of unruly hair, cordovan skin, and a crooked grin, and with each person who passed, he halted his bell ringing and bowed in welcome.

Then he mopped his forehead with a hanky and bared his teeth as he laced his fingers around the rope to begin again. Rudy was deranged, slept on a pallet on the former altar, and when he rang the bell, the whole town heard it.

Pedro's Saloon had five small rooms around a circular, candlelit hallway. But the main event took place in the church, now the bar, a large space with stained-glass windows and the back wall painted with colorful murals of Indian women shouldering water jugs across a peaceful village.

A line of drinkers had already planted elbows on the polished-cherry bar when Will and Merry took a table. The late-arriving band assembled in Rudy's bedroom and made car-wreck screeches on their guitars until they began their set.

Merry sipped three fingers of bourbon and shook her knee to the music. "You do dance, don't you? Please tell me you dance."

Will pretended astonishment. "I breathe, don't I?"

She practically catapulted from her chair and grabbed his hand. Bouncing hats filled the dance floor, and each spin, no matter the direction, sent them crashing into somebody. Between turns, Will talked to Merry about the dancers, telling her how to identify the ones who lived close to town and the ones from way out, beyond where few had reason to go.

The way-outers, making the most of the night and the difficult drive, were better dressed, in spotless once-a-year shirts and brightly colored scarves knotted at the throat.

"Who's this one?" Merry pointed to a stocky, flat-nosed Mexican.

"That's Cuco Muñoz."

"The one who set up your meeting with Marcelino?"

"I hardly recognized him. He shaved."

"With a mirror hanging from a branch, I suppose."

"Word is Cuco had a falling-out with Marcelino and had to get out of Mexico fast."

Merry pointed to a man with his jeans tucked inside his boots.

"Robert Reginald Ashmont III," Will said. "Owns the biggest spread around. He's a dude."

"No good?"

"He's rich. Software." Will sniffed. "He runs home to New York when it gets hot."

Like a lot of newcomers to that country, Ashmont was brilliant at something that earned money and respect outside but paid no dividends on the dirt roads. He understood that and tried to fit in. He was trying to learn how to rope, and wanting to look less like an easterner, he'd let his hair curl out from behind his ears and was working on a walrus mustache. It wasn't good.

He practically bowed as he asked Merry to dance. Ashmont moved formally, rigidly, arms held out. When he freed her, Merry curled a finger at Will, and they were together again.

"I don't even know how old you are," Will said.

"What's this? Did we just meet?"

"I should at least know how old you are."

"Are we being proper now? I just graduated. Take a wild guess."

"I mean exactly. I want to know how much older I am. I figure eight years."

Just then, Will bumped shoulders with a short redheaded man. The collision was no accident. Boone Macklin wore a contemptuous half smile that signaled a man looking for trouble.

"You know who I work for, Zachary?"

Will knew perfectly well but didn't respond.

"She's got a message for you," Macklin said.

"I don't want anything from you or your lawyer friend."

"From what I hear, the bill collectors are getting itchy. She's ready to offer real money."

"Don't care."

"Gotta be smart, slick. Could be you don't know it yet, but your time's up."

"Take a walk, Boone," Will said and stepped away. He lost Merry in the crowd, and when he found her again, she was in

Macklin's arms, looking over his shoulder with eyes that begged for immediate rescue.

Will tapped Macklin's shoulder and cut in. "Call me slick again and I'll knock you down." Before Macklin could respond, Will and Merry danced away.

"You want to tell me who that charmer is?" Merry said.

"Works for a rich lawyer in Tucson named Stacy Queen. She defends big-time drug runners and is buying up ranches around here."

"Do I have to guess why?"

"She has her eye on the Flying Z. Sends that bandy-legged jackass around to scare people. Forget him. You were about to tell me how old you are."

"You are being proper," Merry said. "How funny."

"There are certain things a man should know. Tell me about Ireland."

"You want the basics cleared away before you go any farther. See, it's obvious that you've fallen for me completely and—"

"Wait a minute. Where'd you come up with that?"

"Don't pretend, mister. I can tell by the way you're holding me."

The music and the energy of the crowd combined to shake the old church. It pounded up through the floor.

"See, you've fallen for me," Merry continued, "and you realize there are things you don't know, so you're backtracking to fill in the holes. You're scared because this feeling is new to you and really powerful. And rather than talk about it, you ask questions. The distance isn't so threatening."

Will raised his arm and Merry twirled underneath it and away, hair flying. He pulled her back. Her skin was smooth and sweet smelling. It held Will's eye down through the curve of her neck and onto her shoulder and kept its hold when it went to hide underneath her blouse.

He lost his hand in the tangle of her hair and all he could think was, *That's fine with me, I have another.*

"Okay, we'll do it your way," she said. "Ask me whatever you like."

"Where'd you grow up?"

"Brookline, Massachusetts. My parents divorced when I was little, so during the holidays and over the summers, I lived on my dad's estate in Ireland. It's called Ballyfeard."

"An estate? Is that like a ranch?"

"The O'Haras made their fortune in the 1820s in linen. Father raises horses now and he's good at it. Sorry, no cows."

"Sounds like you have lots of land."

"The green hills go on forever. You've seen the pictures."

"A guy like me, I'd be labor for the lord?"

"If you cleaned up you might get hired on."

Merry settled her face back against Will's shoulder.

"My father's a politician, rising fast, big things coming, all that." She held up her hand to show a dazzling emerald ring. "He drinks and whenever he'd rage around throwing lamps or whatever, I'd go to the barn, saddle one of our horses, and ride. The ring was one of his peace offerings."

She twirled away again and struggled on those Ramírez heels, screeching as she teetered. She took Will's hand and wrapped her free arm around the small of his back.

"All right, my turn," Merry said.

"Go ahead."

"You have this olive skin, nice black hair, and your eyes are really dark and handsome. So far, so good. But something happened to your jaw. I'm guessing it involved a wild animal."

"Can't believe you're asking about my jaw."

"All right, forget the jaw. Aren't you uncomfortable dancing with that gun in your boot?"

As Will had been getting out of the Silverado, he'd grabbed his Smith & Wesson .38 from the glove box and slipped it into his ankle holster. He didn't think Merry had seen.

"Did you have that gun at Zaragoza?" she asked.

"Matter of fact I did."

The band started into a Waylon Jennings song and the crowd roared. Everyone jumped up and grabbed a partner. Merry let the commotion settle before speaking again.

"At first, I thought you were being brave, the way you dealt with Salazar. Now I'm leaning toward reckless."

"That's a lot of word."

"You gave Salazar time to go for that rifle. Like that's what you wanted to happen. What then? Would you have gotten into a gunfight?"

"I know what I'm doing."

The band took a break. Merry and Will went back to their table. The waitress brought a beer for Will and another bourbon for Merry.

She sipped and said, "You had two guns to go riding and now you're carrying a gun at a community dance. That's all I'm saying."

"We carry guns the way you city people carry those Starbucks cups."

"Somehow I don't think it's the same."

Will leaned across the table. "Look around, Merry."

"Huh? Okay." She took in the room, thick with bodies to the four walls.

"Right now, I'll bet there's three guys in this place that work for Marcelino. Scouts, drivers, muscle. His operation extends well north of the border. He's in Phoenix, LA, all over."

More intensely, Merry studied the crowd. Sipping her bourbon, she said, "I thought this was just a cool party."

Harley Jones stopped in front of Merry and asked her to dance. He'd had a run of bad luck lately that included losing his job at El Caballo Blanco, the ranch abutting the Flying Z to the west. He'd been chased off for spending too much time with the owner's teenage daughter, and Will hired him on.

Swaying slightly, Harley pumped his arms in a salsa motion. Merry had started to get up to dance, but Will told him to beat it. Harley left and came back immediately, having forgotten being told to leave seconds before.

He gave a sloppy grin when he remembered, shot himself in the temple with a finger, and was gone.

Merry and Will danced again. No more men came to offer Merry their hand. The way she and Will held each other told them to stay away.

Past midnight, when they'd said their goodbyes and walked outside, it looked as if the year's biggest social event had never happened. All the trucks parked along the street had departed, taking the revelers with them.

But Boone Macklin was still there. He hung his face out the window of his truck as he passed slowly by. On his left forearm he had a tattoo of a straight flush, bracketed above and below by a pair of six-shooters.

He stared intently at Will and Merry, grinning, before passing out of sight.

"Him I'd shoot myself," Merry said.

"Who's reckless now? You really think I'm reckless?"

"Two guns?"

"Got a lot more at the house."

It was a shivering-cold night, their breath visible.

"Dangerous, then. I never thought of myself as one of those women attracted to dangerous men. But here we are."

"Where is that exactly?"

"I don't even know. Seriously. All we do is talk."

"It's been a long time for me," Will said. "I'm not the jumpy sort."

"Do you suppose I can wait forever?"

"Don't know what you suppose. You're bold, you know that."

"It's been building for days. Don't you feel it?"

"I'm a man. Some ideas have presented."

"I was thinking of getting a sandwich board. Why do you think I'm still here? Some ideas." She huffed and looked up at him, a challenge in her expression. "I think you're afraid."

With that, Merry had inched close to the truth. Will was in knots, had been since Morales Road, and kept telling himself, *Hold on. Don't forget Kansas City.* The memory blew through his brain, a woman from his trucking days, beautiful, willing, and all wrong.

The encounter had ended badly and he vowed never to have his head turned that way again. *Don't jump, not with this one. She's too special.* Will didn't know there could be someone like Merry O'Hara in the world.

"When I was a kid, we had a filly like you," he said. "Couldn't keep her in the corral."

"You sure know how to talk to a girl. Now I'm like a horse. Could we just go home before you blow it completely?"

"I'm just saying, she was a good horse."

"First, we need to clear up this jaw business. I can't go another minute until I know what happened."

"You need to forget about my jaw."

"Never. It's a calamity." Merry laughed with a lilt at the end from too much bourbon. "Have you thought of joining the circus?"

"They wired it up tight. A bull kicked me is all."

Merry yelped and jumped in a crazy circle. "A wild animal! I knew it! I so knew it!"

Just then two stragglers emerged from Pedro's, a young couple arm in arm. They passed by without acknowledging Merry's hullabaloo. They were as together as a man and woman could be, lost in each other, lost to the world, and good riddance for this one night.

As she watched them go, Merry bent her head against Will's shoulder.

"If you find it, fight for it," she said, and bounced up on her toes and kissed him on the lips.

Will felt something burst inside, a letting go. He wrapped his arms around the small of her back and lifted her off the ground, and they joined in a second, much longer kiss, until all Will's hesitation was gone, Kansas City was gone, and he knew he'd found it, too.

"There you go," she said upon returning to earth. She cleared her throat and fanned herself. "You needed that in the worst way."

CHAPTER TEN

They climbed into the Silverado. Merry scooched over beside Will until they were shoulder to shoulder, thigh to thigh. She had a funny thought: *Only teenagers do this. But it feels right. No, it feels perfect.*

They drove into the mountains with the lights of town dimming behind them. The houses lining the way became more infrequent and ramshackle as they went. The last one, abandoned, decrepit, overgrown with brush, sat alone on a hill, an outpost, a fort, a marker of civilization's end.

Beyond it the land became raw, beautiful, and merciless. Past this shack all restraint was gone. Will felt that powerfully and knew it would only take the right word, a bump in the road, a jostling, to make the feeling unbearable.

He drove slower and slower. Time was running out. The rumble of the truck made it stronger. The moonlight falling through the trees made it stronger. Merry felt it, too. Her pulse pounded in her ears.

She laid her arm across his shoulder and left it there. "I love my Ramírez boots."

"You danced like a pro in them."

Absently, innocently, she raised her hand to remove a strand of hair from her face, and her fingertips brushed against his ear. He'd never felt anything like the sensation that coursed through him.

"Sorry," Merry said. "I'm clumsy tonight."

"You did that on purpose."

"Do you want me to do it on purpose, Will?"

"I said I'm a man. If you do that again I'll be something else."

"Like this?" She ran the back of her fingernails down along his neck and under his collar.

Will hit the brakes hard, dragging the truck to a stop in the middle of the road. He turned off the engine and the headlights.

"Here?" She looked in his eyes in the mountain dark and got her answer. She leaned her back against the door and thrust one leg across the seat. "They're such beautiful boots. I hate to take them off," Merry said.

"You better take them off."

"Right now. Take them off. Go ahead, pull."

He grabbed the first boot, got it off and over his shoulder and heaved it out the window. The space in the cab was so tight he set off the truck's horn.

"My heart's doing crazy things," Merry said. "It's making me dizzy. Oh, here, here."

She threw her other leg across the seat and off came the second boot, and the two of them came together with the horn letting out alternate blasts from the pressure of one flailing body part or another, until it became obvious that the cab of the Silverado could not contain them, and they hurried outside.

Will jumped into the flatbed and pulled off his jacket and spread it out for her. He reached down to pull Merry in with him. The flatbed smelled of motor oil, hay, and the newborn orphan calf that had hitched a ride a week earlier. Clothing was hastily removed and tossed.

"Hold on, there's something in the way." Will reached underneath Merry and pulled out his riata. She threw her arms around his shoulders and pulled him down. He held on to the rope.

"May I suggest you toss that thing?" Merry said.

"I carry it wherever I go."

They were close together, hands working, kissing, trading breath.

"Wonderful. You have a binky. But you don't need it now."

"I heard a story about a family that got caught in a fifth-floor fire and couldn't get out. They all burned up. Ever since, I'm never without it."

She grabbed it out of his hand and heaved it onto the toolbox. "Are you going to tell fascinating stories about your rope or are we going to do this?" Her whole body trembled. Her voice trembled. She fell into him all the way, and he did the same. Nothing could stop them now.

"Stay cinched, girl."

"Stay cinched yourself."

Merry stretched her arms out behind her head and braced herself with her hands against the spare tire behind her. Her palms turned black from the soot. The heat of their bodies conquered the night cold, and toward the end the forest echoed with every scandalous word in her vocabulary.

Afterward, they heard a horse clopping along the road. They sat up and saw four white socks moving through the trees at a steady trot as the rider bellowed out a song.

When he came closer, they saw that it was Harley Jones, shirtless under his hat, a black Gus. It had a high forward-sloping crown that looked like a loaf of bread with a crease down the middle. He sat erect on the horse's bare back, elbows high as though performing for royalty and honored to be doing so.

The night and drink hadn't been good to Harley. Not only had he lost his shirt, but his truck was missing, too, and he'd found an old swayback to carry him. He clopped along singing in

Spanish, and Will and Merry, sitting in the back of the Silverado, watched him pass within arm's reach.

Harley didn't wave or smile or show any awareness of their presence. He kept intense concentration on the song, belting it out, his mouth round, his shining eyes staring straight ahead.

"Nice voice," Merry said. She was lying beside Will now, her leg thrown across his body.

"He's singing to El Jinete."

"El—what? Who?"

"The Horseman," Will said. "He lives in these mountains."

"Is he like Washington Irving's Headless Horseman? Does he scare people?"

"There's a million stories about what he does. The most common one is if you're lost and sing songs to him, he'll show up and lead you home."

Harley rode on. Even out of sight, his song echoed through the trees.

Merry said, "Shouldn't we follow to make sure he doesn't get lost?"

"El Jinete will get him home."

"I must've lost my marbles there for a second. Did you say El Jinete will get him home?"

"The Horseman is friends with the sun and the stars. They hear his songs and use their power to help him."

"I see."

"The stars guide him at night and the sun during the day," Will said. "If it's cloudy, the stars will shove the clouds aside and show him the way."

"Does this brilliant Horseman have a name?"

"Domingo Opata. Ask Buck about him. He'll go on for hours."

"O-kaaay. Now you have me. I must know more about El Jinete."

"The way Buck tells it, Opata was an Aztec warrior who fought Hernán Cortés and the Spanish down by Mexico City in that big war they had in the fifteen hundreds. After that he rode up this way looking for gold."

"Did he find it?"

"He met a beautiful Indian girl who promised to take him to it, but they got separated and he's been looking for her ever since."

Merry laughed but Will didn't. She put her chin on his chest and looked into his face, which held no doubt or amusement. "Wait, you're serious?"

"Buck started telling me about him when I was a kid. Never lived a minute of my life without him, so yeah, I am. For us Opata's not a story. He's blood and bones."

"You're scaring me, Will. You're supposed to be a regular guy, feet firmly on the ground and all that."

"If you stay around here long enough, you'll believe in Opata, too."

"Let me see if I've got this." Merry sat up and held her hands in front of her face in a steadying gesture. "I'm naked in a pickup truck somewhere in Arizona's backcountry, which I don't mind actually because I'm with you and it's really exciting and lovely, even though it is starting to get chilly.

"Anyway, on this beautiful night, this unforgettable night, I'm with an otherwise normal guy who believes in an Aztec mystery man who rides around trying to find an Indian girl, and he has help in his epic quest from the sun and the stars, good friends that they are. And he's been doing this for, what, four hundred–plus years now?"

"That's it."

Merry wrinkled her face and thought hard for a minute. "This girl, he loves her, right? Tell me he loves her."

"Very much. She's called Kazoh."

"Ahh. So he's not looking for the gold, he's looking for Kazoh?"

"Some people think one way and some the other."

"I get it now," Merry said. "It's an allegory and the answer says everything about you. Whether you're romantic or not, whether you let your heart speak to you or you don't listen. For me, the answer's easy. It's got to be Kazoh. He needs to be reunited with his true love. What do you say, Will? Is it love or is it gold?"

"Gold doesn't last forever."

"That is so freaking the right answer." Delighted, excited, Merry put her finger under Will's chin and turned his face to hers and kissed his lips.

Much later, after coming together and making the night warm again, they searched the dark brush beside the road to retrieve a tossed boot and random articles of clothing hanging from tree branches.

In the morning Will got up and was in the kitchen when Buck came out wearing slippers, a tattered nightshirt, and baggy pajama bottoms. He couldn't find his hearing aids. He often forgot to remove them before going to sleep.

After returning home, and with Merry giggling beside him, Will had tiptoed into his room and removed them to keep him from hearing the goings-on in the next room. Will held the hearing aids in his palm.

"How come you got 'em?" Buck asked.

"I wanted you to sleep good."

"Sleep good?" Leaning forward, confused, Buck put his hands on his hips. "What noises am I gonna hear, middle of the dern night?"

Showing her unmatched skill at timing, Merry emerged from Will's bedroom in a robe, her hair a mess. Suddenly aware, Buck rolled his eyes and grinned.

"Oh, lordy!" He clapped his hands. "Lordy! Lordy!" He was beaming. "We been needing a woman round here." He smiled at Merry with his old-man teeth. "This is great news, girl. You don't know how bad Will needs someone to talk to that don't have four legs and a tail."

"You always know just what to say, Buck," Will said.

He cupped a hand behind his ear. "What's that?"

"How about making us pancakes?"

Buck clapped again. "Great idea, boy. We'll celebrate with my special pancakes. They'll fatten you up, Merry."

He motored around the kitchen while Merry, sitting at the table, rubbed her eyes with the heels of her hands and groaned. "I have a screaming headache."

"He's right," Will said. "You need to fatten up."

"Stop it, you, I do not. Actually, I used to be bigger. I was a pudgy kid. That must never leave this room."

Will told Buck of encountering Harley in the mountains. "I wouldn't expect him to be doing much work around here today."

"Drunk, was he?" Buck said.

"Sorrowful. Riding along half-dressed singing to El Jinete. I introduced Merry to the Horseman."

Surprised, Buck turned from the stove. "You told her everything?"

"Not quite everything," Will said.

"You're sure learning a lot about this place, Merry," Buck said. "Well, we've got our stories and we've got our secrets, that's for sure. Beautiful and dangerous secrets."

"Ooooh," Merry exclaimed. "I love secrets. Tell me, tell me."

Buck had a question on his face. *Should I reveal it all? Should I throw open the door to our private world?* Will thought it too soon.

Putting the topic away, he said, "Let's fill up with pancakes." The secrets of the Flying Z would have to wait.

The coffee maker growled, filling the kitchen with the smell of fresh coffee. The fireplace in the living room blazed. Will had stoked it with piñon logs from southern New Mexico, the best for making a fire.

Jorge the woodcutter drove them into town with his whole family on the truck, the logs stacked high in back and his kids hanging on any way they could. Folks lined up for hours waiting for Jorge to arrive. Everybody loved the homey scent of a piñon fire.

Buck put a steaming plate of pancakes on the table. Merry rubbed her hands together. "Let's eat and get fat. I need to remember what it's like being a big old fatso."

They all laughed. They were happy that cold Saturday morning in the borderlands.

CHAPTER ELEVEN

Next morning, Will, Merry, and Buck had chores to do, and Hector came, too. They were searching for a lost cow in Rebel Canyon. It was a beautiful morning, cloudless and Arizona bright.

Will's plan for Buck didn't come out of any medical book, but he knew it to be true. Keep him on horseback as much as possible, riding the land and working it as he had for all of his eighty-two years. Riding kept him in touch with the instinct of a lifetime. Will's desperate hope was that he'd find restoration in that, and his mind would come back.

They left the ranch on the main trail, Buck in the lead. He wore a misshapen gray felt hat with turquoise studs on the band, and a beat-up wool coat. Like Will, he carried his .30-30 Winchester. It was flat and short barreled and fit nicely into the scabbard under the fender of the saddle.

Merry rode alongside him. She had her hair in a ponytail, accentuating the strong line of her jaw. She wore black gloves, the same oversized canvas jacket from the first day, and a white straw hat that had belonged to Emma. It had a silver band and purple roses embroidered on the underside of the turned-up brim.

Buck had given the hat to Merry. She looked genteel, like the new lady of the ranch.

They departed the main trail to bushwhack through a small canyon and up onto a broad table of burned-up pastureland. A portion of the barbed-wire fence around it had been cut.

Scanning the bone-dry ground. Buck shook his head. "Ain't enough grass to pick your teeth," he said. "But I seen it worse."

"No good for my flowers this year," Hector said.

"That's why you wanted to come here first, ain't it?" Buck said. "Never seen a man crazier about wildflowers."

The blooming of the Mexican poppies made winter Hector's favorite season. He photographed them during the day and at night he sketched the prettiest scenes, with the faces of his three grade-school daughters set among the flowers.

With a kerosene lamp burning beside him, he went through reams of paper to get the images right. He drank whiskey while he worked, and in the morning the floor beside his cot would be covered in balled-up pieces of paper. He gave copies to his daughters' teachers in Nogales for posting in their classrooms.

It made him proud to know the whole school could look at his work.

"Maybe they come late this year, Señor Z," Hector said.

"Don't count on it. No rain in October means no Mexican poppies in December. If they was a-comin', this ground'd be yellow all through by now."

Buck got down from his horse and inspected the fence cut. "All right, Will. Let's fix this here while Hector dries his tears."

As they worked, Hector wheeled his horse east toward a mesquite flat.

"You won't find nothing thataway," Buck called.

"Be right back, Señor Z." Hector waved over his shoulder and was gone.

"Hector's thinking about wildflowers 'stead of that calf," Buck said. "He's gettin' all misty-eyed."

"I need him to keep his mind on business," Will said.

"Don't you know Hector's got the soul of a poet." Buck laughed. "He feels more than what's good for him. Can't hardly fault a man for that."

With the work done, Will, Buck, and Merry rode south into Rebel Canyon, a landscape of giant cottonwoods and gnarled mesquites. Boulders like dead elephants lay all over the ground.

As they neared a cluster of rocks, a man sprang up from behind a tangle of fallen trees. He was no more than thirty feet from Buck, and he had a rifle. Buck saw him first.

"Shooter!" he yelled. "Look out, it's a shooter!"

Still trailing, his head down looking for tracks, Will looked up and saw Salazar, the boy from Zaragoza, shoulder his weapon, aim straight at him, and fire. The bullet passed through Will's jacket, inches from his ribs.

Lobo reared and kicked, and Will lost the reins and flipped over the saddle cantle to the ground. Salazar fired at Will again. He heard the *whiz* of the bullet's passing but wasn't hit.

"The wolf's out, Merry!" Buck's voice was strong but calm and not panicked. "Take cover! It's apt to get loud!"

Buck's horse had spooked, too. As he fought for control, he reached back for the Winchester, and with the hurricane raging beneath him, pulled it from the scabbard and tried to find Salazar in his sights.

He squeezed off three fast shots and missed with all three. He settled in the saddle the best he could and fired again, this time hitting Salazar in the leg.

Lobo had run off. Will crawled on his elbows toward the rock cover. Merry had jumped off Candy and had already taken shelter behind the rocks. Amid the chaos, Buck saw movement in the trees lining the ridge ahead. He fired in that direction and the men in the timber fired back.

Buck dropped to cover and rose again to shoot. He did that three times before a bullet struck his right shoulder. At impact his face looked puzzled, as though he'd heard a sound he couldn't identify.

He blinked rapidly and said, "They shot me. They shot me, by dern." He dropped the rifle and fell forward, cracking his head against a rock.

"Buck!" Will shouted. "Stay down! Stay down!"

Salazar fired at Will, who dropped as low as he could, his face in the grass. As Salazar hobbled forward toward the rock fort, Merry lunged for Buck's Winchester and got hold of it. But in her excitement and fear, she lost her grip and the weapon exploded in her hands, sending a round harmlessly away.

Bleeding from the wound on his thigh, swinging his wounded leg in wide, struggling steps, Salazar kept coming. Hatless and with a gash on his forehead, Buck recovered his senses and sat up.

"Give it here, Merry." She tossed him the Winchester and Buck leveled it and squeezed the trigger just as Salazar came around the rocks. The blast hit him in the chest and lifted him off the ground.

Buck fell on his back. More shots came from the men on the hill. Will reached the rock fort and grabbed Buck's rifle and walked toward the shooters firing multiple times. They retreated at his advance, two of them helping a wounded man along.

Will hurried back to Buck's side and got down on his knees beside him. He put his hand behind Buck's head and raised it.

"It's over now," he said. "They've had enough. It's all over."

Blood ran down Buck's face onto his chest. His eyes were spinning. "I seen him point his rifle at Merry," he said.

"Take it easy," Will said. "Don't talk. We'll get help."

Breathing hard, Merry said, "Salazar shot Buck and was going to shoot me. The look on his face, Will, I've never seen anything like that. It was—wicked."

Merry pulled off her jacket, rolled it up to make a pillow, and placed it behind Buck's head. She stayed cool. She used Will's bandanna to wipe the blood from his face and apply pressure to the wound.

"Believe I got that fella good," Buck said. "Think so, anyways."

"His name's Salazar," Will said. "He's dead all right."

Buck's words barely crawled past his lips, but they were full of pride. "He was spoiling for a fight and got it, by dern."

"Another one was hit up in the timber and limping bad," Will said. "You wounded him."

"Guess I oughta work on my aim."

Hector rode up. He saw Buck on the ground bleeding, looked away, and pounded his hand on the saddle pommel. Will told him to ride until he got a cell signal and call for help. Hector tossed his canteen down and went.

Will unscrewed the cap and held the canteen to Buck's lips. Water leaked down his chin.

"That tastes awful good," he said, as his eyes rolled up and closed.

CHAPTER TWELVE

When County Sheriff Levi Johnson got to the scene, Merry and Will told him everything they knew, including the details of Will's encounter with Salazar at Zaragoza. A Border Patrol chopper evacuated Buck to Holy Cross Hospital in Nogales, where a doctor sewed twelve stitches into his forehead and removed the bullet from his shoulder.

The doctor declared him the luckiest man in the state of Arizona.

"Two inches left and that would've been it," he said.

Late the following day, Will brought Buck home. The doctor argued strenuously against it, but Will insisted, saying he needed to be in his own bed. He promised that Buck would be well cared for by Henry Gonzáles, a doctor and Buck's close friend.

He'd driven to the Flying Z from his home in Nogales, Sonora, and was waiting on the porch, alongside Levi, when Merry and Will pulled up to the house.

Merry and Doc each took an arm and got Buck out of the truck and into bed. Hector watched from the bedroom doorway. His breathing scented the air with whiskey until, distraught and mumbling, he put his hat on and left.

After a while Will came out and joined Levi at the kitchen table. They'd been best friends since grade school, had played high school football together. Will was the quarterback and Levi his best offensive lineman.

"Between the bullet and that rap on his head, I'd say Buck's a lucky man," Levi said. "I need to hear what he has to say for my report. The FBI is sending a couple of agents by tonight."

"Merry and I talked to them at the hospital. What else do they need?"

"They want to hear Buck's side. Best I talk to him before they do."

"He's still doped up," Will said.

"I'll ask them to hold off." Levi opened his notebook and read, pondering. "Hector's pretty shook up about this. I need a statement from him, too."

"Don't bother. He wasn't there."

"What do you mean? Where was he at?"

"Went off looking for wildflowers just before."

"That man and his wildflowers." Levi shook his head. His face was boyish, honest, and untroubled. He wore a red long-sleeved snap-button shirt. His neck was wide under the ears, pushing out against his collar. He stood six feet four and had big arms and legs.

"Wouldn't matter anyway. Hector won't talk," Will said.

"I don't need much."

"You're missing the squirrel, Levi. He won't tell you anything. He makes his living on those trails."

"You're talking the cartel scouts."

"They got eyes all over. They know his kids' recess times."

"Makes you sick, don't it?"

"Hector sees what he has to see to do his job, and for anything else he needs glasses."

Will got up to get another beer. Levi didn't drink alcohol and Will kept an emergency six-pack of Dr Pepper for him in the fridge. Will got one out, poured it into a glass with the required two ice cubes, never more, never less, and set it down on the table in front of Levi.

He sipped. "On this Zaragoza business, I don't understand you, Will. You've lived out here your whole life. You know better than to mess with a load. Old Buck's one thing, but you?"

"It's starting to look like I got no sense at all."

"You mess with these drug pushers, they'll come back at you for sure. That's what today was about, getting revenge for Zaragoza. That's what we figure happened to Jimmy Benson. He messed with Marcelino and that was it."

Benson was a neighbor found dead on his ranch two years before. Will asked if he'd made any progress on the case. "Can't close it and likely never will. No one's talking. They'll pull something else on you now, just watch."

Levi sipped his drink and put it down. He fiddled with it to make sure it sat perfectly in the same moisture ring.

"Trouble is, we're dealing with a whole new breed," he said. "Wasn't long ago these guys wouldn't shoot at anybody, and all of a sudden, they try to kill Buck and now this. You can't fight these killers alone, Will."

"Your guys and Border Patrol are too far away to help."

"You got Marcelino on one side and Stacy Queen on the other. You think they're working together to squeeze you out?"

"I don't know what they're doing."

"What's Queen offering, anyway?"

"Haven't met her. She sends her muscle guy to stare at people."

"Ugly?"

"As a snake's rear end. Boone Macklin's the name."

"Seen him around," Levi said. "Drinks at the Remuda. His spurs get loud late in the afternoon. We've had to send deputies to quiet him down."

"Got anything on him?"

"The car he drives is a loaner from Stacy Queen, but his driver's license says he's from Reno. I can make a call. The Washoe County Sheriff is a friend of mine. If there's anything on him, Ralph Reyes will know."

"Doesn't matter what Queen's offering, she's not getting this ranch."

"I know that." Levi started to say something, stopped, tried a second time, and finally came out with it: "I know you don't want to hear it, Will, but these bills you got, say the word and I'll loan you the money. I got a little extra in my poke. Might give you room."

"Appreciate it, Levi. But you know I don't like being beholden."

"You like doing things the hard way, that's what I know."

"Best part is it comes natural."

Levi scratched his whiskers. It made a sandpaper sound. "There's another problem you need to consider." He leaned forward and spoke in his confidential voice. "What're you going to do about that gal you got back there?"

He tilted his head toward Buck's bedroom. "You can't protect her all the time, not with this kind of trouble brewing. I heard about that souped-up Mustang she was driving when she showed up. Over these roads? Holy smokes, she don't belong in this country."

"I make my own decisions, Sheriff Johnson. All by myself."

Merry was standing in the kitchen doorway.

"I don't mean to intrude, Miss O'Hara," Levi said. "All I'm saying is this place makes for hard living. Harder than you know."

Merry got a bottle of Seagram's 7 from the kitchen cabinet and poured two shots. She sat at the third space at the table, putting the extra glass down at the fourth, just as Doc Gonzáles emerged from Buck's bedroom. He was tall, dignified, white-haired. His cookie-duster mustache was white, too, and he walked in short, shuffling steps.

"He's sleeping," Doc said. "Best thing for him."

"No way he's going to let you treat him, Doc," Will said. Even though Buck and Henry had been lifelong friends, Buck had never taken medical advice from him or any doctor. From his years at Rancho Dolores, he'd relied only on the herbs of a *curandera*, a Mexican healer, to tend his ailments.

"The man's got his ways." Doc shook his head in frustration. "I know that better than anyone." He pulled out his chair and took up his whiskey.

No one spoke as the minutes fell away. Will thought about what the doctor in Nogales had said. Two inches and Buck was gone. Levi and Doc Gonzáles thought the same thing.

The kitchen door swung open and Lucy came in. The night wind tossed the curtains over the sink. Lucy paid no mind to the somber scene at the table as she rummaged through the refrigerator, collecting leftovers in plastic containers and two cans of Pabst Blue Ribbon beer, stashing one in each coat pocket.

Cradling the food in her arms, she flew out the door again, leaving behind the smell of grease, body odor, and cigarette smoke.

CHAPTER THIRTEEN

On the wall behind Buck's bed hung a beautiful oil portrait of John Wayne. Sadness in his eyes, gaunt with sickness, he'd agreed to sit for an artist on the set of his last picture, *The Shootist*. He autographed the painting, "To my great friend and saddle pard, Buck Zachary."

Buck had handled the stock in some of Wayne's movies and they'd grown close. Buck always said he felt safe knowing Duke was there.

Now he had Merry O'Hara watching over him, too.

All through that first night she kept vigil from a bedside rocker. Buck's rhythmic snoring and the creaking of the chair made the room's only sounds. When he grew fitful, she held his hand and sang songs. She didn't know if they reached him until he awoke late the second day and said, "Sing me another one, Merry."

He wanted to hear George Jones and Sinatra. He loved "New York, New York." He took Merry's hand and sang along, his voice gravelly and barely audible over the painkillers.

Over those two days, Merry never left Buck's side. He gradually came around as the drugs wore off, and she was there when Levi took his statement.

"I killed a devil, how's that?" Buck said. "Shot 'em deader 'n wood. That's my true and accurate statement."

Levi paused, tapping his pencil on his notebook. "Be careful how you put things, Buck. When the FBI comes around, don't make any big statements. Just answer the questions as short as you can and leave it there."

"FBI? What do those guys want?"

"They're looking into possible civil rights violations."

"Hell, I didn't do nothing wrong."

"They're aware of your prior, ah, activities, menacing folks with that rifle of yours. Thought it best if we talked first, squared things up."

A white bandage covered Buck's forehead. Lying on his back, he looked as if the mattress might swallow him. He stroked his chin in mischievous thought.

"No big statements, eh? How about this? I lived every day the past few years thinkin' about havin' to fight those men and I'm de-lighted I got the opportunity. Hope I live long enough to have another go at 'em."

"I see this as a plain case of self-defense," Levi said. "But it doesn't pay to say things that might excite the feds."

The more Levi tried to confine Buck's thoughts to the specifics of the incident, the more he ventured off into all the slights the smugglers had visited upon him over the years, and his desire for revenge.

When Levi left, Buck looked at Merry and at Will. "How come you people are makin' faces at me? I ain't afraid to tell Levi or anyone else what I think."

"You need to be smart," Will said. "Don't say more than you need to."

"Wish I could've gotten all of 'em. Whether it'd be a proper killing to the law don't matter to me."

"Oh, Buck," Merry said. She shifted in her chair in discontent.

"That's what I mean," Will said. "Keep that kind of talk to yourself."

Buck grinned. "Did you get a load of Levi's face? Like he swallowed somethin' hot and hairy." He chuckled and coughed hard, and when he came out of it his voice sounded wet. "The good Lord nearly made me an angel many times over the years, and he put me in another tough spot out there in Rebel Canyon. By dern, he must like me okay 'cause I'm still here."

He folded his hands on his big belly. "He'll judge what I done when the time comes. But I'll say to him and Levi right now, it felt awful good puttin' Salazar down that a-way."

"It was justified, there's no doubt," Will said.

"Justified? Why, that's law talk. It's what you do with a rabid dog."

"I know you don't mean that, Buck," Merry said.

"Don't I? Let me tell you something, dear. All our people have had to defend this ranch one time or another, going all the way back to Silas Pearl Zachary. You best believe there's bodies buried on that range."

Merry gave Will a look that begged for an explanation, some softening words. He gave her nothing.

"I'm thankful I got to add to the register before my time run out," Buck said. "Will's turn's comin', too, and he's looking forward to it, ain't you, Will?"

Merry's eyes snapped toward Will.

He said, "Let's drop it, Buck."

"Tell me I'm wrong," Buck went on. "Tell me you don't wanna have a go at one of them outlaws, put 'em down like a big old Kaibab elk?"

"You've talked enough for now."

"It's hygiene. We need more of it, good old-fashioned hygiene." He ran a finger under his nose, scratching vigorously. "Say, can you get me a taste of whiskey, some whiskey in a glass?"

"No liquor," Will said. "Doc says no liquor."

"Henry." Buck scoffed at his childhood friend. "Henry's being difficult like always." To Merry: "Run and get me a drink, dear. I need a swallow to help me sleep."

With Merry in the kitchen, Buck waved Will closer and whispered, "She don't look good. What happened out in that canyon, it ain't settin' with her. In her gizzard. You need to look after her proper."

"I am looking after her."

"She's hurtin'." He tapped his heart. "Inside. Do you see?"

"You make it worse with your talk about killings. She's scared enough."

"She ain't like us, she's nice." His nasal laugh sounded like cicadas. "But she's here, so she best know the truth, the whole history, all the nips and tucks of real life."

Merry returned with a cup. Buck held it with two hands and let out a long "aggghhhh" after each sip. "That hit the goddamned bull's-eye." He didn't cuss in front of women, and when he realized his mistake, he said, "Forgive me, Merry. I'm *corriente*"—common.

He let his head fall back on the pillow and continued: "Those drug men, at least they're up front about what they're doin'. They want our land and they're tellin' us, 'Okay, let's see you fight for it. Let's see what you got.' That gives us a chance to fight back."

The whiskey had rekindled his fire.

"FBI, my neck. And the whole blame government, too. They don't do their job and it's us that's gotta live with the consequences. It's never been different with Washington. Am I right, Will? You've lived it, too."

"You need to get some sleep."

"In my day we took care of our own problems and they had the good sense to look away. The drug smugglers, hell, I can fight them. But these government lawyers with all that money and time on their hands, they come after me over this, settin' us down in a meetin' room, one of them big, long tables with pretty gals that smell good bringin' us coffee, why, we got no chance. No chance a-tall."

He wiped whiskey from his lips with the back of his hand. The speechmaking had drained him.

"Save your energy, Buck," Will said. "The FBI will be here soon."

"Wish I was younger. Nobody trifled with me twice when I was younger. Emma, too. We made a winnin' team." He closed his eyes and drifted away on the whiskey. Opening them again: "Say, where'd my Emma go off to now? Diggin' in her garden probably."

Will and Merry traded worried looks. They sat at Buck's bedside until the FBI agents arrived, two blank-faced men with business school haircuts. Too tired for more theatrics and with Will standing alongside, Buck gave them a straightforward version of what had happened.

When they left, Will said, "It's going to be sunny tomorrow, Buck."

His saggy face brightened. "How about we put on layers and go out and listen to the mournin' doves? You know how much I love hearin' them sing in the mornin'. Them cute little critters, I hope it ain't too cold for 'em."

Will leaned down and kissed his forehead. "I can't wait, Buck."

CHAPTER FOURTEEN

Levi said he'd return at seven the next morning to cook breakfast. He walked in the door exactly on time, emptied a sack of groceries, and got to work. He didn't knock or call out a greeting and didn't need to. The rattling of the pans was the only announcement required.

It was a morning for visitors.

Harley Jones came, looking better than he had the night of the dance. Tall, more bone than meat, he had sandy-blond hair and a long neck, and his blue eyes looked unusually sharp against sunbaked skin. He'd let his beard grow and the result was stringy and unkempt.

He tossed his Gus onto the steer horns on the wall by the door, nodded proudly at his success on the first try, and sat at the table sipping coffee.

Lucy walked down from her bunkhouse in the upper canyon wearing her sidearm under a fringed buckskin jacket that she claimed had been owned by a packer for George Armstrong Custer. They all knew that wasn't true but pretended otherwise to avoid a conflagration.

Sweetie Taylor from the feed store came right after Lucy. The Taylors were the closest thing to royalty that southern Arizona could claim. Ebin Thomas Taylor, born in Limerick, Ireland, arrived as a cavalry lieutenant in 1856, the first of the clan to set foot on American soil.

With the Chiricahua Apache in firm control, it was a bloody time. But Ebin survived several lethal skirmishes and stayed on after his enlistment to establish a ranch, from which he sold hay to the government at Fort Crittenden.

His remains and those of his ancestors, and the stone remains of the fort, lay in the grass outside Patagonia.

"Hope I'm not intruding," Sweetie said.

"Not intruding at all," Levi said, and happily set a fifth place.

"I got my antenna out, Sheriff. Anything turns up on them shooters, I'll let you know first thing. Count on it."

Nothing happened in the county without Sweetie hearing of it at the store. She was lanky, all limbs, and had snow-white hair cut in a bowl. She was built like a man and wore a baggy blue work shirt. She said hello to Buck in his bedroom, came back and scraped her chair up to the table, and grabbed a fork like it was trying to get away.

"Don't this look scrumptious," she said.

At first it didn't feel right to have a gathering, an impromptu party, three mornings after Buck's wounding. But with each person who came the sentiment in the kitchen shifted. It became a way of being together against the enemy each of them faced daily, the smugglers, the violent advance team of a multibillion-dollar international business.

They all lived on a modern frontier, on the bull's-eye between Americans who wanted drugs and would pay anything for them, and the cartels that fed them. That fact defined their lives, dictated the course of their days, and it was in the room with them that morning more than ever.

The day was especially difficult for Will. He felt sick about his deal with Marcelino. Not even Lucy or Levi knew, and he dreaded the eventual telling. The agreement led directly to what had happened, and for that reason he steered the conversation away from Rebel Canyon.

Happily, no one else wanted to talk about it either, so they engaged in pleasant morning chatter instead.

The *chug-click, chug-click* of a diesel truck announced a new arrival. Based on the sound alone, Sweetie knew who it was.

"There's our mystery man now," she said and kept eating.

Cuco Muñoz stepped inside, said *"Buenos días,"* made no eye contact with anyone, filled his thermos with coffee, grabbed a muffin, and without another word, went back out to work on Will's windmill.

Days before, Will had mentioned to Elena, the postal clerk, that his windmill needed work. Elena told Sweetie at the store, who sent it out on her all-purpose, never-fail, lightning-fast, occasionally juicy underground chat network, and that meant Cuco knew within an hour at most.

As well-known as he was around Patagonia, Cuco's previous life in Mexico was the subject of much speculation, including his split with Marcelino. The scar on Cuco's neck added credence to the theory of bad trouble, as did the scout knife he carried under his belt.

One story said he'd used the knife to lethal effect in Caborca, Sonora, prior to leaving Mexico, and that explained why he could never return, at least on the roads or through the ports of entry.

On his frequent trips back to Mexico, he always went alone and over mountain trails. No one knew his purpose and Cuco wouldn't say. He came from a world where talking could get you "disappeared."

All anybody knew for sure was that Cuco Muñoz grew up as a vaquero in the old Sonoran tradition, and when a neighbor needed help, he came. Nobody could outwork him. He never tired, never stopped moving, and never slept more than two nights in the same place.

He was the best windmill man in the county.

After breakfast, with the visitors gone and Merry staying behind to watch Buck, Will and Lucy rode out to check the trails near the house. For the first time in weeks, the Canyon Trail showed no evidence of a morning crossing, but one canyon over, on the Peck Trail, they found fresh tracks.

"Buck gets shot and all they do is move a mile east," Lucy said.

All Will could think was that there wasn't supposed to be traffic on any of the trails across the Flying Z, except at Zaragoza, and that made him feel foolish all over again for believing Marcelino would keep his word.

As they patrolled, he considered telling Lucy about it. But he knew she'd react badly, and rather than endure the inevitable scene, he put it off for another time.

The next day they checked the same trails with the same result.

On returning to the ranch, having just come off Morales Road and started down the spur, they saw a white GMC Yukon Denali parked beside Will's Silverado. A blond woman stood beside it. Although he'd never met her, the city clothes and the $85,000 truck told Will it was the lawyer Stacy Queen.

Bud Tisdale's red Dodge Ram was there, too, and he and Boone Macklin were standing nose to nose trading angry words. By the time Will had dismounted, they were grappling in the dirt, and Tisdale was taking a thumping.

Will wrapped his arms around Macklin's neck and dragged him away. Tisdale scrambled to his feet and was ready for more, but Lucy held him back. Leaning against her Yukon, arms crossed, Stacy Queen stood by, untroubled, as if she were at a Saturday picnic.

Macklin continued trying to get past Will, his eyes fixed on Tisdale. Merry had stepped outside and was helping Lucy control him. Only after they hustled him into the kitchen and shut the door did Will let Macklin go.

"Don't ever put your hands on me again," Macklin said.

"Pull yourself together, Boone," Will said. "You're acting like a butthead."

He stepped close to Will, eyes hot. "I repeat, never touch me again, Zachary."

Stacy Queen said, "Boone, that's enough. Step back by the truck."

Macklin acted as if he hadn't heard her and continued glaring at Will.

"Boone," she said with more authority. "This isn't how we do business. I'm telling you to step back." Reluctantly, he did as ordered.

"I apologize for my investigator," Queen said. "He handles difficult men for me and sometimes has trouble finding the right gear."

Queen looked to be in her late thirties. She was pretty in a too-much-makeup way. She had smooth white skin, thick dark eyeliner, and pink lipstick, and her hair was back in a ponytail. She carried too much weight for tight jeans. She wore pointy-toed boots and walked in them the way city people do, like she was balancing on a high wire without a net.

"I thought it was time we talked," she said.

"Folks usually call first," Will said.

"I was told you don't have a phone."

"That's right."

Queen gave Will a wide smile but her eyes stayed icy. "I've left messages for you with Sheriff Johnson, but I guess you didn't get them."

"What is it you want?"

"I've been in the area looking at property and heard about the trouble with your uncle. Such a dangerous place to work." She pointed at the front door. "Are you going to invite me inside, Mr. Zachary?"

"Nope."

"I came in person to let you know I'm ready to make an offer."

"Buck's hardly quit bleeding and here you are."

She nodded in unspoken apology. "I admit my timing isn't perfect. But I'm heading home to Tucson this morning, and it's an hour's drive to come back down this way."

"We have nothing to talk about."

"Your place here, it's going to get harder and harder to work being down a man. There's bills to pay, taxes to pay. Running a ranch is one bill after another, am I right?" Queen rocked her head. "I might have a solution for you."

Macklin had been fuming nearby. "Is that your wreck, Zachary?" He pointed to Will's Silverado. "Even if I couldn't pay my bills, I wouldn't drive a wreck like that. Looks like hard times on the old spread."

The truck had body rust, a bent rear fender, and dirt caked over the sides. It didn't look like much next to the Yukon and Tisdale's new truck.

Queen jotted on a business card squeezed into her palm.

"This might not be the best way to do it, but it's looking like the only way I can put a number in front of you." She handed Will the card. "That's a cash offer and a good one. Say the word and you can have the money in your hands in a matter of days."

Will took the card. Without looking at, he said, "Tell me what you know about Rebel Canyon."

Queen looked puzzled. "You mean the shooting? I'm sorry, Mr. Zachary. You must be unclear what it is I do for a living. I don't know anything about the shooting."

"Got a pretty good idea what you do."

"I'm a lawyer. I defend people at the worst time in their lives."

"You represent sleazeball dopers. You take piles of money to get 'em off and use it to buy up land to put them back in business."

"Everyone deserves an appropriate defense."

"Does your business include Marcelino?"

Queen's half smile couldn't have been emptier. "I might be able to answer your question if I had any ties to the Mexican underworld. But I don't. And for the record, I want to say that I'm sorry about your uncle."

That made Will mad. Without looking at the card, he ripped it in half and pressed the pieces into Queen's hand. "Don't come around here again."

"Hey, whoa there," Macklin said. "That's no way to talk to a lady. She come here to see you all polite and you talk that way."

"There's no words could come out of you I want to hear, rooster," Will said.

Stiff-necked and scowling, Macklin stepped aggressively toward Will. Queen gave him a withering look and said, "Boone." When he didn't stand down: "Boone! I'm talking to you."

Macklin kept on glaring at Will. Pointing, he said, "You and me, Zachary. It's coming and I can't wait."

Turning back to Will, Queen said, "Perhaps we can do business at a better time. I'm sure we can come to an agreement. I'll say good afternoon and leave you to your day, Mr. Zachary."

Will watched the Yukon travel up the spur. When it was out of sight he went inside. Tisdale was sitting at the kitchen table. He had a bloody lip and his shirt was torn.

"Sorry, Will," he said. "Lost my goldarn temper."

"You were fixing to lose more than that. What were you two beefing about?"

"He was going on about Buck Zachary getting what was coming to him. I couldn't abide him talking that way at Buck's own house."

"If I'd known that, he wouldn't have left here standing up."

Tisdale dabbed his split lip with a napkin. "Anyways, I had time and thought I'd give the old wrangler a holler. Brought some of my jerky for him." He dropped a plastic bag of it on the table.

"Buck's gone back to sleep, Bud," Merry said, and put a cup of coffee in front of him. "Let me get you ice for that lip."

"Thank you truly, young lady." Tisdale drank his coffee. He wanted to talk about what had happened in Rebel Canyon. He asked Will if he had noticed much traffic there prior to the incident, and how Border Patrol might respond.

"It ought to be simple enough," he said. "Put agents in that canyon and stop it quick. Have you talked to Border Patrol, Will?"

"The sector chief came by," Will said. "They're promising to put a team in Rebel to shut it down and see where the traffic moves from there."

"Any idea where that'll be?"

"How would I know?" Will wanted to get off the topic. "Wherever Border Patrol ain't. You know how it works."

"I hear that." Merry handed Tisdale a washcloth with ice rolled up inside. He alternated between sipping his coffee and dabbing his lip. "What about Marcelino? Border Patrol give you any read on the big man?"

"You ask a lot of questions, Bud."

"That's because I'm in the lion's mouth next few days. Doing well work for Macho Tapia down at the Double R. He gives me a couple of days on, a couple off." Tisdale shrugged. "Gives me the chance to make a little scratch."

Tapia was Will's second neighbor to the west. His ranch house sat a hundred yards north of the line and drew heavy cross-border traffic.

"Keep your skin on tight," Will said.

"I get wind of anything, I'll let you know. Gotta get moving." He checked his watch, tapping the crystal. "No wonder I'm always late. Darn thing keeps quitting on me." He slapped his palms down on the table and stood.

Merry said, "Take the ice with you, Bud. You're going to have bruising there."

"Thanks. Tell ol' Buck I was asking after him. Sure hope he's gonna be okay."

"The way things look now, he'll be fine," Will said.

"By God, it was only one bullet." Tisdale let out a growly laugh. "That old bellyacher."

CHAPTER FIFTEEN

Buck rebounded that night and insisted on getting up and moving. Will walked the floor with him, but he weakened quickly. They managed a couple of turns before he had to stop. Merry administered another round of pills, and Buck was back under the covers.

Over his growling snores, Will and Merry talked over what to do next.

Will understood that the episode in Rebel Canyon had only made the target on Buck bigger. Killing one of Marcelino's men couldn't be tolerated. The only possible way out was to make sure Marcelino knew that Buck had acted in self-defense.

That might dampen his desire for revenge. It wasn't much, but it was the best that Will had to work with.

Merry thought a return to Nogales, Sonora, too risky. "Are you forgetting, Will? You're the one Salazar was trying to kill out there."

"But he missed and Buck didn't."

Will had another goal in mind, and that was finding out if Marcelino and Queen were working together. It made good business sense. If Queen owned the Flying Z on the north, and Marcelino controlled the traffic immediately to the south, they could print money.

By sunrise, Will had decided that he had to try. He told Merry, "Stay close to Lucy and Hector and do what they say."

❖ ❖ ❖

Will arrived in downtown Nogales just after 8 a.m. He parked on the Arizona side and walked across the border and down three blocks to the Gran Hermano Hotel. The elegant lobby had a cherry-wood check-in desk, a copper-plate ceiling, and a winding marble staircase up to a first-floor dining room with big chandeliers and white tablecloths.

The cattlemen of Sonora gathered there each morning. That it was also Marcelino's place meant he'd gained control of the trails across their land, bossed the entire *plaza*, and now the cattlemen smiled and drank coffee with Marcelino's lieutenants because they were partners, whether they wanted to be or not.

The loud voices echoing across the dining room stopped when Will walked in. Word of the Salazar shooting had crossed the border. Nogales, Arizona, and Nogales, Sonora, are different countries, but the same neighborhood.

He stood by the entrance waiting for a table. The maître d' wore a red vest and looked like one of the munchkins from *The Wizard of Oz*. He scooted around the room doing his best to ignore Will.

When a table cleared, Will raced to it and sat while the busboys were still working. He spread out three $20 bills and waited. It didn't take long for Munchkin to catch the scent, and when he motored by and reached for the bills, Will snatched them away and handed him a note.

"See that Marcelino gets this."

The note disappeared between the buttons of Munchkin's red vest. Will handed him the bills. "You get double when I hear back from him."

Will drank coffee and waited. An hour later, Munchkin handed him a paper with the number fifty-three written on it. By the time Will had reached the elevator, men were walking at each shoulder with another behind him. As the elevator doors closed, they pushed his palms against the wall and searched him for weapons.

The fifth-floor room had been cleared of furniture except for a bare table with a chair on each side. Sunlight leaked in around the curtains, but otherwise the light was low. Bodyguards stood at each end of the table. Marcelino sat behind it facing the door, Will opposite him.

"I must know," Marcelino said, "how is Cuco?"

"He's well."

"I'm glad. We miss him. Dear Cuco." He put his palms flat on the table. "You seem to think we have more business."

Marcelino was in his early thirties and good-looking enough to be an actor or soccer star. He had short black hair perfectly trimmed, a straight-razor goatee, and he wore a blue jogging jacket open at the neck.

At his hip sat a panting bulldog with a mashed-in black snout and two stiletto teeth jutting up from either side of an oversized bottom jaw.

Will said, "I want you to know that my uncle killed Salazar because he had to. Salazar shot first."

Marcelino looked Will over as if he were unfamiliar with the species, seeing his kind for the first time. He tilted his head one way and the other. Rumor had it that Marcelino had eye problems, and his vision was limited.

He gave Will a long look in the low light. Satisfied, he waved his bodyguards away. They stood with their backs to the window, hands clasped in front of them.

"After what happened, it's brave of you to come here, Señor Zachary."

Marcelino's eyes stayed on Will as he petted the dog's head. The animal yawned. The opening and closing of its mouth sounded like someone pulling a boot out of the mud. "Am I supposed to forgive you for burning my property?"

"Regret doesn't suit me," Will said. "That's not why I'm here."

Marcelino didn't expect that. He stared, waiting.

"Salazar didn't belong in my cemetery," Will said. "He was trampling it. His men were trampling it and had been for a while. There was trash all over and they were using other trails across my place, too."

"Are you saying I broke my word?"

"Certain promises were made."

Marcelino's mouth got thin and angry. "For that, for trash, Salazar is shot down, murdered?"

"What happened in Rebel Canyon was no murder. Salazar tried to kill me and Buck shot him to save my life."

"So you are here—why? To beg me for a second time to spare your uncle?"

"I don't beg."

Marcelino's eyebrows rose in surprised admiration at Will's boldness. "I speak to many men who beg and they bore me. Go on."

"The kind of man you are, you would've done the same thing to defend your family. Wash your hands of this. Buck Zachary doesn't have much time."

"You want to go back to where we started? Impossible. Nothing is the same. Your uncle has a bill to pay."

"God will mark the ledger when the time comes," Will said.

Marcelino's catlike stare returned. This time the target wasn't Will, but his silver belly cowboy hat, upside down on the table in front of him. He waved to one of his men to open the curtains. With the light flooding in, Marcelino's eyes fixed on the hat's inside brim.

Underneath it was a prayer card depicting the Virgin of Guadalupe, the patron saint of Mexico. As he stared, Marcelino's face softened. He closed his eyes and spoke in a whisper: "For every beast of the forest is mine."

"And the cattle on a thousand hills."

"Psalm fifty." Marcelino nodded reverently. "You read the Bible, Mr. Zachary?"

"I do."

"I'm impressed. There are so few of us in these difficult times. A shame, isn't it?" In the space of a minute, he'd gone from menacing cartel boss to a preacher mourning the passing of devotion.

"I want my uncle to die naturally on the land of his birth," Will said. "If that happens, I could think about selling to Stacy Queen."

That was a lie, and Will practically choked on the words. But he wanted to say Queen's name to see if it drew a readable reaction. There was none. If Queen meant anything to Marcelino, he didn't show it.

"My preference is a trade," Marcelino said. "Salazar's life for your uncle's. But since you showed courage in coming here and didn't bore me, I will think about your proposal."

Marcelino waved his hand in a motion of dismissal. Will pushed his chair back and stood up to leave. He put his hat on and walked to the door.

"Señor Zachary," Marcelino called. "I've completed my deliberations and decided you are right, I would do the same for my family. Do you know who Salazar was?"

"No idea," Will said.

"My nephew."

The shock hit Will like a punch.

"My sister cries for Vicente all day," Marcelino said. "He was twenty, a wonderful boy, but he could not be controlled. Vicente wanted revenge for the burning of my property. I would not have approved. But he had courage and you are lucky to be alive, my friend. Now you come here and tell me his mother gets nothing in return for his death? Is that what you suggest?"

Standing in the doorway, Will said, "It sounds like we read different Bibles. Mercy is no stranger in mine."

Marcelino's jaw clenched. The veins in his neck bulged. "My sister understands nothing of your mercy. She is heartbroken, and she asks me, 'Brother, how will you right this terrible wrong?' She loved Vincente with all her heart, in the same way you love your uncle, but because of your uncle she only has his memory."

The ugly dog yawned again, an elaborate exercise that produced hanging spit trails and ended with the loud clacking of teeth.

"So, it is up to you whether your uncle lives or dies," Marcelino said. "Can you protect him until his last day? If so, your uncle lives. If not, I will soak the ground in his blood. That, my friend, is the only deal we make here today."

The words stole the air from Will's lungs. To his face Marcelino had threatened Buck again, turned his life or death into a contest. Will imagined going over the table at him. Straddling him, grabbing him by the shoulders and banging his head against the floor over and over. Any other man in the world and he'd have had him on his back.

But he wouldn't have made it out of that room alive.

As soon as Will walked outside, three of Marcelino's men began following him. They walked close behind mumbling taunts under their breath. Will wanted to turn on them and start something. He wanted to tell them his name, shout it in their faces so they'd never forget.

Hard as it was, he resisted, telling himself he had to be smart.

They trailed him all the way to the border, calling out to him even after he'd crossed into Arizona.

Back at the Flying Z, Will found Merry sitting on the porch. She stood when he pulled up. "Been waiting for you," she said.

"It was only a few hours. I hurried back."

"With Buck sleeping and you off seeing that monster, it was lonely around here."

"You could've talked to Lucy."

"There's an idea. What would we talk about?"

"She's smart once you get past the bad mood."

She held up a tattered copy of *Shane*. "Been reading this. Went all the way through to the end and I'm starting again on the first chapter."

"Great, isn't it?"

"*Shane* is the first fiction I've read in ages by somebody who didn't live in Brooklyn." She fanned the pages. "You know, I think I'm in love with this mysterious Shane fellow. He's quite the renegade."

Will didn't respond.

"He reminds me of somebody," Merry went on.

Again, Will let the remark pass. He walked toward her. She could see by his face that his mind was far away, and said, "Are you going to tell me what happened in Nogales or do I have to guess?"

"Let's go inside. I'm hungry."

In the kitchen, Will fixed two plates of cold chicken. He poured iced tea for Merry and got a bottle of beer for himself. He'd decided to tell her everything. Since Rebel Canyon, she'd been unable to close her eyes to sleep without seeing Salazar and the shooting all over again.

As much as he didn't want to make things worse for her, she needed to know. They talked across the kitchen table.

"I can't tell if Marcelino's hooked in with Stacy Queen," Will said. "But if he has a shot at Buck, he'll take it. He told me that to my face."

"My God, not again. Why can't he just let it go? What're you going to do?"

"Same thing we've been doing. Make sure Buck never leaves our sight. Harley, Lucy, and Hector can help with that."

"And me. Don't forget me."

Something had nagged at Will on the drive back and he wanted to bring it up. But he struggled to begin. There was a long silence. He thought more about what he wanted to say, then jumped in.

"Look, I don't want you to misunderstand what I'm telling you, Merry. I want you here with me. I want you at the Flying Z."

She reached across the table and touched his hand.

"But with what's coming our way, I can't ask you to stay on."

The surprise left Merry staring, open-mouthed.

"You can still get to Stanford before the semester starts."

"I can't believe what I'm hearing."

"I have no idea how this is going to play out."

"With you and me together, here." She looked shocked and confused. "Go to California now? What about Buck? He needs me. Am I supposed to leave and wait for a call that something bad has happened to him? He saved my life in that canyon. And who looks after you if I'm in California?"

"I look after myself, like before."

"Oh, Will, don't you understand? Stanford is gone. I've stopped thinking about it even, and do you know what? I don't care. It was a long time ago and a different time." She shook her head stubbornly. "No, I'm staying right where I am."

She marched around the table, took his face in her hands, kissed him on the mouth, and sat down again, as if done with the topic.

But Will kept going. "I saw your reaction when Buck was talking about shooting those smugglers."

She waved him off. "That was the dementia talking."

"His mind was clear as a stream."

Shocked, Merry said, "You're telling me Buck really wanted to shoot those men?"

"Yes."

"Okay, now I'm upset. Buck? Seriously?"

"'Want' has nothing to do with it."

"Sorry, Will, but you're going to have to explain that to me."

He drained his beer and put the bottle down and began speaking slowly. "Buck has always said that with each man born into this family there's a killing born with him. And it hunts you down. And sooner or later, at some time in your life, it'll find you. Buck's an old man and it finally found him. His prophecy came true. That's what he was talking about."

"That's so dark, so Shakespearean. Like the fates are closing in and there's nothing you can do about it. You don't believe that."

"I believe in this ranch. I believe in these mountains." Will shrugged. "I believe in our lives here and what we've worked hard to build. I don't believe in making trouble for people and expect the same in return."

Staring, Merry's face became intense. "But what Buck said about you being just like him and wanting to shoot those men, like they were elk or something. That's not part of what you believe, is it?"

Will stared at his empty beer bottle.

"You're supposed to say no, Will. But I get it. Because of where you live, sometimes you get into these situations you can't avoid. I understand this is a complicated place."

"Actually, Merry, it's simple. Do whatever it takes and don't be sentimental. If you want to survive on this border, it's a mistake to be sentimental about anything or anybody."

"This from the most sentimental man I've ever met." She smiled, expecting Will to do the same, expecting some recognition that Buck's time, and the frontier itself, had long passed.

But he just stared blankly across the table.

Seeing no room for agreement, Merry gave up and said, "No sentiment." Then she nodded absently and looked away. "I'll remember that. Not one inch of sentiment."

CHAPTER SIXTEEN

Levi came to the Flying Z to make breakfast every morning that week, arriving at the same time each day. He had a big block head and his hair in a crew cut, the lines of it looking like they'd been carved into his skull. He was an immaculate dresser—no one had ever found a spot of dirt on Levi's clothes—and his habits were written on rock.

On Sundays, he went to an 8 a.m. church service, then drove to the shooting range to take target practice. That was his relaxation. He fired the same number of rounds each time. After shooting, Levi had his Tahoe washed and detailed, and in the afternoon, he cooked.

Cooking was Levi's passion. He often came to public events wearing his splendid white Stetson and carrying one of his Sunday casseroles. Voters loved his dishes and loved him, often remarking that he should've been a minister.

At thirty, he was the youngest man ever elected county sheriff.

Doc Gonzáles had practically become a tenant at the Flying Z. He'd turned the living room into his private quarters, sleeping in Will's easy chair by the fireplace. He was present for those breakfasts, too, as were Merry and Lucy.

Harley had begun taking his meals at the ranch. He accepted whatever wages Will could pay, and sometimes that was nothing. He parked his truck beside the corrals overnight and slept in the flatbed.

Buck's condition improved to where he was able to move around on his own, but his mind stayed shaky. Merry shadowed him in daylight and sat in the bedside rocker at night, and Doc Gonzáles shadowed them both.

His long-term prognosis for Buck wasn't good. Even before the shooting, Doc had tried to convince Will to move Buck into a care home, and his injuries at Rebel Canyon had made the issue more pressing.

Doc waited until they could talk alone and found Will at the corral brushing Lobo. Will saw him approaching and guessed the topic.

"The answer is still no," he said.

Doc frowned behind his white mustache. "Hear me out. I'm familiar with these facilities and they're excellent."

"I won't do it. Buck wants to die right here at the Flying Z."

Out beyond the canyon, a Border Patrol agent stood next to his truck scanning the mountains with binoculars. Another Border Patrol truck sped along Morales Road.

"La Migra likes you today," Doc said.

"I don't even have to look. Border Patrol trucks all rattle the same way."

"I'll bet there's been a lot of agents around here since Salazar."

"They're doing their best to help us, but it won't last. Something will happen someplace else and they'll have to leave."

"They're outnumbered."

"That's it right there."

Doc rubbed his hand gently along Lobo's back. He explained that Buck would continue to recover physically and might be as strong as before Rebel Canyon. But his mind would lapse into confusion more often, the bad days outnumbering the good, his episodes becoming more frequent and severe.

"I can suggest less expensive homes in Sonora," Doc said.

LEO W. BANKS

"Leaving here will kill him quick," Will said. "Besides, if Marcelino finds out he's in Mexico, he won't last a day."

"Okay, then Tucson."

"You don't think Marcelino's people can get to him in Tucson?"

"He needs specialized care that he can't get here."

"Do they have *curanderas* at those places?"

Doc rolled his eyes. "You've got to talk him down from that. I've tried and he won't listen. I can't deny a psychological benefit for believers, but he needs modern medical care."

"Buck and modern medicine, I'm afraid those words don't go together. I got too much respect to talk him out of what he believes."

"This is his life."

"No, Henry. It's his death. It's a gift knowing where you want to take your last breath."

Doc knew that Will was unmovable on the topic and left it there. But he had more on his mind and switched to Spanish, as he did when he wanted to get the words right. "I know this isn't my business and Merry isn't my patient."

"Doc, you brought me into this world. Speak your mind."

"Merry is a marvelous young lady. She's strong, surprisingly so. I admire her very much. But she's too connected emotionally to Gibson." Buck's given name was Gibson Franklin Roosevelt Zachary.

Will explained about Merry leaving home just before her grandpa Cornelius had died, and her guilt at not being there. She didn't want to do the same with Buck. Doc nodded in understanding and continued.

"She's taking on all his stress as her own. She needs relief. She saw a terrible thing in that canyon."

"What do you suggest?"

106

"You're having a problem with that wild bull."

A bull had been coming across the border through a fence cut. Will and Hector had pushed him back several times, but the smugglers kept cutting the fence and the bull kept crossing. The animal had gotten to the heifers they'd sorted for replacements and bred with them before they were a year old.

"You bet we have a problem," Will said. "Some of them are bagged up so tight they could start calving any day."

"Working first-calf heifers is a round-the-clock job. As soon as they start springing, you'll need extra hands, won't you, Will?"

He knew what Doc had in mind. "Merry working my heifers?"

"She wants to be a ranch woman. How about letting her be one? Lucy's in charge of the heifers, right?"

"Nobody I trust more. She's got them penned up at the Horseshoe."

"If Merry can stand getting blood on her hands, I'd say she has what it takes to stay on," Doc said. "It'll be a good test for her."

The plan gave Lucy indigestion. "Miss Mustang's gonna help midwife my calves? Now I've heard it all."

"She needs something to do that isn't worrying about Buck," Will said.

"Get her a library card."

"She's tougher than you think."

"If she breaks a nail, what then? You thought about that?" Lucy laughed, a screeching cry that sounded like a billy goat stuck under a gate.

CHAPTER SEVENTEEN

The road to the Horseshoe started behind Will's barn and curled up the hill to a horseshoe-shaped canyon. Lucy lived there in a long-abandoned, flat-roofed stone bunkhouse with five rooms set in a row.

Two of them no longer had doors, and busted furniture was visible inside. On two others, the doors were hanging loose on their hinges. The only working door led into Lucy's room. She had a bed and a table and candles for lighting. She hauled water for drinking and washing. An outhouse stood beside the bunkhouse and it didn't have a door either.

Within the horseshoe itself was a corral and squeeze chute, and three calving pens inside rail fences. The pens had tin roofs, open sides, and wood floors covered with hay. The job was to monitor the heifers and wait for them to begin calving.

The ones that were bred by that bull were bound for trouble. His calves could weigh a hundred pounds hitting the ground and split the heifers in half. Without help, they could lose any number of them.

Lucy made a delivery the first day. The heifer had fallen down in the struggle, and Lucy got her standing again and pushed her into the corral. The heifer kept falling under the weight of her heavy load, and each time Lucy stood her up again.

After an hour, when it became clear the heifer wouldn't be able to drop the calf herself, Lucy pushed her into the squeeze chute and reached inside her to see if the calf's parts were turned the right way.

The easier method was to attach chains to the calf's legs and use a calf jack to pull it out. But Lucy wanted to make Merry's training as grisly as she could.

The heifer didn't take to Lucy's intrusion and banged against the rails. She tried to raise her hind legs to kick Lucy, but she was too heavy, and the chute didn't leave enough room.

"Is he turned right?" Will said.

Lucy had on a white sweatshirt stained with red paint and her snow-white hair up in a messy bun that accentuated her bloodless face. She plunged her arm in up to her elbow. "Can't tell yet, William."

As she reached in, she looked back at Merry. "You ain't squeamish, are you, girl?"

Merry wore one of Emma's old shirts. None of her Stanford clothes were fit for ranch work. With Buck's blessing, she'd taken over Emma's wardrobe.

"Not a bit," Merry said. Her face was a sickly gray, but pride wouldn't let her turn away.

"You gotta have nerve to do this here work." Lucy stayed put with her hand inside the animal, her face scrunched up and her tongue sticking out. "The trick is to feel for the two front feet and the nose."

When it happened, it happened quickly. Lucy gripped the hoofs and pulled and the calf came sliding out, slick as a seal. Lucy jumped back and shook her hand to clear it of blood and discharge. The calf lay on its side, head raised, spying the world for the first time.

"Hello there, Silly Sally," Lucy said. "That'll be your name. That's what we'll call you, all right. Silly Sally."

The work at the corrals drew friends and neighbors. They came to watch and help and eat good food. Will had set up a table of tortillas, *carne asada*, rice, beans, salsa, chips, pitchers of lemonade and iced tea.

Bob Ashmont rolled up in his red Hummer. He helped where he could and was curious about everything, but mostly he served refreshments. Rudy, the bell ringer from Padre Pedro's Saloon, came with him. He followed at Ashmont's heels, repeating whatever he said, and at any excitement in the pens, Rudy exclaimed, "Whoopee!"

Cuco Muñoz never missed a moment and never got there later than 7 a.m. The only one to arrive earlier was Harley Jones. He came with the runaway teenager Lovesome Magdalena Bravo, daughter of Wiley Bravo.

Harley had whisked her away from her El Rancho Caballo home in a midnight horseback escape, and her father was said to be armed and on the hunt for her and Harley.

Lovesome had chubby cheeks and a toothy smile. She was long-legged, high-stepping, and spirited. At lunchtime, proudly declaring her allegiance to George Strait, the King, she played his songs on her cell phone and sang along in a loud voice.

Any mention of King George set Lucy off. In a passionate voice, she made known her preference for older-style country music.

As she made her case, Lucy became red-faced, and redder still because through all of Lucy's pleadings, Lovesome sang louder and louder. Harley, wearing his signature black Gus, couldn't stop staring at Lovesome, clearly enthralled.

Buck came, too, still bandaged, glad to be out of the house, but he tired easily and only stayed through the mornings. When it was time to go back, Will drove him down the road to the house, or sometimes Hector did, and when it was Hector, his orders were to not let Buck out of sight for any reason.

✤ ✤ ✤

Merry delivered her first calf on the third day. She led a heifer into one of the calving pens to give the mother time to drop the calf herself. She hadn't left the enclosure when that calf came into the world like a thunderclap, landing hard on the hay.

"There it is!" Merry cried. "My first one!"

But the calf didn't move or make a sound and wasn't breathing. Merry wrapped her arms around the newborn's midsection to stand it up. Lucy, Cuco, and Will and the others watched from behind the railing, arms resting on it.

Lucy barked, "That won't help! Not a tiny little bit!"

"I know horses, not cows!"

"Whoopee!" exclaimed Rudy.

Merry pulled the newborn off the ground, but the weight was too much and she had to let go. The rail oglers shouting advice only added to the noise and confusion. Merry pushed down on the calf's ribs, trying to get the breathing started manually.

"He ain't having a heart attack, girl!" Lucy hollered.

"Help me, for God's sake! He's not breathing!"

Lucy didn't move a finger. "Don't you remember what I told you?"

The mother cow reared angrily. Merry was in the line of attack. Lucy saw and jumped the railing, knocking the mother away with a swing of the hips. The animal went down on bent forelegs and, although weak, rose and stepped toward Lucy with mayhem in her eyes.

With her mouth wide open, she let out a high-pitched bawling as she plotted the defense of her young. Lucy nodded to Will, indicating she had the mother covered, and he bounded over the railing and handed Merry a strand of straw.

But Merry was still unsure what to do.

Lucy let out her cackling laugh and said, "That calf's only half alive, and if you don't hurry it up, he's gonna be all the way dead."

"The straw!" Will said.

Lucy used her hip to keep the mother cow back. "Don't help her," Lucy shouted. "She needs to do it herself."

Then Merry remembered. She leaned down and tickled the straw up the calf's nostril and it sneezed. That cleared its lungs and the calf began to breathe. His head came up off the hay, his big black eyes looking around. He sat up with his weight back on his rump and got his forelegs out in front, stiff and angled.

He straightened one of his hind legs, then the other, and fought to stand all the way up, all four legs trembling and shivering across his whole body.

The mother still fought to get around Lucy's hip. Lucy held on as long as she could, and yelled, "Here I come!" and sailed headfirst over the railing ahead of the chasing mother. Lucy yelped as she landed. Will grabbed Merry and they jumped the railing, too.

The excitement over, Lucy, breathless, bloody, happy, brushing hay from her clothes, said, "Let momma alone now. She'll mother him up good."

CHAPTER EIGHTEEN

With the work done, they went back to the house and Merry made hot dogs and beans for supper. Buck wanted to stay up. He settled in front of the fire in his reading chair under the saguaro-rib ceiling. Will sat in the chair beside him, Merry opposite.

All three sipped whiskeys, the bottle standing on the center table.

Filled with exhausted energy and soaring pride, Merry chattered about all she'd done that day. She'd saved a calf, helped bring a new life into the world. That mattered, and made her feel as if she mattered, too.

"You'll remember it forever, I guarantee," Buck said.

"Do you think Domingo was watching? Do you think he saw me?"

"I bet he did, uh-huh. Ain't much he don't see."

Merry loved the story of Domingo Opata. She loved it as folklore, a worthy legend. She didn't believe it the way Buck and Will did. That was too far to go. But with all the formerly unmovable parts of her life shifting and re-forming, she wanted to know more. She wanted to know the unrevealed secrets from their pancake breakfast.

She began slowly, gently pushing the topic along and hoping it all would spill out. She asked Buck when he'd first heard about Opata.

"I remember it plain as can be." He sipped his whiskey and smiled with all the warmth inside him. The fireplace and a massive maple bookcase covered the entire wall behind him.

"The whole story is as much Emma's as mine. She grew up with him at Rancho Dolores and so did the whole Carrillo family going back to, well, forever. He was part of their lives and part of the land, like the grass and the trees, all the way back to the Spanish days."

"Will says you started working at Dolores as a kid," Merry said.

"First rode up to that grand hacienda at fifteen, and there was Emma Carrillo on the porch looking right at me. She was sixteen and, by dern, I was a goner. An older woman!" He belly laughed. "Oh, we was in love the way teenagers get. Grabbed every chance we could to go off on our own. So we'd ride out looking for Domingo, his tracks, the cave he lived in, anything a-tall."

"It was a way of being alone," Merry said. "That's sweet, Buck."

"Neither of us had any idea what we might find, but it didn't matter. We knew he was out there and that belief was in Emma's heart and it got into mine. We rode all over, never tired, never knew what a bad day was. It was me and Emma and Domingo Opata and the land."

"And Kazoh," Merry said.

"Oh, she was a beauty. Like you, dear."

"Why, thank you. You talk like you've seen her, Buck."

"When a story's real, you see people clear. That's how come stories have so much power. I can see Domingo right now. What a horseman he was. Had to be, ridin' this wild country, makin' new trails lookin' for Kazoh."

"Will tells me lots of people around here know about Domingo."

"They talk like they do, but they's just repeatin' an old story they heard. They don't know him the way I do. I sat by the fire with him, many a time. Talked with him, too."

Merry sat quietly, surprised at such a claim.

"Even when he don't show himself, you know he's there by his sword banging against his saddle riggings," Buck said. "I've never been lost in all this country since I was a boy, and Domingo's the reason. Follow that clangin' sound and he'll lead you right where you're a-going."

"Has anyone checked Spanish archives for his name, I mean like a historian would?"

"You mean the spectacle people?" Buck flapped his lips in disgust. "They get owl-eyed and ask if I've been to the barrel. Tell me there's no record of him. That don't mean shucks. I know what I know. Will, too. Even though he's never seen Domingo, he knows if he needs him, why, he'll be there. Ain't that right, Will?"

"Yup, ever since I was a kid riding alone," Will said.

"All those times you rode up to the Split thinkin' I didn't know where you was a-goin'. Hell, I knew."

"I got back all on my own, Buck. I didn't need anybody's help."

"But if you did, Domingo would've been there. That's why I never worried and never came a-lookin'."

Talking about Opata made Buck feel good. It gave him energy, more than he'd had since his wounding, and he wanted to keep going.

"If you wanna know the truth about Domingo, Merry, I'll tell you about Golanta. That's where it really begins. See, when Domingo come to this country it was all new to him and he couldn't have survived without Golanta."

Will startled at the mention of that name, for Buck had walked right up to the door behind which lay all the beautiful and dangerous secrets of the Flying Z.

Golanta, the shaman boy!

Golanta, the key to it all!

Buck had told the story of Domingo and Golanta to only one person in his life, and only once, and that was Will when he was a boy. He'd held it close from the day his own father had handed it down to him.

Now Buck was ready. He looked at Will as if to seek permission.

But what Buck was really asking: Is it okay to let Merry inside? He was asking Will if he loved her. They'd had a wonderful day and it had become a consequential night, and now Will felt the weight of it as much as Buck.

He grabbed the whiskey bottle and poured three more drinks around and offered a toast.

"To Domingo Opata," Will said.

The glasses clicked, and they all three drank.

"Go ahead and tell her."

He loves her! Buck silently rejoiced. *By dern, he loves her!*

Thus freed, the long bonds severed, Buck told the story of Golanta and Domingo Opata.

Opata had fought so well and bravely, killing so many Spanish invaders, that when the Aztec cause was lost, the conquistadors tried to find him and kill him out of revenge. He escaped north and met Kazoh.

They rode together and camped together, fell to their knees and drank from the same waters together. She taught him about the land, how it was in different seasons, what the colors of the sky meant, how to hear the songs of the rain, and what the land taught those who knew how to listen.

She told him there was gold waiting under canyon walls and promised to take him to it. All the while the conquistadors kept after them, and one day, with the enemy close, riding hard, horses lathered and straining, Opata and Kazoh separated.

Opata hid until the conquistadors had given up and left. And when he was safe, he began his long search for Kazoh. For years he found nothing, until coming upon a group of Indians from Kazoh's band. Thinking they'd come to kill him, Opata drew his sword.

He was going to kill them first. But he saw that they were peaceful and didn't kill them.

They were five in number, three captives from a northern tribe and a lost white child with no eyes who couldn't find his way home. Their leader was a cripple, a shaman boy with a shriveled leg who used a crooked cedar crutch to walk.

He was called Golanta, and he could hobble through the toughest terrain as fast as anyone with two good legs and not make tracks. The chief of the band was afraid of Golanta. He thought the boy was a witch, so they left him and his followers alone.

But Golanta wasn't a witch, only wise.

On the day he encountered Opata, Golanta wore a yellow vest and a long-sleeved white shirt and a straw hat with a black band that looked like a derby sitting high on his head. Underneath was a red bandanna that covered his forehead right above the eyes, so Domingo couldn't see any hair, except that which hung against his back.

It was silver, like an old man's.

That was an important power Golanta had. He could make his face look old or young. He'd made himself look like a sweet boy for Opata, his face wide open, his eyes happy, so he wouldn't use his sword.

But Golanta kept his hair all white in back to give him the wisdom of age to ward off enemies coming from behind.

Golanta explained to Opata that they were friends of Kazoh's and that the chief, her father, was looking for her and would kill her if he found her rather than let her be with Opata.

The warriors were out looking for her and they were looking for Opata, too, and Golanta and his people had come to teach him how to survive until he found her. They taught him how to gather berries and fruit. They brought him a deerskin to sleep on and taught him how to build a shelter and a fire that couldn't be seen.

When his boots wore out, they brought him cowhide to make moccasins and leggings, and taught him to put sand and rocks in his moccasins to toughen his feet for long hunting trips. They taught him where to dig in the ground to find water, not the bitter kind that made you sick, but water that bubbled up from the underground springs and was sweet and gave strength to anyone who drank it.

They took Opata to an unknown mountain and showed him a cave where he could sleep cool in the summer and warm beside a fire in winter and safe from his enemies, with only peace in his dreams, because he was protected by the Way.

Golanta showed Domingo the paintings on the cave walls and said the stories they told constituted the Way. Golanta explained that these images had been there forever, before time, before the sun, before snow, and before the first cactus ever flowered in the spring.

And those pictographs were the teachings of the Way. They told the story of the world and its beginning, and the truths that the first people lived by, and if Domingo studied those stories and learned what they had to teach, he could survive to continue his search for Kazoh.

Golanta taught him how to ride without leaving tracks, taught him the prayers that the people had said since they'd emerged from the cave on the first day. He taught him how to summon help from the sun and the stars.

He taught him the language of the coyote and in return the coyotes would howl in warning when danger came near. Opata became friends with the coyotes, and they protected him and told him when the owl was scheming against him.

That is how Domingo had survived for so long to continue his quest.

When Buck had finished, his eyes were as bright and clear as they'd been in a long time, and his voice had regained its power. He nodded in contentment, awaiting Merry's declaration of shared belief.

"That's a beautiful legend, Buck. It really is."

"Legend?" The word stung him. "Domingo's as real as you and me. Kazoh, too."

Merry said nothing. But there was doubt all over her face.

Buck saw and said, "Emma and me, when we were on our rides, we found Opata's cave. I never told this to nobody outside of Will, but we found the cave and we found proof."

"Proof?" Merry managed only that word. Whatever additional words she had planned fell apart on her tongue.

"I'll show you, by dern." Bent over and grunting, Buck struggled to his feet and went to the bookshelves behind him. There were narrow vertical compartments on both ends. He opened the right-side compartment, took out a sword, and unsheathed it.

Merry put her hand over her mouth in gasping surprise. "Is—is this—?"

"It's Opata's sword," Buck said. "Emma and me took it from his cave. We didn't want to but didn't want nobody else taking it either. We left everything else right where it was. There was jewelry and strings of beads, Mexican saddles and blankets, all kinds of pots and silver goblets and a chest full of gold coins, amulets and fetishes, a leather satchel with all of Opata's possessions inside. It's all still there, a king's treasure."

Buck handed the sword to Merry. The blade was thin, three feet long, sharp on both sides, and finely pointed at the tip. It had a wrapped wire handle and floral patterns stamped into the steel by the hilt and the tip, and in between, written in an elaborate scroll, was the name Opata.

"I can't believe you have this," she said.

"You're holding something special, and nobody knows it's here," Buck said. "Nobody knows about Opata's cave. If it gets out, treasure hunters will swarm this place, and the feds will step in and make it into a monument with them rangers in their funny hats tellin' their lies. That's after they take your money and tell you where to park."

His face had reddened. He gave himself a moment to control his breathing. Feeling his anger ease, his voice soft, he said, "You see, Merry, the paintings of the Way will rewrite history. They'll tell the whole world a new story of life and time, and they can't have that."

"I'll never tell anyone, I promise."

Merry was hypnotized. Wary of even leaving fingerprints, she held the sword across her open palms as she would a sacred object. She never touched the handle and extended her arms to give it back, relieved that it was no longer in her care. He returned it to its compartment.

The closing of the narrow door put an end to the discussion, and with nothing more said of Opata, they all had another drink and another as the fire burned. When the alcohol had made Buck sleepy, Merry helped him into bed.

Returning to the living room, she stared into the fire, a look of amazement on her face.

"I feel completely different," she said. "Like I'm connected to a whole different way of thinking. It's powerful and so far away from everything I thought was true. I'm trying to understand, to think all this through."

"It falls apart if you think," Will said. "You have to just believe."

"I'll try that with my academic advisor." Merry made her voice sound important. "'I've decided not to think. There's nothing in it for me. No wisdom in thinking. No truth in thinking.'"

Bewildered, Will said, "You held Opata's sword and still don't believe?"

"I want to believe. But I've always lived in a world of scholarship, of hard evidence."

But the story of Opata and Golanta was about love, and love cannot be seen, touched, or analyzed. Love is beyond the evidence that Merry O'Hara lived by, and yet in her time at the Flying Z, she'd come to believe in it completely.

She sipped her whiskey and stared at the fire and thought, *I love Will Zachary, so yes, I will try to believe.*

CHAPTER NINETEEN

Merry delivered two more calves. She'd passed Doc's test. He was impressed. Lucy was impressed, too, but didn't like being wrong and hid it behind a sour expression that was, as Merry joked, like her regular expression.

With Buck improving rapidly, Artie Avila wanted to take him into Nogales for Fajita Friday at the VFW. Will thought it too risky and called Artie off. Hector stayed at the ranch with Buck while Lucy, Merry, Harley, and Will worked the heifers.

Early that afternoon, Hector flew up Horseshoe Road in his pickup. When he fishtailed to a skidding stop beside Lucy's corrals, the dust at his back overtook him, and he vanished behind the swirling cloud.

But his voice boomed all the way through it: "Buck's out! Will! Come quick, Buck got out!"

All work stopped. Will sprinted to the truck. Hector slid across the seat to let him drive. "You were supposed to watch him!" Will shouted. "Why didn't you watch him? How could you let this happen?"

"I watch him close. I turn around, that's all."

"You're not supposed to turn around."

"He's riding Slim and has the Winchester, Will. Buck has the rifle."

That conversation, shouted over the roar of the engine, took place during Will's breakneck ride down to the house, with

Merry and Lucy struggling to hang on in the flatbed. Working quickly, Will saddled Lobo, and Lucy saddled her horse.

Scattered across the floor of the barn, they found the burlap that Hector had collected at Zaragoza. Will had ordered him to dispose of it and wanted to know why it was still around. Hector said he'd stashed it in the trash bin and secured the lid.

"I meant burn it, get rid of it completely," Will said.

"Burn it? No, no."

"You should've burned it. It should've been gone a long time ago."

Seeing the burlap had been Buck's trigger. His mind exploded. Will heard Buck's voice in his head: *By dern, I won't let them drug men tromp over my Emma! If it's a fight they want, they'll have it!*

Will ordered Hector to stay behind to guard the ranch and watch over Merry. Lucy rode out first. Merry held Lobo steady. Will took his riding hat off the pommel and slapped the dust off against his thigh. He jammed his boot into the stirrup and legged up.

"Do not leave," he said to Merry. "Marcelino's making his move and that means his scouts might be watching. I want you here where it's safe."

Will looked past her to Hector standing on the porch and said, "Hector?" His stern tone conveyed a clear message—keep Merry safe. Hector signaled his agreement with a single up-and-down nod, though his eyes told of his disgrace.

Lucy pounded down the trail ahead of Will, the fringes on her buckskin coat flying, along with her long white hair. She looked like a ghost rider on the landscape. Will caught up with her and together they rode a hole through the wind all the way to the prominence above Zaragoza.

The day was gray under thick clouds. Will glassed the cemetery as Lucy's horse tossed his head and danced, eager to run again.

"No sign of him," he said.

"He definitely come this way," Lucy said as she studied the ground. She had excellent tracking eyes. They say the best trackers can see through the hills, and that was Lucy. "That's Slim's hoofprints for sure."

They rode down the hill with the bleak wind beating at them.

"You ever have a premonition?" Lucy said.

"If you got something to say, spit it out."

"There's a bunch of turkey buzzards circling down south a ways."

Will hadn't looked, but he knew they were there, for he'd caught the same scent of death in the air. "You don't need a premonition when it comes to vultures. They don't hide what their business is."

"You want me to go across alone?"

"Are you really asking me that?"

"Nothing I could ask would make this situation any better."

"Then don't ask it."

They pulled up at the cemetery's edge. Studying the ground, Lucy could see that Buck had been riding hard, as if on the chase. Will knew it, too, and knew that he had to follow him, and what he'd find. He knew it in his heart and in every other part of him.

He didn't pray or give in to hope, because he knew, and that knowledge was complete.

His urgency gone, Will dismounted and walked into the cemetery. He stopped beside the flat headstone of Buck's great-aunt, Alma Louise Romero. She'd lived from 1885 to 1889 and was known in the family as Baby Louise. She was gone before Buck's time and long before Will's, taken by the fever.

THE FLYING Z

But she was as much a part of the family as anyone, a prominent character in stories still told, as though all had known her
and loved her. Now her grave was covered with shards of glass
where someone had broken a beer bottle.

"Cleaning up won't change nothing, Will," Lucy said.

"See what they did? They poured beer on this baby girl."
Anger made his neck burn.

"They're sonsofbitches, all of them," Lucy said. "Downright
and no doubt. But there ain't nothing you can do for her now."

"I'll tell you what I can do. I can not leave her like this. I can
show her respect, that's what I can do." He picked up the glass
shards one at a time and put them in his pocket. He took his time
at Baby Louise's grave. He needed her then because he knew he
no longer had Buck.

With Will's cleanup complete and the breath torching out
of them in the bitter cold, they rode south on the smuggler trail
through a cut in the barbed-wire border fence into Mexico. Slim's
tracks showed that Buck had ridden along the creek into a grove
of willows that marked the beginning of Yaqui Canyon.

Knowing this place would be the end of his search, Will
jumped down and let go of the reins. With a hole in his gut, he
walked through the trees into the wider canyon, and there was
Buck, on his stomach, facedown in the grass, arms stretched out
in front of him.

He had been shot in the chest. The bullet had exited his back
and left a bloody starburst hole in his coat, between the shoulder
blades.

Will sat on his heels, but there was nothing to check. No
pulse, no life, only a cold corpse. Buck's pockets had been turned
inside out, and his keepsake watch was gone.

Feeling no shock, only a sickening calm, Will took Buck by
the shoulders and rolled him over and sat him up, He held him as

one would an infant, and spoke to him softly, his palm cradling the back of his head.

He told him he loved him and that he was sorry. He told him he didn't deserve it. Will held him tight against his coat so that Emma, looking down, couldn't see his face. In death it looked like a stone, like it had been a stone and nothing else for a thousand years.

Wings wide, the turkey buzzards swooped low, commanding the air, watching.

"You can help me now and I'd sure appreciate it," Will said.

Taking Buck by the shoulders and Lucy taking his legs, they lifted him off the ground and laid him facedown over Will's saddle. The buzzards screeched in anger at a planned feast gone awry. "I'd like to bring him home alone," Will said.

Lucy studied the ground for tracks leading south. "I'll warm up this trail here and be back soon." She looked at Will. "You okay?"

He didn't answer. There was nothing to say. She clicked her tongue and rode away.

Will reached the Flying Z at dusk. Merry had been waiting and worrying, and at the sound of a rider she hurried outside. She couldn't make out what she was seeing at first, only a shadow coming down the trail.

But the shape wasn't right for a horseman riding alone, and something told her it was going to be bad.

She ran toward the figure, still unsure, still hoping, until Lobo entered the glow of the fading sunlight. Seeing Will, and seconds later realizing that Buck was facedown across the saddle, Merry fell to her knees and filled Cabezas Canyon with a horrible wailing.

CHAPTER TWENTY

Will carried Buck's body inside and laid him down on his bed. Merry pulled a sheet up to his shoulders and folded his hands on his stomach. She worked deliberately and without comment, each passing second its own perfect agony.

Doc joined the vigil. He stood at the foot of his best friend's bed, heartbroken in the half darkness.

Sheriff's deputies, Border Patrol, and FBI agents swarmed the Flying Z. The county attorney and the coroner were there, too, along with two representatives of the Mexican federal police. They'd been in Phoenix at the time of the shooting and drove down to the Flying Z to help with the investigation.

They all made a silent procession into the bedroom and asked Will questions in solemn voices. With his hand resting on Buck's bedpost, FBI agent Hugo Suarez did most of the talking, saying he intended to lead a group of investigators to Yaqui Canyon.

Young and eager to impress, Suarez sometimes interrupted the Mexican policemen as they asked questions and tried to explain aspects of Mexican law.

When he couldn't stand it anymore, Will went outside and stood at the corral gate. Levi followed and they waited together shuffling their feet and not talking. Suarez stepped outside and walked straight for Will.

"I know this is a tough night, Mr. Zachary. But I need you to understand what's going to happen now."

He explained that the State Department in Washington was preparing a diplomatic note asking Mexico's interior minister for permission to allow FBI investigators into the country. The investigation would be a joint effort.

But at the moment the two parties were arguing over whether there should be legal consequences for Will's violation of sovereign Mexican territory when he crossed the border to retrieve the body.

"That's a crime you committed, and Mexico is considering prosecution."

"Is that a joke?" Levi said. His normally calm demeanor broke, and with his voice rising, he said, "Do they not get the irony there?"

Suarez held up his palms. "I've managed to talk them out of it for now." Looking directly at Will: "Our Mexican partners would have a better opportunity to solve this crime if you hadn't disturbed the scene."

Will nearly came out of his boots. "What did you just say?"

"As you know, Mr. Zachary, given the nature of that landscape, Border Patrol's cameras don't have eyes on Zaragoza and due south. It's out of their view shed so we're working blind. That makes the scene all the more important and the scene was contaminated. Evidence was compromised."

"I was supposed to leave my uncle there?! On the ground like an outlaw?!"

Neither man backed down, and there was a scuffle. Dirt got kicked up, but it didn't last long as Levi and others intervened.

When Lucy returned from her scout, she told investigators that she'd found nothing. They talked to Harley, too, and he said he knew nothing of what had happened between Hector and Buck, either that day or any other time, and he knew nothing of Hector's whereabouts.

Hector had ignored Will's order to stay at the ranch, and in a fever, talking rapidly and reeking of whiskey, he'd ridden away from the Flying Z saying he was headed to Zaragoza to help Will. Hours after nightfall, Hector still hadn't returned.

First chance she got, Lucy pulled Will and Levi aside and announced that she knew who'd killed Buck. She'd found the sniper's perch on a hilltop just south of where the body lay and hoofprints leading south from there.

"It's Abrazo, Will," she said. "Abrazo's prints are all over that ground."

"Same ones we've been seeing at the Mogollon and the Canyon Trail? You're sure about that?"

"Sure as I can be."

They talked in low voices amid the hubbub around the house.

Addressing Levi, Lucy said, "I wasn't going to tell them badges nothing." She waved toward the men on the porch. "No offense, Sheriff, but I got no use."

Levi stood with his arms folded on his chest. He nodded solemnly.

"There's more," Lucy said, and motioned for them to move farther from the house. Whispering now: "Hector lied. I picked up his tracks before it got dark, and I can tell you for sure he didn't go nowhere near Zaragoza. He rode straight east on the De Anza Trail and disappeared. Adios, amigos."

"He's off on a spree," Will said. "It'll be like always. He'll come back and apologize, say it'll never happen again, and that'll be it."

"I believe your heart's talking louder than your brain," Levi said.

"Do you know something I don't?" Will said.

"I've gone over this in my mind a thousand ways," Levi said. "How could Buck get a saddle on Slim without Hector stopping him? Impossible. And I don't believe Buck found that burlap in the barn on his own. Way it looks to me, Hector used it to get Buck fired up."

No one spoke as they pondered that.

Levi continued: "Abrazo knew Buck would ride to Zaragoza and was waiting for him. Hector was working for Abrazo to set Buck up. Don't forget, he went looking for wildflowers just before you got to Rebel Canyon. He knew what was coming and didn't want to see it."

Will didn't believe a word of it and said so, and the matter stayed there as investigators worked through the night. The following day, Suarez returned with more questions, most centered on Hector's whereabouts. Even if Will had known, he wouldn't have told Suarez, while to Levi and Lucy he never wavered in his opinion that Hector was innocent.

Day after day, Will waited and watched for Hector's return, insisting the funeral couldn't happen without him. After five days he could wait no more, and Buck Zachary was buried at Zaragoza.

The coffin was placed in the bed of a four-wheel-drive truck and driven to within a mile of the cemetery. The road was too rough to go any farther. Artie Avila enlisted his old highway crew to carry the coffin on their shoulders the remainder of the way.

They also wheeled in a compressor and a jackhammer to dig a grave. It took a long time and great effort because of the hard ground. Three sheriff's deputies with rifles guarded the laborers as they worked.

The proceedings felt solemn and strange with everyone standing around watching the work in silence.

Lucy wore her Custer buckskin. Bob Ashmont wore a scorpion bola tie and wept like a boy. Levi stood alongside Doc, his face sunken to the bone. The only one of Buck's friends from

Mexico able to reach the site was Tampico Calderón, an old hand from Rancho Dolores.

He followed Buck's coffin on horseback, and when it came time to say goodbye, he tapped on it with his cane and spoke the greatest compliment he knew: "I never saw this man quit on a lost cow. He'd ride clear through the night until he found her."

Harley Jones wore a long tan coat and he'd slicked his hair with some kind of cream. He was badly hungover and so undone by grief that Lovesome Bravo had to hold him up. But when it came time to sing "Amazing Grace," Harley pressed his black Gus against his stomach and gave it all he had.

Merry wore white sunglasses and Emma's black felt hat. She had on brand-new Wranglers and a belt, Emma's favorite, decorated with silver and turquoise studs.

She and five of the men took hold of the coffin ropes and pulled them tight. They firmed their grips and set their feet, and at Will's signal they lowered Buck into the ground beside his beloved Emma Mendoza Carrillo Zachary.

His headstone was a large square of oak, the inscription elegantly carved in block letters: *Gibson Franklin Roosevelt Zachary. Loyal husband, father, friend, and cowboy. Still ridin'.*

CHAPTER TWENTY-ONE

After the service, Will hosted a reception at the ranch to accommodate friends unable to travel to Zaragoza. Buck's favorite cowboy songs and George Jones played on a loop in the kitchen while old stories were told and retold.

A former Arizona governor attended, as did an ex-senator, three sitting Arizona mayors and a famous Hollywood producer who'd befriended Buck during the filming of one of his movies at the Flying Z.

But most of the visitors were common Arizonans, and they came from all over—from the deserts around Yuma and the posh enclaves of Scottsdale and Paradise Valley. From the Tonto Basin country around Payson, from San Carlos, Fort Apache, and Whiteriver on the Apache Reservations.

From John Slaughter's old ranch and the grasslands of the San Bernardino Valley, and from the Ponderosa pine country around Flagstaff. A medicine man from Window Rock, on the Navajo Reservation, was there. He had a long silver ponytail, dressed in a velveteen shirt, and knew all the healing chants.

Also present was the artist from Prescott, in Arizona's Central Highlands, who'd painted the portrait of John Wayne that hung over Buck's bed. He was ninety-nine years old and still physically hearty.

But the emotion of the day kept him calling for tissues to dry his leaking eyes.

For that one day, Morales Road had become a thoroughfare.

In the midst of the gathering, Will pulled Levi outside to tell him of his deal with Marcelino. Levi looked confused at first, as if he couldn't believe what he was hearing, then, the words penetrating, his face turned red.

Sputtering, he said, "You figure that was a mistake or do you still hold with it?"

"You know it was a mistake. The deal, burning Salazar's load, all of it."

Levi nodded hard in agreement. He was grinding his teeth, struggling to hold himself together. He gazed at the pitying sky. "It's been a day, hasn't it?"

"It's done now," Will said.

Levi laughed without pleasure. "Long as you live it won't be done."

After seeing his guests off and going back into the house, Will felt the dread he knew was coming, the awful sensation of a house permanently without the man who'd spent his life occupying it, all his things in place, his clothes hanging in the closet, his books in the living room, his bedroom as it was on his last night.

At the burial, Levi had told Will that he had news about Hector, and they agreed to talk later. With Lucy and Merry sitting at the kitchen table, Harley and Lovesome nearby, and everybody talking in their funeral voices and the silences in between long and dreadful, Will couldn't wait anymore.

"Okay, Levi, what have you got?"

"Sorry to have to say this, but it's like I figured. Hector saw to Buck's murder, might as well have pulled the trigger himself."

"You know this for sure?" Will said.

"Hector's three daughters," Levi said. "He pulled them out of school in Nogales. No notice, no explanation. They're gone. His wife, too."

Merry spoke up. "He was protecting them. He loves those kids more than anything. What matters is when he pulled them out."

"The day before Buck got killed," Levi said.

Those words landed like a hammer on an anvil. A long and terrible quiet followed.

"I asked Harley to stick around," Levi continued. "Turns out he knew Hector was pulling his kids out before all this and kept it to himself. You want to tell us why you kept that to yourself, Harley?"

All eyes in the room went to Harley. Lovesome stood at his shoulder, her arm through his. "Like I told you, Sheriff, I never talk about other folks' business. You live around here, you learn to keep a lid on."

Will said sharply, "You talk enough when you're drunk."

"Heck, I do." Harley drew back, highly insulted. "I ain't no drunk talker. Everybody knows I sing."

"We're all better off for it, too," Will said. "You should've come to me."

"I didn't know he was plotting this manner of evil."

Lovesome said, "That's the Lord's truth, Will. My Harley woulda spoke up, sure enough."

Levi asked Harley why he thought Hector was running. Harley stroked his scraggly beard to concentrate his thinking.

"I'll tell you, he was always going off by hisself, and he knows all the drug pushers out there, so I figured he was filling his wallet. He could buy plenty of presents and make it look real nice under the Christmas tree. Maybe some trouble come outta that situation and it got too hot for him."

"Has he taken money before?" Levi said.

"Yes, sir. When I was working at the Seventy-One, me and Hector talked plenty. He told me about working at Bandera and making a good bit of foldin' down there. Told me so himself."

Rancho La Bandera was in Sonora, east of Rancho Dolores. Hector had worked there before throwing in with Buck and Will at the Flying Z.

Offering a quick clarification, Harley said, "Let me say I never seen Hector take no money, Sheriff. Actual in his hands take it. Sometimes my words come out crooked after a night such as I've had. But he give his girls things he couldn't buy on horseback pay. That I know."

"What about you, Harley?" Levi said. "Do you take bribes? Is that why you got fired at El Caballo Blanco?"

"I didn't get fired, no way. I left 'cause of boss man Wiley Bravo. He didn't like me and his daughter having—I guess you'd call them romantic adventures."

Lovesome looked up at Harley and smiled. He stroked her cheek and they touched noses.

Levi rolled his eyes. "All right, that's enough you two. Don't make me see something that'll torture my sleep. Harley, pay attention now. How old are you?"

"Twenty-eight, near as I can tell."

"I can see Mr. Bravo's point," Levi said and pointed at Lovesome. "Girl, you can't be more than sixteen."

"Seventeen in six days, Sheriff. And I can't wait for the big day. And I ain't going back to Caballo Blanco no matter what my daddy says." She made a pouty face and tightened her grip on Harley's arm.

"See, Wiley was endeavoring to acquaint me with his thirty-aught," Harley said. "So, he didn't fire me, not hardly. Just the same, we skinned out of there pretty quick."

That had the ludicrous ring of truth.

Levi said, "Fact is, Harley, you've moved around a lot."

"Yes, sir. I worked with Jimmy Calderón on the Santa Cruz. I was with Bob Westinghouse, too, and like I said over at the

Seventy-One. Name a spread in this old parcel and I put down tracks."

"You take bribes at any of these places, Harley?" Levi said.

"Not a one. I get hot-footed is all."

"I'm curious why you didn't mention the Tres Vacas," Levi said. "You worked there, too. I believe Stacy Queen owns it now."

"That rich lady from Tucson? Heck, I didn't see her there but one time. Bumpy Rodriguez runs that ranch and he's got himself a temper. Fired me quick but calmed down and asked me to come on back. I would've, too, but I already put my gear up at the Seventy-One."

"If you had to guess, where do you figure Hector run to?" Levi said.

He answered immediately. "Bandera. He's got friends there. Francisco Perez still runs that place. Believe you know him, too, Will."

"He was foreman when I was sixteen and breaking horses for him."

"Francisco and Hector is old friends," Harley said. "So he coulda got his horse took care of, water and feed, anything you like. Yup, Bandera's my guess."

Lucy jumped in. "I tracked him east from here before losing him. Sure looked like he was headed for Bandera Road, but I can't find tracks."

"If I'm runnin' with a corpse on my back trail, I ain't gonna travel Bandera Road either," Harley said. "Too wide open. Folks can see you for miles around."

Bandera Road began on the southeast corner of the Flying Z and crossed onto Bob Ashmont's ranch. But Harley described an alternate route running through Sierra Gap, a narrow passage between Cinco Lanas Mountain on the east and Burro Mountain on the west.

The land was so broken up that Border Patrol's cameras couldn't get any coverage, and at its southern end the gap opened to a meadow that led right up to Bandera's hacienda.

"I'm betting he holed up at Bandera overnight," Harley said. "Francisco woulda took him in no question, and in the morning, why, he coulda kept going anywhere he wanted in all of Mexico. If that's what he done, there'll be no finding him for looking."

Harley was making sense. Will and Levi nodded at one another.

"Something tells me you're smarter than you look, Harley," Levi said.

"I wouldn't count on it, Sheriff." He put his hat on and tugged down so hard it squashed his ears. "Okay if Lovesome and me get back to the Horseshoe? We got tons of work to do."

They went out the door. Immediately, Harley poked his head back inside. "I'm sorry as I can be about this, Will. I don't object to a man making his way, but Hector shouldn'ta done what he done. Old Buck oughta be alive and setting here with us yet."

Levi knew before anyone what Hector had done, but part of him had held out against it. Now he felt sick. Buck had been an important part of his life for all of his life. When Levi returned from his mission to China, the three people waiting for him at the airport were Will, his mom, and Buck Zachary. Will, too, had exhausted his ability to resist the truth.

"Eight years Hector worked for Buck and me," he said.

"Money can clear away a whole lot of years," Levi said.

"Looks like there's more killing coming."

Merry shifted uncomfortably in her chair. "Let's take a breath here, Will. You're hurting, we all are, but we have to handle this the right way."

"The right way?" Will's words came quick and angry. "That's a helluva pretty notion. You mean with the FBI cooperating with the Mexicans to solve this?"

"Won't they?" Merry said. "Isn't that what they promised?"

"Go ahead, Levi," Will said. "Tell her."

In his slow, even voice, Levi explained that the promised cooperation between Mexican investigators and the FBI wouldn't happen. Marcelino was too powerful. He owned too many high-level Sonoran officials and wouldn't turn over one of his men.

"Now, understand," he said, "I'll use what influence I have to see that this is done proper, and I know some fine Sonoran policemen. But you never know who's bought and who isn't, and the higher up you go, the better they are at hiding it. Especially on a high-profile case like this."

"What does that mean for us?" Merry asked. "What do we do, Levi?"

Will answered for him. "We catch a killer."

Merry's eyes darted from Levi to Will and back. "Is that true, Levi?"

"Sorry, Merry, but the truth ain't helping us right now."

Will said, "What he's trying to say is Buck's murderer walks unless I set this right. If Hector went to Bandera, Abrazo did, too. First thing I need to do is sit down with Francisco Perez." He turned to Lucy. "It's a full day's ride. I could use the company."

She smiled with every tooth she had left. "I can be ready in twenty minutes."

"Bring your phone," Will said. "You got the number for Bandera?"

"Sure do."

"We'll need it when we get there. We leave first thing in the morning."

Increasingly unnerved by the conversation, Merry said, "Buck hasn't been in the ground three hours, Will. Shouldn't we talk this over?"

"Just did," he said.

Merry turned to Levi with a plea. "Can't you do something?"

"I've never known anybody could talk Will Zachary out of anything. That's as true a statement as I know how to make."

CHAPTER TWENTY-TWO

Toward evening, Levi left, Lucy left, and the tortures of burial day worsened in the darkness, becoming bitter memory. Merry had gone to bed. Will sat alone at the kitchen table drinking a beer. The night wind drummed against the little adobe.

After a while he walked out to Hector's apartment in the barn.

The single room was a crude build-on, made of rough wood slats. The bed was a thin blanket covering a mattress of hay. On the wall were photos of his kids and a framed photo of Hector's wife on a horse, smiling, the wind tossing her hair. His sketches of Mexican poppies hung there, too. Even his prized camera, which could easily have fit into a saddle bag, was there.

Will studied the place and thought: Eight years. *Eight years!*

He remembered the day he and Buck had gone with Hector to Tucson to finalize his application for citizenship. Buck had done all the legwork, hired the lawyer, loaned Hector the money, and helped fill out the endless papers.

The ceremony was at the old Spanish mission at Tumacácori south of Tucson, and afterward Buck bought lunch at Zulas restaurant in Nogales. He was so excited he couldn't sit still. He took Hector from table to table, arm over his shoulder, introducing every stranger there to the new American.

He was beaming, as proud as Hector was. "I want a man working for me that's got a stake in the ranch and a stake in the whole dern country," Buck said.

Hector's room looked as it always had, as if nothing had changed. His break had been clean and remorseless. How could he just leave it all behind? Even in a bad fire he'd have shown indecision. Picked up an item, dashed around, thought about it, dropped it and grabbed something else.

But he'd done none of that. It was as if no part of his life at the Flying Z had been worth saving. He'd erased eight years on the ranch, erased his entire past with Buck and Will in the few minutes it took to ride away.

"How do you murder the man who gave you a home and a living?" Will said aloud. "How do you do that, Hector? I really need to know."

But it was too late. The time for talk had passed. The rage came fast. It raced up Will's spine as he ripped down Hector's sketches and photos and tore them to pieces.

Will was at the corral early next morning. He had Lobo saddled with several days' supplies in a sack and his Winchester in the scabbard. He'd dressed for concealment in a black jacket, a black bandanna, black gloves and hat.

Lucy had on a long brown trench coat, double-breasted with wide lapels, a high collar, and a belt through loops. She'd plucked it from her junk collection. It might've been spotless two decades ago. Her white hair hung beneath a black knit beanie that accentuated her bony face.

Merry came out wearing Emma's white robe. During the night, she'd again tried to talk Will out of going. That went as Levi had predicted, but she wanted to try again.

"Even if you find this mysterious Abrazo," she said, "what're you going to do with him?"

"Tie him up and bring him in."

"The killing was in Mexico, Will."

"I know good and well where it happened."

"What about Hector? If he's there, too, what're you going to do?"

"Don't know exactly. Believe we'll have ourselves a talk."

She pointed to the Winchester. "You need that to talk?"

"Maybe Buck was right after all and it's my turn to defend this place."

Lucy was mounted nearby, smiling, joyful. "I'll snap a picture for you, girl. That's after we're done with him."

"You go on ahead," Will said to Lucy. "I'll catch up."

Lucy trotted off. The canyon was silent in the predawn dark. Merry folded her arms on her chest. "Please tell me you won't hurt Hector. That's not you. You're not like Buck."

"I need to make sure Hector never comes back here."

"He's gone for good. He's not coming back."

"How do I know that? Like I knew he wouldn't kill Buck?" Will tugged on the saddle to square it on Lobo's back. "I could wake up one night and there he is standing at my bedroom door in the dark. No one on the Flying Z is safe with Hector out there."

"Give me time to get dressed," Merry said. "I'm going with."

"I've lost more than I can stand already. You're staying right here."

"If you're riding into trouble, I want to be with you."

Will came around Lobo, patted the animal on the rump, and looked Merry straight in the eyes. "I've been thinking a lot about this and I don't believe this life is for you."

The breath caught in Merry's throat. "Did you really just say that to me?"

"I was born to this fight. You landed here after driving your car into a ditch."

"I'm here because I love you."

"You think this is Cambridge?" Will swung his arm. "Out in these mountains?"

"I was at Rebel Canyon. I know exactly what this place is."

"You can't pick up the phone and here come the cops. Don't you get that? There's nobody to call. We do it ourselves, always have."

"I'm sure they threatened Hector's family."

"They threaten everyone's family," Will said. "Do you think this was the first time? I'll be sure to ask him why this time was different."

Cuco drove through the gate. Lucy had summoned him to watch the place in their absence. He didn't wave or acknowledge them in any way. Carrying a box of cartridges and a rifle in the crook of his arm, Cuco walked on parentheses legs into the darkness behind the barn.

"This is crazy." Desperation had crept into Merry's voice. She swept her hair off her face. "You don't have to do this, Will."

"I don't have a choice. This is my home."

"It's mine, too."

"Won't be for long if you don't fight for it."

"I'm fighting for it right now. I'm fighting for us."

Will untied Lobo's reins from the corral post and mounted up. The saddle squeaked and cracked from his weight. He kicked the horse into a high-stepping walk. Merry grabbed his boot in the stirrup and walked alongside, stumbling, regaining her balance, walking some more, grabbing at his boot again.

"Will, please, please. Don't do this."

He glanced around Cabezas Canyon and down at Merry and saw everything good the world had to offer and felt foolish for believing he could have it.

"If there's any trouble, you do what Cuco says."

He rode off, never looking at her again because he couldn't.

CHAPTER TWENTY-THREE

Will and Lucy rode over bare ground into the iron dawn. At the Mogollon, they found the wire fence unbroken, no tracks, and kept going over hills that dropped into canyons of white oaks and black oaks, and around impassable ravines, no sign of water in the drainages or creeks, the canyons becoming steeper and rockier as they went.

The land leading to Cinco Lanas Mountain from the east was difficult to get through. Bob Ashmont's cowboys called it the wait-a-minute, for the claw-shaped prickles on the catclaw bush that caught on a rider's clothes and caused him to hold up until he got unstuck.

They struggled through it one step at a time, turning sideways and back again around the rocks and brush, and at the base of the mountain they pulled up to get a breath. The sun hitting the scattered clouds made shadow monsters on the ground.

Lucy arched her back, stretched in the saddle, and gazed up at the silent mountain. "It's gonna be a trick getting over this puppy.."

"We can do it."

"Once we get down into Sierra Gap the map shows an easy run across the border. Ain't never gone through it myself."

"Me either," Will said. "I know outlaws used it in frontier times as a getaway. It was either climb Cinco Lanas or get shipped to Yuma."

"How is it you know such facts, a law-loving man like yourself?"

"They called it the Bandito Trail in the old days."

"Let me guess, Mr. Tom Zachary told you about it, am I right?"

"Matter of fact. The kind of man he was, he knew all the back trails."

Will rarely spoke of his birth father. Tom Zachary liked to drink and brawl, quote Shelley, Harry Crews, and Edward Abbey, with whom he shared a great friendship. He read and raged at Abbey's writing about ranching in the West, but they drank that disagreement away behind their shared motto: Take your hat off to no man.

Tom Zachary could ride any animal with hair and made good money doing it. He traveled the jackpot rodeo circuit in Mexico and sometimes had to get out of the country fast, with determined men hunting him.

With Will leading the way, he and Lucy struggled up Cinco Lanas on a deer trail, a slow, foot-by-foot climb, the horses stepping high, their heads thrusting up and down to gain purchase. From the peak they rode single file down the eastern side, leaning back in the saddle to handle the steep descent.

Sierra Gap might've been two hundred yards across. The bottom of the slopes on both sides were clogged with rocks that had rolled down, and farther back came trees with their branches twisting up and sky in between and the leaves gone.

Back of the trees were ridges that went up to clouds that obscured the peaks. The clouds were gray and moving. The ground was hard and not green, and all the land looked dry and cold.

Eager to know if Harley had been correct about Hector's escape route, Will got down to track on foot. Lucy joined him and together they walked south, leading their horses and straining to read the ground in the dying light.

Not far along, they saw the tracks of Hector's horse, and Girl Dog's pawprints alongside.

"Jackpot," Lucy said. "Man and dog. Got 'em both right here. Hector couldn't go nowhere without her following. Never seen such a loyal dog."

Will spotted a stain on a boulder, dry to the touch. He licked his fingertips and touched it again and his fingers came back red. "Blood," he said. "Either Hector's or Girl Dog's, can't tell which. But we know they were both here."

"How could it be Girl Dog? She didn't betray nobody." Lucy studied the ground closely, her face knotted in concentration. "These tracks go ever' which way, some real deep. His horse was jumping and kicking something awful. Could be another ambush happened right here."

She wiped her hand across her mouth and thought a minute. "I'm thinking Hector died right where we're standing. Yes, sir."

"Unless they wounded him," Will said. "If they did, he's bled out by now."

"So we're looking for a body?"

"Likely, but we won't find him."

"Lions would've winded him for sure. Had themselves a feast."

Will thought things over. If Hector was dead, then Marcelino had eliminated two problems the same day. He'd gotten Abrazo to kill Buck in Yaqui Canyon, after which Abrazo rode to the Gap and shot Hector out of the saddle there.

If he had it right, Will knew that Abrazo's hoofprints would be close by. He walked farther down the trail and found them.

"No need to guess anymore." He pointed to a spot on the ground marked by the distinct Abrazo hoofprint, the tracks of Hector's horse following close behind.

Lucy put her nose to the ground again and eyed the tracks sideways and up and down. Turning her head to change the view and the light, she touched them to gauge their depth. "These horses had riders, both of 'em," she said. "Can't tell if Hector was dead across the saddle or riding wounded."

Twilight was in the gap. Deciding it was pointless to move any farther, they hobbled their horses and tended their outfits. Lucy gathered dry oak branches and built a smokeless fire. They sat on either side of it eating hard-boiled eggs and canned peaches with coffee.

Lucy had beef jerky in a pocket on her chaps and she got that out.

"Back there was the first time I ever heard you mention your father," she said. "Whatever happened to him?"

"Tom went into Mexico one time and never came out. Disappeared and presumed dead. I was seven."

"Come to think of it, you never said nothing about your mother."

"Never met the woman."

"You never met your own mother?"

"Got an old photo in my stuff. She was pretty. Sometimes I look at it and wonder what she was like."

The sky had clouded over as the sun set and the wind came with it blowing cold.

"Was she a ranch woman, your momma? Did she ride?"

"Sang in nightclubs in Mexico. Sold herself. That's all I know except she was Yaqui."

"That means you're Indian, too."

"I bet you never miss the rooster crowing in the morning."

"So you're a mutt, a half-and-half man?" Lucy clucked her tongue. "Can't believe I'm eating my supper with a mutt. Hope it don't disable my digestion."

"You're cranky enough on a good day. How about more coffee?"

"I'm told I make the best camp coffee there is, and I believe that's a true fact."

Lucy came around the fire with the pot. Her bones creaked and she answered them with a moan. Will held out his cup and Lucy poured. She put the pot down and got on the ground against her saddle.

"Yaqui," she said. "My, my. I gotta say, you never was my idea of normal. Well, it don't change nothing. You're still Will Zachary to me."

"Never been anything but." He sipped. "Happy about it, too."

They sat for a moment listening to the wind. Lucy sipped her coffee and said, "You think your blood makes you?"

"Makes you what?"

"I don't know, the way you are, day to day. Get up in the morning and do this instead of that."

"I always felt different."

"On account of your mom?"

"Suppose so. I just knew there was something in me that wasn't in other folks."

"Ornery's in you. You got a wagonload of stubborn, too. Them two things are in you for sure."

The gray clouds had bulked up. They hung low over the camp now.

"There's a lot of centuries behind that blood, a lot of habits and ways of living," Will said. "And being border people, that makes us different, too. Being born in a place like this, the ground, the air, it gets inside you."

"Sounds like it didn't get inside Tom."

"He was Buck's wild brother. Somebody should write a book, only it'd be full of lies."

"You recall much about him?"

"Some. He couldn't stay in one place for long unless it was jail and couldn't tell the truth for money. If anybody asked him he'd say he was part Apache and the next day he'd swear he was descended from Thomas Jefferson. Most of what I remember is him being gone."

They opened their bedrolls. The cold wind blew harder, and thunder boomed somewhere beyond Sierra Gap. Will lay down with his hands folded behind his head and looked at the sky. He thought that with the thunder and the clouds, there had to be rain somewhere, and it was hiding from him.

He'd seen rain plenty of times during the relentless drought. Sometimes, he even watched it fall, a silver curtain in the distance. But for months it hadn't fallen where he was. He wondered how that could be, if the weather had moods and vendettas and wanted to torment him by putting empty clouds at the treetops, almost close enough to reach up and shake.

He lay there letting his head fill with the sweet smell of somebody else's rain and trying not to think about his deal with Marcelino, and what happened at Zaragoza. Lucy needed to know and he couldn't hold it in any longer.

"You awake over there?"

"No."

"Yeah, you are. I can tell by your breathing."

"Ain't you clever."

"When you sleep, you wheeze like a stopped-up pipe."

"Keeps the boys away. You know they can't resist my ways."

Will waited. He thought about whether he should say what he had to say or take the easy way and let it drop, as he'd done many times before. He decided, finally, that he'd delayed long enough and would come out with it.

"Got something I need to tell you, Lucy. That is, if you're still talking to me, seeing as how my blood troubles you so much."

"That thunder's put me in a good mood, so I'll make an exception."

"With this thing going the way it is, it's best you know it all."

"Oh, crap. Those words bring me no comfort." Lucy sat up in her blankets. "Do I need to roll a smoke?"

"I think you better."

She got out her papers and tobacco pouch. She rolled and stuck a wrinkled cigarette on her bottom lip, dragged a stick match across a rock, and puffed like it was her last one before the gallows. She shook the match dark. "Get to it, why don't you."

Will told her about his deal with Marcelino. As he spoke, he could hear Lucy's breathing gathering steam as she fussed around in rising anger. She cut him off before he could finish.

"You and Marcelino? That's a terrible thing, Will. I can't believe you done it. You shoulda told me. Why the hell didn't you tell me?"

"Embarrassed. But I couldn't see another way out."

Lucy's voice thinned to a squeal when she was upset. "We could've figured something out. We coulda come up with a plan. Me and you together, like we always done. Does Levi know?"

"Just did tell him. He didn't like it much either. Turned colors, actually."

"You can't make a deal with a killer, Will. You should know that." Lucy flicked her cigarette away. "Damn it all. Hold on. Gotta pee."

She walked into the brush, dropped her pants, and squatted. Two-day-old colts made less noise. She came back. "I don't know what to say to you, Will. I'm outta words. My bucket's empty. You got no idea how many ways this ticks me off."

"I can guess."

"You can't count that high." Lucy thrashed under her blankets to get them right again. "You gave away Zaragoza, the place all your people is resting at. You turned your back on Emma, on Baby Louise, all of them, and let Marcelino have their graves, their bones, let him have the resting place of their livin' spirits."

Will didn't speak and he didn't get angry. With someone else, he would have. But Lucy said what was on her mind, and she was right. He'd betrayed them all and there was no taking it back and no making it better, only living with it.

"They're cryin' out right now," Lucy went on. "Asunder they go, flying around and wailing something awful. Nobody's ever dead, you know that. They carry on throughout the different worlds. They're gonna be screamin' in my head all night long now."

The fire was good and warm. It snapped and burned and Will struggled to see Lucy on the other side of the flames leaping like swordplay.

"This talk of spirits," Will said. "We don't believe in spirits."

"You wanna try that again? Are you forgettin' El Jinete? You and Buck talk to the Horseman like he was your bartender."

Lucy only knew about Domingo Opata what everyone else knew, the songs and common legends that lived in the borderlands. She didn't know about Golanta and the sword and the cave filled with Opata's treasure, and the paintings of the Way.

Will didn't expect Lucy's objection and produced a weak evasion. "Opata's not the same thing. That's different."

"Like hell and beefsteaks it's different. How's it different?"

"It just is. Can I go to sleep now?"

"You gotta fix this, Will. Buck's out there flying across the sky and wailin' something terrible, and he won't quit until you handle Abrazo."

"That's what I'm here for, isn't it?"

"Ain't sure no more. Making deals with killers don't exactly give me confidence. You either want to fight or you don't. Can't have a single doubt about it. Are we gonna tree this cat or ain't we?"

The storm got louder and closer. The sky cussed and boomed and threw down forked lightning that filled Sierra Gap with a brilliant light, but only for an instant, then darkness again and no rain.

"Nobody's getting away with killing Buck," Will said.

"Good."

"Good. This is why I waited so long to tell you."

"What is?"

"All this agitation. God, just go to sleep."

"I'm going, I'm going." But Lucy wasn't done. She drank her coffee, making loud slurping noises with each sip. "Know what the worst part is?"

"Listening to you to start with."

"The worst part is Miss Mustang knew before me. Can't abide that. You shoulda trusted me, Will."

"Wouldn't be riding with you right now if I didn't trust you."

"Wanna know what I really think?"

"Because I don't know already?"

"That gal back at the Flying Z can trace her blood back hundreds of years. She's got money and people and a whole long story. I bet her family's writ up in books with pictures. You got nothing but a lying father and a whore for a mother. What does that make you?"

"Cowboy."

Lucy let out a high-pitched hoot. "That's it right there, the whole bag of nails. But our way of being don't mix. Cowboyin's a beautiful thing, and you and me both got a blood claim to it. We was born with a horse underneath us, and for us that's plenty. That's the best life there is. I just hope it's enough for her."

"I'll pay you to stop talking. Cash money."

"Talking ain't what I'm doing."

"Sure sounds like it."

"What I'm doing is being mad and trying to let it burn out so's I can sleep. But you keep blabbing and I'm wondering when you're gonna quit."

"How about right now?"

"Right now is good for me. The way you carry on, it's boogerin' the horses."

Lucy said no more and settled under her blankets as the lightning struck again and again.

CHAPTER TWENTY-FOUR

No rain fell through the night and in the morning the cloud cover was gone. Will and Lucy set out down the gap, staying in the shadows until the sun rose over Cinco Lanas, bathing them in its light. As he rode, Will held the Winchester across his saddle, searching the higher ground for signs of movement. If scouts had alerted Abrazo to their pursuit and wanted to stop it, this was the place to do it.

Lucy followed Abrazo's tracks and Hector's right behind those. Spots of discolored ground underneath Hector's horse told her he was dripping blood from the saddle as they rode.

"From what I'm seeing, I'd say Hector's a goner," she said.

Girl Dog's pawprints dotted the ground alongside Hector's horse until they veered off into the hills fronting the mountain. Lucy thought that was unusual and followed the tracks up through the rocks and brush out of sight. Will waited, not moving, eyes roaming the hills, the butt of the Winchester resting on his hip.

Lucy came back grim-faced and holding Girl Dog under her right arm. The dog had been shot and had gone off alone to die. The carcass was frozen stiff. "She stayed with Hector as long as she could," Lucy said and climbed down from her horse and got on her knees.

Using a branch, she dug at the frozen ground, attacking it with downward thrusts, as if splitting wood with an ax, spit trails hanging from her lips, her grunts growing louder with each swipe. She gouged out a shallow hole and covered Girl Dog with dirt and brush.

Looking down in disgust at the makeshift grave, she said, "I never had to say words over a dog that got killed."

"I never did either," Will said. "It's not right."

"I have to say something. Come on, gimme some words, Will."

"What am I supposed to say? I'm no good at this."

"I can't just leave her in this hole without no send-off."

"Say she was a good ol' girl."

"That's it? That ain't enough for all the years she's been riding with us."

"Okay, then say, ah …" Will thought it over. "Say she looked out for her people, the way she was supposed to. How about that?"

"Oh, hell, it'll have to do," Lucy said and repeated those words exactly. She scooped more brush onto the grave. "Happenings such as this challenge my good nature."

They remounted and rode south. The farther they went, the higher they went, and the more the path through the gap narrowed, the ground bending around rock overhangs and then back the other way until the next turn.

Where the gap ended and the view opened, they crossed into Mexico and it felt as if they'd traveled a hundred miles to a place far away. Riding on, they could see Bandera Road to the west and stayed parallel to it, concealed by brush, until reaching a cottonwood grove that Will knew from his time breaking horses for Francisco Perez. They dismounted and tied their horses.

The grove was lower than the ground around it and covered with rocks and the twisted roots of the cottonwoods bulging out of the ground like muscled arms. The place gave them a good view beyond it to a flat meadow that ran for a long distance before rising to Bandera's hacienda. They could see portions of it through the bellota oaks that lined the sides of the path leading to the gated courtyard in front.

Having Will ride unannounced to the house wasn't an option. He was well-known in that area, and with so much trouble afoot, his appearance might compromise Perez with anyone watching, or anyone on the ranch payroll who might be working for Marcelino.

That was why he'd wanted Lucy to bring her phone. With their plan already set, she pulled it from her pocket and punched in the number for Bandera's hacienda and handed the phone to Will. A female voice answered.

"I need to speak to Francisco," Will said. "It's important. Tell him it's Will Zachary."

After a minute, Will heard voices and footsteps and then Perez came on the line. In a booming voice, he said, "Am I hearing this right? It's William Juan Zachary from Arizona's legendary Flying Z?"

When Will explained the situation, Perez's attitude became serious and without hesitation agreed to meet. He drove his truck across the meadow and walked under the hanging branches into the enclosure.

"This is something I never expected," he said. "My daughter is home for the holidays and now I have the pleasure of seeing Will Zachary again. It's a merry Christmas already."

"How is little Juana?"

"Not so little anymore."

Will pointed toward the hacienda. "I taught her to play checkers on your front porch."

"She was five. She still beats me." The two embraced the way men do. Thumb locks, backslaps. Looking into his face, Perez held Will by the shoulders. "The last time I saw you, why, you were a teenage boy. Wild as a wolf."

"A lot of years have passed, Francisco."

"Perhaps not so many. You're hunting someone."

Perez was short and deep chested under a denim jacket. His face was dark brown, his age lines deeply carved. He had a firm jaw slightly raised in a proud expression, alert brown eyes, and a black quarter-moon mustache. He wore a straw cowboy hat.

"I need answers and know you to be an honest man," Will said.

Perez accepted the compliment with a nod.

"I heard about Olivia," Will said. Perez's wife had died a year ago. "I wish I could've made it to the service. My sympathies, Francisco."

"And to you, Will. We bear our burdens together. My mother used to say that makes them lighter."

Dappled sunlight filtered down through the branches, making pockets of warmth. Will motioned to some rocks and the two men sat. "You showed discretion meeting me this way," Perez said. "With the situation at Bandera, I appreciate that."

"I know you have traffic, too."

"So far, they've stayed out of our way. If they start coming to the house and making demands, I don't know what we'll do. Juana attends Tejas Academy in Austin." He paused, shrugging thoughtfully. "Maybe we'll move back to Texas."

He pulled his phone out and showed Will a picture of his daughter. Will remarked on her beauty, as the situation required, and handed the phone back. He explained about Abrazo and finding two sets of tracks and a blood trail in Sierra Gap, and what he thought had happened.

"Let me say first that Buck Zachary's name will be spoken on these ranches for many years to come," Perez said.

"He loved Mexico, Francisco. He loved Emma more than anything and she was Mexico all the way through."

"And he was loved here. Do you suppose Hector's dead?"

"It looks that way."

"I've known him all my life. I never thought him capable of what you describe."

"Marcelino bought him, Francisco. There's nothing more to say."

"That Satan has brought hell to us all."

"I need to know if you've seen Hector or any sign of him," Will said. "We know he passed close to Bandera, but did he stop here?"

"I can assure you he didn't, and I'm glad. I would've welcomed him, never imagining what had slept under my roof." Perez removed his straw hat. He rubbed his hand back and forth through his hair. "As for this Abrazo, I might be able to help you."

Will and Lucy alerted, listening with great interest.

"The shoe he uses, I've seen it, the abrazo weld," Perez said. "In the Carranza Hills a week ago. My men have been seeing that track there for some time. He's working that area, there's no doubt of that."

The Carranza Hills were split by a series of deep draws that allowed the smugglers to walk unseen for long stretches. The hills bordered the west end of La Bandera land and fed right across the line onto the Flying Z.

"You saw the man himself?" Will asked.

"He wore dark clothing and his horse was dark, black or brown, I couldn't say." Perez threw his hand forward to indicate distance. "I was too far away to see anything more. I tracked him, but he knows how to hide, even trailing a pack mule."

At Will's first sighting of Abrazo's tracks at the Mogollon, he'd been trailing a pack mule then, too. Will had Lucy sketch the Abrazo print on a piece of paper, alongside Lucy's phone number, and asked him to post it in Bandera's bunkhouse.

"The next time one of your hands sees that print headed for the Flying Z, I want to know right away," Will said.

Lucy handed the sketch to Perez. He drew his head back and squinted as he studied it. He tapped his finger on the paper. "This is your horse for sure. I'll tack it up today." Perez stood and they shook hands. "You're going to the Carranza?"

"I'm going to find this Abrazo."

"The smugglers run several shipments a week through there. Some of them are armed and some not. But if it's Abrazo, he'll definitely be carrying. Be careful."

"How can I thank you, Francisco?"

"You can do me a favor. Wait for dark to leave here and don't return until this trouble passes. I've enjoyed seeing you after so long, but the risk is too great, for my daughter and for you as well."

Will and Lucy camped in a wash that night, and in the morning, they rode to the top of Mormon Mountain overlooking the Carranza. Less than an hour later, they saw the first group of the day walking north. The guide wasn't armed.

Making sure her holstered sidearm was visible, Lucy rode up on them and ordered the mules to line up, while Will walked back and forth in front of them like a drill sergeant.

"You all know me," he said. "My name is Will Zachary. I own the Flying Z right across the line. You cross my ranch even though you got no right to. But that's not why I'm talking to you."

The men didn't look at each other or at Will. They stood stiffly, staring past his shoulder. Lucy had done another sketch of the abrazo print, and he held it up and asked if anyone had seen it or the rider.

No one had and he continued: "If you see this track, I want you to come to my house right away. It's important and I promise no *chili verde*"—smuggler slang for Border Patrol, for their green uniforms. "You have my word on that. All I want is information. I'm offering a reward and it's good money."

Over the next three days, Will and Lucy confronted forty-six men. Three of the groups were led by guards with rifles. These men knew Lucy and relaxed when they saw her coming, allowing Will to disarm them.

It was dangerous work in bitter cold as winter fell hard over the borderlands. But it yielded nothing. No one admitted to knowing Abrazo.

CHAPTER TWENTY-FIVE

They returned to the Flying Z at 11 a.m. on a sunny Wednesday. Will was eager to see Merry and expected her to step onto the porch to greet him. He tied Lobo at the corral and hurried inside, but the house was empty.

Merry had packed her belongings and left. Some of her things were scattered across the floor, and on the nightstand, forgotten in her rush to be gone, was the emerald ring her father had given her.

No letter, no explanation, no goodbye.

Levi said that Merry couldn't find Lucy to retrieve her Mustang and had asked him for a ride to the bus station in Nogales. She was in a rush to get to Stanford in time to register for the coming semester.

"I tried to get her to wait for you, but you know how she is. She's got her ideas about things and that's that."

"There's nothing you could've done, Levi."

"I called her cell a bunch of times. I'd say she's good and gone."

"Looks like it."

"Sorry about this, Will." Levi looked uncomfortable. "You think maybe we should sit down and talk about it?"

"No."

A week passed during which Will and Lucy continued scouting trails and stopping smuggler groups, to no avail. In the evenings, they ate a quiet supper together, after which Lucy went to her bunkhouse up the canyon and Will spent the nights alone.

The old adobe house had never been so silent.

One night Lucy fired up the propane heater and sat in her rocking chair on the porch. The sky was clear and the stars sent down enough light to see past the gate, to the horses in the corral and a good portion of the canyon.

Will came out and sat beside her. He hadn't shaved or slept and looked as pale and awful as he felt. He'd made a decision.

"You're going to be running this place for a few days," he said.

"Hang on a minute." Lucy sprang out of the chair and hurried to her truck. She came back with a box covered in green-and-red wrapping paper and topped with a red bow. She dropped it in Will's lap.

"Go on, open it." Lucy jerked around in the rocker, girl-like in her excitement.

Will shook the box. Something heavy thumped around inside. He ripped the paper off and opened it to find a brand-new ball-peen hammer.

"Wow," he said, in a tone that meant he had no idea what to say.

Lucy pointed like it was a roll of hundred-dollar bills. "You can pound fence all day long with that. It's tungsten. It's your Christmas present."

"Thanks." Will tried it on an imaginary target. "Son of a gun's heavy." He was embarrassed. He hadn't gotten her anything and said so.

"You still got a few days," Lucy said.

"Forgot all about Christmas."

"That's because your mind's all cattywampus. Never seen you in such a state." Lucy rocked while JB and Bond snored beside her. "Heard you packing in there. Let me take a wild guess. California."

"The way Merry left here was all wrong. That can't be the end of it."

"So you're gonna chase after Miss Mustang. My question is, what took you so long?"

"I wanted to settle up with Abrazo first, but I can't wait any longer."

"Running off like a lovesick teenager. That's something I never thought I'd see from Will Zachary."

Will knew this was going to be a difficult conversation.

Lucy had been at the Flying Z eleven years, longer than Hector, and from her first day she'd made Will the center of her existence. She'd do anything for him. She'd guarded his life as well as her own, and in her way, and as Merry had recognized early, she loved him.

Will knew it, too, and left it unspoken, as did Lucy. She was content to be at his side, the person closest to him apart from Buck. Now Will was holding her Christmas gift, having forgotten to get her anything, and about to drive to California to bring back Merry O'Hara, the one Lucy saw as taking her place.

"There's another way of going about this situation," Lucy said, rocking. "If you can handle it and the good Lord wants it, we can go back to punching cows together just you and me, building water tanks and such as that, making all that cash money us ranchers have been burdened with, lo these many years."

"Something tells me the prosperity would wreck us."

"Know what I think? I think you got too much man in you and I got too much woman." Lucy gave him a side look. "Do you think I'm right about that, Will? That you and me don't mix up right?"

"I believe that's true."

"Is that it, then? We're all through?"

Will thought about what to say and couldn't finish his thinking before Lucy spoke again.

"Forget it," she said. "You don't have to say nothin'. I'll spare you that." The dream that she had lived only in her mind since her first day at the Flying Z had officially ended.

The porch bulb had blown and Lucy was barely visible beside him, small in her sadness.

"That settles it then," she said. "Go fetch Merry O'Hara back here. It's all you been thinking about, so go on and do it."

"How do you know what I'm thinking about?"

"You can't work, can't remember nothing. Important stuff like where you left your razor. That beard you're working on, it's an abomination. Looks like a upset varmint. Just say I'm guessing."

"I like my beard. It's a work in progress."

"And spare me the nonsense about Miss Mustang not having the right blood for this place. It ain't in my blood and I do fine."

"Where'd you come from, anyway?"

"That's my business," Lucy snapped.

Will had broached that topic before, but she'd always shut him down. She guarded her past like a strongbox.

"You know all about me but you won't give up a thing about yourself," he said. "The only thing I know is Buck pulling you out of that jail."

Will remembered the story.

Lucy had drifted into town and was sleeping wherever she could lie down. Big Mike Lindsey, owner of the Remuda, had hired her on and made the mistake of trying to explain how he wanted things done. She broke a bottle over his head.

In the lockup, she made the jailers' lives miserable, and one day a rattlesnake got into her cell and bit her. No doctor could explain it, but the snake died and Lucy's hair turned snow-white. She threatened to sue.

When Buck heard, he offered to pay her fines and court costs, and in return she'd drop the suit and go to work for the Flying Z. At the marshal's request, actually his begging, for they were desperate to be rid of her, the magistrate accepted the deal and Buck brought Lucy home.

"I'm guessing you come from Texas," Will said. "When folks around here act sketchy, it usually means Texas."

"You never mind about that."

"I'll bet the law's looking for you."

"I'm tired of you folks was born here thinking you're special, 'cause you ain't. Who do you think you are, the king of England? You think being born on the Flying Z gives you a fancy title? You're no different than anybody else."

Lucy rose in her chair in excitement and turned to face him.

"This country's always been about whether you can stand the heat and the cold and the wind and the lonely and not go chicken-crazy. Can you get up in the morning with all the muscles in your back on fire and still do what it takes to work the land and defend the land and stay alive on top of it instead of underneath? Blood don't play a part except what you leave on the ground by accident, bad fortune, or a combination."

"The king of England?"

"I said it and I mean it." Lucy rolled a cigarette. She used a stick match, protecting the flame inside her cupped hands. She tossed it away and watched the flame arc to the ground. "The way you been actin' makes me sick."

She puffed grandly, theatrically. "Morning to night you mope around like a lost puppy. Can't tolerate it another day."

Lucy's anger masked the hurt she felt. But she was right. Will was a different man, separated from his old life, detached even from the land he loved.

With Buck gone, the ranch had lost its voice, its virtue, its history and purpose, and Will had lost those things, too. And now Merry. He missed her terribly, ached for her.

"Miss Mustang can take it and that's enough for me," Lucy said. "Go fetch her back here so's we can put this family back together."

"You'll watch the ranch?"

Rocking, smoking, unbearably sad: "Never take my eyes off it."

Will went inside and got Merry's emerald ring off the nightstand. He grabbed his overnight bag and his rope off the bedpost and put them on the front seat of the Silverado. Lucy was still making her rocking chair creak when he sped over the cattle guard and up the spur.

CHAPTER TWENTY-SIX

Will drove through the night and arrived in Los Angeles with the sunrise. The light was different in Southern California. Everything hidden behind a gray haze, the feeling of the ocean just beyond, of something better just beyond, and everyone rushing to get there amid choking traffic, the fury of metal in constant movement.

He mashed the accelerator and continued up the coast, the Silverado straining to keep going. He stopped only for gas and to catch his breath at the side of thundering highways.

By the time he'd reached Santa Maria, the old truck had lost two dashboard dials, shaken free by the vibration. But he couldn't stop. If Merry had gotten to Stanford and found her spot gone, what then?

How would he find her again? She'd be out of his life for good.

In Palo Alto, he followed the red-tile roofs to Stanford. Looking him over with suspicion, the secretary in the administration building had nothing to say on the whereabouts of Meredith Breck O'Hara.

Disheveled from the drive and still unshaven, Will held his grungy range hat against his leg. Reinforcement secretaries emerged from adjoining offices to lecture him on their privacy policies. He got the same treatment in the English Department.

As he exited down the hall, the pop of his slant heels drawing curious eyes, a female voice called to him from behind.

"Hey, Arizona!"

She was running after him. Stout, glasses, a pale, pudgy face. She'd witnessed the scene in the office. "I helped Merry register when she got here. I'm Joanie."

"She made it in time?"

"Yes, sir, she made it. Barely." Joanie fingered her glasses back off the tip of her nose.

"I really need to find her."

"They don't want us giving out, like, addresses."

"But she's my girl." Will said this as if no further explanation could possibly be needed. The simplicity left Joanie without a response. She melted and scribbled directions on a piece of paper against the wall.

Will found the house, a wood-and-brick bungalow with a ground-to-roof brick chimney on the driveway side. The porch pillars were painted green and the lawn perfectly kept. The front door was open and a student with a pointy-nosed bird face sat on the steps with a laptop open on his knees.

At the squeal of the iron gate, he raised his eyes to study the ragged-looking visitor. Huffing in annoyance at the interruption, he snapped the laptop shut and came down the steps, shouldering past Will as if he were invisible.

From the sidewalk, he turned and hollered, "Hey, Merry O'Hara! There's a Civil War reenactor here to see you!"

When she stepped outside, Merry froze on her feet. "Oh." she said, blinking several times in shock. She sputtered two more "ohs" before swiping a nervous hand across her face to straighten her hair. "Hello there, Will."

Merry looked drawn and exhausted. She shook her head at the sight of him. "You really need to shave. You're scaring people."

She sat down on the steps. She wore her deplorable Santa Fe snakeskins. She wrapped her arms around her knees and looked out absently, her face framed by that beautiful chestnut hair. The hair had always done things to Will, and so did the shape of her, the way she moved, so perfect in its balance, her slender arms out from her hips, swinging as she walked.

He thought of their nights together, the wind blowing outside, the coyotes screaming in the darkness of the mountains and JB and Bond giving it right back. His brain swooned with the smell of her, with wild memories of how they loved.

He shut the gate and sat beside her. "I came to bring you back."

"I'm not a stray cow, Will."

"I know that."

"Did you bring your rope? In case I break off from the herd."

He threw his chin. "Front seat."

"You said I wasn't cut out for the Flying Z. That I didn't have the hide to live there. Do you remember that?"

"Turns out it's me that doesn't have the hide to live there without you. When I got back and found you gone, it felt like I'd lost everything."

Turning to Will, Merry's eyes flared, showed anger, and settled again. "You said I didn't belong." She felt the hurt of those words all over again. "You practically told me to beat it."

"I got scared." Will hung his head. "Couldn't keep on living."

"I cried all the way here. On the bus. Couldn't get my car back from Lucy and didn't care. I needed to get away." Merry laughed crazily. "I practically sailed across the desert on my tears. Now you track me down and say you want me again?"

"It's what I want. You're what I want."

She closed her eyes and moaned. "What're you doing to me, Will?"

"I don't want to live out my life wondering what our lives together would've been like."

She blew out an exasperated breath. "I can't believe this. You need to understand, I didn't leave Arizona because I was afraid. I left because of what you were going to do."

"I didn't know what I was going to do. I told you that."

"What happened with Hector? Did you find him?"

Will explained about the blood and the hoofprints in Sierra Gap. "Looks like Abrazo killed Buck in Yaqui Canyon and Hector in the gap."

"Jesus." She took a moment to breathe and think. "It's hard for me to think about Hector. I liked him. I mean, I hate what he did, but I'm so sorry to hear that."

The afternoon was quiet. Parked cars lined the street on both sides. Will wondered if he could fit his five-horse slant trailer between them. For some reason that seemed a worthwhile topic at the moment.

"This is something I need to know," Merry said. "Can you please tell me what you were going to do if you'd found Hector alive?"

"What does it matter now?"

She persisted. "Kill him, right? Put another body on the range like Buck said. That's basically what you said at the corral that morning."

"Told you, I don't know."

"You need to answer me. You said you were different, but ever since Buck's been gone you've been sounding an awful lot like him. You asked me to come back to the ranch with you, so I have a right to know."

"I need to protect myself and the Flying Z, whatever it takes."

Her eyes widened in surprise, and she tried again. "But if you'd found Hector alive, is there a chance you wouldn't have done something awful? I mean, after thinking about it?"

Will considered that thoughtfully.

"My God, I'm giving you an opening," Merry said. "Take it, just take it. Is it possible you would've walked away?"

"It's possible."

"Possible. That's, what, ten percent? There's a ten percent chance you would've backed off when your temper cooled. You're a humanitarian after all." She threw up her hands and turned toward him. "You're unbelievable. All you had to do was say no and I would've gotten into your smelly old truck and gone back to Arizona with you. But you didn't say no."

"If we're going to start our lives together, we have to do it on the square, everything in the open."

Merry gave him a round-eyed stare. "Our lives together? You think I'm going with you now? I'm supposed to take my work here, my future, and throw it away for a guy who says, 'Yeah, I might've killed a man who was a brother to me. Why the hell not?'"

"At Rebel Canyon you had Buck's rifle in your hands and were going to kill Salazar," Will said. "When you love somebody, you do what you have to do."

"That was self-defense. This—this is nothing but revenge."

"Sometimes revenge is all you've got."

She grinned unhappily. "That's the wrong thing to say, Will."

"I'm no killer. Is that what you think? That I'm a killer?"

She didn't respond, and that lit a fire. Will wanted to talk. She needed to understand, even if she judged him badly. He wasn't going to shield her from the dark corners of his nature, from the truth, for all its costs.

"It was an evil thing Hector did," Will said. "He led Buck to his death for money, sold himself like a sack of grain to get it." He tasted the venom in those words. They made his jaw tighten. "Do you get that? He murdered the man who gave him a life in

Arizona. Gave him a job, a home, gave his kids and his wife a home. Treated him like blood."

Merry looked away, her face ashen.

"All I ever wanted was to grow cattle and live on the only home I ever had. My life is the land under my feet and my stock and that's it. And these drug men are trying to take it away from me. A regular thief steals your money and that's one thing. The Zacharys never had much.

"But these smugglers don't stop with your money. They take everything you have. They pull your heart out and fill it with hate and hand it back to you. They steal your whole way of life and turn you into one of them, and that's the cruelest crime of all."

Listening, Merry's attitude hardened. She wanted to sprint away.

Will pressed on: "Hector and those men he's in with need to know I can't wait for them to come and take all that we've worked for, and I can't walk away. That's not how we're made."

"That's enough," Merry said. "I've heard enough."

Talking so much made Will uncomfortable, but he couldn't stop.

"What kind of man would I be if I gave up? What if Buck ran when it got bad on him? Right soon or down the road, I'll be resting with him at Zaragoza, and that's going to be a tough enough conversation as it is, explaining my deal with Marcelino. If I quit on the ranch now, he'll be giving me hell into eternity."

She couldn't look at him, and her voice had become a soft monotone, gone of argument. "I'm going inside now."

Will knew his words had frightened her, but they had to be said. Sitting on those steps, he felt despair, failure, loss, and when he turned his face to the sky to search for a better realm, he saw only that choking haze hanging like a shroud.

He shut his eyes and murmured, "I don't know how you can live in a place with no sky."

In a thin whisper, Merry said, "Goodbye, Will."

The front door closed and she was gone.

CHAPTER TWENTY-SEVEN

Will got on the Pacific Coast Highway and drove down the blue coast. Somewhere along the way he began hearing a rush of air, as though he were falling through a deep chasm, a dark hole apart from this Earth. It wanted to swallow him and he had nothing to grab on to, no way to stop the headlong plunge.

The sound got louder, a tremendous *woooshing* that stayed with him as he drove along the edge of the world.

Past Monterey, past Carmel, past Big Sur.

Stunning landscapes right outside his window, but all he could see was Merry's face, and all he could think about was life without her.

At San Luis Obispo he pulled over and the sound stopped, and he realized that he still had Merry's emerald ring in his pocket. Staring at it, he thought of the night at Padre Pedro's Saloon, and what Merry had said just before she kissed him the first time: "If you find it, fight for it."

She had said goodbye, firmly and finally. But now, clutching the ring, he couldn't accept that. If he was going to fight for the ranch, he had to fight for Merry, too. He turned around and drove back to Palo Alto. He got no response to the doorbell or his hard knocking.

But the curtain at the window moved and he saw the tip of Laptop's long nose. Will hammered on the door with his fists.

Cracking it an inch, Laptop said, "Merry O'Hara's gone. She left, okay?" He tried to close the door. Will shoved it open, almost taking off Laptop's head. "Where'd she go? I have something valuable of hers I need to give back."

"I didn't ask. If you don't mind, I have things to do."

Thinking Merry might've left behind a clue to her destination, Will bulled past Laptop and bounded up the stairs to her room. "Ah, sir, excuse me. You can't be in here. This is what's called a home invasion."

"Close the hole, Chester."

"I'm calling the police."

Will found Merry's bureau drawers pulled out and empty, the closet empty, too, and papers crumpled up on the floor. The place looked as if burglars had swept through. He opened the papers one at a time, inspected them, and tossed them aside.

He went downstairs. Laptop was standing in the doorway. "They're coming, you know, the police."

"How'd Merry leave without a car?"

He refused to answer until Will took a menacing step toward him. Encouraged, Laptop said, "I drove her to the bus station in San Jose."

"And you don't know where she was going?"

"I told you, I didn't ask. She jumped out at the curb."

"When was this?"

"I don't know, three hours ago."

"She must've said something."

He rolled his eyes. "She said she was withdrawing from Stanford because she needed to go back to her real home. I didn't ask questions, okay? Now I have to pay the rent on this house by myself, thanks to you."

Will left and drove to the bus station in San Jose. His description of Merry O'Hara didn't register with the man at the ticket window. In the previous three hours, nine buses had departed for various destinations. Merry was on one of them.

If he knew which one, he would've sped to that city and met the bus.

All he could do was guess. The hub was Los Angeles. Most buses went there eventually. He knew he needed good luck, but he was desperate. Driving the way Will drove that night, he made it to LA in four and a half hours.

The Silverado began to throw out smoke, little wisps curling up through the hood cracks. He followed the 101 freeway down through Hollywood into downtown. He walked into the bus terminal and looked at the faces. The place had the feeling of a cemetery a little early.

When he didn't see Merry sitting there, bags at her feet, his stomach sank. He went to the window and watched the buses pulling in and unloading. He studied the passengers as they stepped off, and after an hour he accepted the hopelessness of his mission and left.

With the truck throwing out even thicker smoke, he got directions to a nearby Walmart, and, driving along, thought more about where Merry might've gone. Probably Brookline. She'd said she needed to return to her real home, and Brookline was where she'd grown up.

She might've already called Glenna Hannon, her mother, to say she was on her way.

Will parked in the Walmart lot and on his way into the store passed a window poster advertising cell phones. *Call anywhere, anytime!* He found the hose he needed for his truck, grabbed a Tracfone, paid for both items, and returned to the truck.

Sitting behind the wheel, he called directory assistance to get the number for Boston University. He followed the prompts to the office of Professor Glenna Hannon. He knew there'd be no answer late at night in Boston, but he wanted to be sure that he had the correct number.

When her message came on, he hung up. If Merry hadn't contacted her mother, Will leaving a message that he couldn't find her might cause undue worry.

His second call went to Levi Johnson at his home in Arizona. "The moon's gonna fall clean out of the sky," Levi said. "Will Zachary's got a cell phone again. I thought you were done with the world."

"It won't quit coming for me, Levi. It's like a predator."

"I'm betting it makes you feel like a whole different man."

"It'll send me down a bad road for sure. Maybe tomorrow I'll rob a bank."

Levi chuckled. "Where're you at, anyway?"

"In LA, a Walmart parking lot."

"What the heck? Why are you all the way out there?"

"Just bought a hose for my truck and I'm about to rig it up."

Will stepped out of the Silverado and stood with his back against the grill, the phone to his ear.

"That old wreck," Levi said. "I'm surprised you got that far." He yawned. "By the way, your birthday party's all set. The whole crew's coming."

Will's friends had a years-long tradition of gathering at the Flying Z to celebrate his birthday. They called it a birthday party, but with Buck as the main organizer, and now Levi, it had become a combination community get-together and Christmas party.

The parking lot was busy. Drivers inched along hunting for spaces, and farther out, up under the night, three highways crossed at a busy intersection.

"Forgot all about the party," Will said.

"Day after tomorrow. Got a big feast planned. I'm cooking."

"I don't know, Levi."

"You need it. We all need it. Can't call it off now anyway."

"Is this where I say the call's breaking up? Isn't that what people do?"

A woman passed by pushing a loaded shopping cart. With her free hand, she gripped her young son's shirt and was pulling him along, the boy squealing and wind-milling his arms. When he got free, the kid took off running. She screamed at him to stop. He ran as if on a motor, with no thought or purpose and no idea where he was headed.

He darted around one parked car and another, pumping his arms and making train noises as he went. The woman's face turned red yelling at him.

"Get back here, Edward! You'll get run over!"

Will couldn't hear Levi over the noise. "Hold on a minute."

He put the phone down on the hood and went to the passenger door and reached inside for his rope. He waited until Edward had made his speedy way between the Silverado and the next car over, the mom frazzled in pursuit without a chance of catching him.

Other passersby stared as Will twirled the rope over his head. Several of them held up cell phones to record it. When Edward chugged into the clear, Will threw the loop over the boy's head, pinning his arms to his ribs, and reeled him in.

Having never witnessed such a thing, the crowd let out a collective cheer, and Edward, shocked at his sudden imprisonment, ceased his antics. His mom hurried to his side, all the while glaring at the strange man with the rope. She threw it off Edward's head, freeing him, and wrapping her arms around his shoulders, pulled him away.

Will rewound the rope and looped it over his shoulder and picked up the phone and heard Levi saying, "Will, are you there? ... Are you there?"

Will said he was there.

"I'm trying to tell you, I got a call from that jughead Boone Macklin," Levi said. "He wants to meet with you."

"What about?"

"Don't know. But he says it's important, a matter of life and death."

"Got anything on him yet?"

"Ralph Reyes in Reno tells me there's nothing under the name Boone Macklin. I told him about that six-shooter tattoo and he's gonna check on that. What is that racket out there?"

The mother was talking loudly to a policeman and pointing at Will. Edward gripped her leg with the expression of a freed hostage. The policeman approached Will, asked a few questions, and went back to the outraged mother whose boy wasn't run over to explain that he wouldn't arrest Will.

Hearing everything, and rather than listen, Will looked up at the web of highways and the unbroken lines of traffic zooming by under a black sky. The city night was an endless roar of motors, and there was nothing to see, no good air to breathe, and no place for a man like Will Zachary to be.

"People are strange out here, Levi," he said.

"Heard so. Did you know you woke me out of a sound sleep?" He yawned again. "If you've got yourself a new phone, I'm guessing it's because of Merry O'Hara. Things ain't good, are they?"

Will said nothing. The policeman was trying to calm Edward's mom.

"She's one of a kind," Levi said. "But you're no follower either."

"We're different kinds."

"That might be it right there. What I'm thinking about is the night we lost the state championship, the feeling we had. The world ended for us boys."

"It did."

"Took a while to get over it, but we finally figured out it was just football and got ourselves stood back up."

"I haven't thought about that in a long time."

"That's my point. Stuff goes away after a while."

Will leaned against the Silverado and thought, *If you think this is going away, Levi, you don't understand. This is never going away.* He said, "I need to find her, Levi. I called Merry's mother figuring she's headed east."

"Makes sense."

"She got on a bus, that's all I know."

"She hasn't been picking up for me. Maybe you'll have better luck. You're really going all that way?"

"Got an emerald ring to return."

"You might not be thinking straight right now, Will."

"If I can rig this hose up, I'll be all right."

"I didn't mean your truck. You can send the ring in the mail easy. The mails still work okay."

"I need to talk to her. Nothing came out right before."

"It's quite a thing you're proposing, talking to a gal like Merry O'Hara."

"Never talked so much in my life. I'm no good at it."

"Not even a little." Levi gave an easy laugh. "You wouldn't be you if you were, so there's that."

"Talking doesn't pay my bills. Rain does. These days, we got too much of one and not enough of the other. All this jaw flapping, it's giving me a headache."

"I'm starting to feel woozy myself."

"But I've got to keep trying. I'm going to leave here in a minute and start driving east."

"To Brookline, Massachusetts? That's a whole continent you're talking about." Levi thought that was a bad idea but he knew that speaking up any further wouldn't change anything.

"Call me once in a while on your new cell phone. You'll be driving along seeing the land and talking on your phone like all the other dunderheads out there. You know that's illegal in a lot of places."

"Sorry, but you're breaking up."

They laughed, and neither spoke in the long quiet that followed. The deepest communication between men often happens that way.

"I know you think I'm crazy, Levi, and maybe I am," Will said. "But it's something I gotta do."

CHAPTER TWENTY-EIGHT

From his days of long-haul driving, Will could figure travel times to the hour. Forty-five hours and he could be in Massachusetts. He got on the freeway and drove through the night and into the next day, calling Glenna Hannon repeatedly on the way.

He was passing through Topeka when his cell rang. It was Hannon.

"I'm getting calls from this number. May I ask who this is, please?"

Will identified himself. She didn't recognize his name. When he told her Merry had stayed at his ranch on her way to California, she said, "Oh, yes, the gentleman with the gun in his boot. She's spoken extensively about you. Is there a reason you haven't left a message?"

"I can't find Merry and didn't want to worry you."

"She's not missing, if that's what you're suggesting. I talked to her last evening."

"Is she all right?"

"She's fine, Mr. Zachary, but I'm not. She informed me that she's left Stanford, and I must say, I'm sick about it and so is her father."

"Did she say where she was headed?"

"Back to your little—I don't know what you'd call it—outpost there in Panorama, Arizona."

"Patagonia."

"I'm sure it has certain rural charms, but we didn't raise our daughter for that kind of life. She's a special young lady with a wonderful future and we feel strongly that she needs to be in a more enriching environment, more intellectual. You understand."

"Sure." Will considered telling her that he kept a gun in his glove box, too, and in his saddle bag, and multiple hunting rifles in his bedroom closet and that he reloaded his own ammo to save money. Brass casings only, of course.

But all he wanted was to get off the phone and get home.

"The call was not the most pleasant," Hannon went on. "But Meredith had made up her mind. She was on a bus. My word, a bus of all things!"

As soon as he could, Will ditched Glenna Hannon, turned around, and mashed the gas pedal to get back to Arizona. He kept hitting redial on Merry's number, but she didn't pick up. He drove all night.

The Silverado broke down twice on the way. He got it going again, but across New Mexico black smoke started pouring out from the radio and the glove box.

He had to wind his neck out the window to breathe. It got so bad he stopped in Tucson and jerry-rigged a new hose for the remainder of the drive. He arrived at the Flying Z late that day. Merry wasn't there, and Lucy, who was sitting on the porch smoking, hadn't seen her.

Thinking Levi might know something, he walked up the hill behind the barn with his cell phone and called him.

"I'm here right now," Levi said. "Look over your shoulder."

Levi's Tahoe had just turned off Morales Road and was inching down the spur. Will hurried down the hill and could tell by Levi's face that something was up. He wore his biggest grin, a real face breaker with lots of teeth.

"You look like you won the lottery," Will said.

"I would've called but I wanted to surprise you," Levi said.

Merry O'Hara stepped out of the Tahoe's passenger door. She stood in the perfect sunlight and made it better.

Being able to speak at all was a triumph. Will managed three brilliant words: "You came back."

"Yes, I did. I came back to the Flying Z."

She wore blue jeans and the Ramírez boots they'd bought in Pitiquito. She had on a long-sleeved white blouse with turquoise scrolling at the cuffs and neck. Will recognized the shirt. It had belonged to Emma.

Merry was disheveled from the bus. She tried to straighten herself, tugging the wrinkles from the shirt and smoothing her hair.

She stood uneasily, not certain what to do with her hands. Finally, she jammed them into her front pockets, thumbs out, and hunched her shoulders.

"It took me a long time to decide."

Will nodded toward Levi. "I see you had an escort."

"Picked her up at the bus station in Nogales," Levi said. "Pulled up and there she was, standing right there."

Will looked at Merry in disbelief. "You called the county sheriff for a ride?"

"Once I made up my mind, it was kind of an emergency."

Levi looked happier than any man in history. Will wanted to talk to Merry alone, and Merry wanted the same, but Levi wasn't going anywhere. After a long and awkward silence, during which his smile stayed glued on as he savored his role in the reunion, he emerged from his oblivion and said, "Oops. Anyway, errands to run."

He climbed back into the Tahoe and leaned out the window. "Don't forget the party tonight, Will." He pushed a plastic super-market bag out the window and called to Lucy. "My chilis. Put these in the fridge right away." He U-turned and stuck his head out again, hollering to Lucy, "Not the regular fridge, the crisper!"

Lucy gave him a get-out-of-here wave and carried the chilis into the house, and Merry and Will were alone. They stood together by the porch watching Levi's dust cloud. Both of them wanted to talk, but the surge of emotions made it hard to find a place to begin.

Will held up his TracFone. "Bought this evil little item in LA. Levi gave me your number but you didn't pick up."

Merry held up her own phone. "Bought a new one myself, and got a new number, too. Levi kept calling and I was afraid if I picked up, I could never make the break."

"But here you are anyway."

"I changed my mind. I do that sometimes. Is that still all right, for a girl to change her mind? I just couldn't stand the way things ended in Palo Alto."

"Me either."

Cabezas Canyon was calm and peaceful with night coming on. No wind and all was silent but for the horses nickering in the corral.

"I know the kind of man you are, Will, and what this place has made you."

"Tell me." His eyes met hers. "Tell me what I am."

The challenge took her by surprise. "I wish I could put a word to it. I know who you think of yourself as. Shane. The righteous man standing up for what he believes." Merry paused and breathed heavily. "There's the other part of Shane and you're like that, too. You don't mind fighting. Sometimes I think you like it."

"You can't stand it that you could love someone like me."

"You know what? You're right, someone like you. I love someone like you and it—it really ticks me off."

Merry threw her head back dramatically. "How the hell did this happen? How did I end up falling in love with you? I've tried to trace it back, to figure out the exact moment. It was the night of the Thanksgiving dance, when you said I reminded you of a filly you had. That was so wrong it was irresistible."

She fingered a strand of loose hair behind her ear. "Love makes you say really dumb things and do really dumb things."

A truck bounced along Morales Road with another following close behind.

Will held up the emerald ring. "I turned around in San Luis Obispo and drove all the way back to your house. It wouldn't be right for me to keep it."

"Oh, thank you. My father's ring, thank you. It's good luck."

"Drove like a maniac. Chester told me he drove you to the bus station."

"His name's Phineas. Seriously, it's Phineas. He's a genius. He'll own the internet in two years." Merry let out a long sigh. "I rode all around California on the bus. For two days including Christmas. There's an experience for you. People with plastic bags for luggage singing 'Silent Night' in the dark. But I had this."

She fished around in her backpack and pulled out her beat-up copy of *One Hundred Years of Solitude*. "It kept me going. I read it three times."

"I figured you were headed to Brookline."

"I can't be in Massachusetts anymore. I couldn't stay in California either."

"Does that mean you're here to stay?"

She waited before answering. She gazed around the canyon. "I'm lost. I'm a lost girl, Will. I thought I knew my place in the world and it turns out I don't know anything. Not one little thing. But you can figure out a lot by riding the bus around like a crazy nomad. Like a modern-day Kerouac."

She tipped her head back. Happiness spreading across her face, a giddy laugh: "If this is going to work, there are certain books. It's been on my mind, so I have to ask. It's been killing me, actually. Have you read Kerouac?"

"Of course."

Her face lit up in happy surprise. "I have to say, that's a good sign. That's like a requirement. *On the Road* is my second all-time fave."

"*The Dharma Bums* is better. It's about the land and freedom, the only things that matter."

"You've read that, too? Wow. Impressive again. Wait, you didn't like *On the Road*?"

Will made a face. "Narcissists in a car."

"Seriously? Oh, my." Laughing: "We're going to have to come to some sort of understanding about certain books if this is going to work."

The two trucks had turned off Morales Road and were starting down the spur. Harley Jones's blue pickup was in the lead with Bob Ashmont's Hummer following close on his bumper. They were coming for the party.

"I've had time to think about what I am and where I belong," Merry said. "The thing is, I never actually liked school. It was expected of me, the family business. But there was nothing to really love about it. Then I met you and saw you struggling to save your home, and it's dangerous and hard, but it's something worth living for and worth fighting for."

The trucks made a racket as they neared the house.

"What I decided is to go with the ten percent," Merry said. "That's all I have, a ten percent chance you wouldn't have done something awful. I begged you to give me more, but you couldn't. Who knows? Maybe having me in your heart will change things, for you and for me."

She lost herself in a private thought. The windmill clicked and banged and the sound brought her back.

"Anyway, I had to travel back to a different century to find what I want. Oh, and there's one other thing. I'm definitely, infinitely, and stupidly in love with you. You already know that, but I wanted to say it. It's one of those things you don't get to say too often. There. I said it. God, I'm babbling. Dear me."

She swept her hair back off her face. "You really should stop me because I'll go on and on. Okey-dokey. Uh-huh." She pointed at the windmill. "It's making a racket again. We need to get Cuco back out here."

She waited for Will to talk. In the time they'd been apart, he'd assembled his thoughts in his head, all the words he'd wanted to say in perfect order, and they were all gone.

"Don't just stand there," Merry said. "You must have something to say."

"I wish I had more to offer you. I know I'm not much to boast about. I'm a common man and this old place is all I have."

"Don't. Don't talk like that. That's not what I meant."

"When I think of the men you must have met back east. Smart, from old families, cash in their pockets, big futures."

"I don't miss a single one of them. All I want is right here."

"You better be sure about that, sure as the sun."

"I am. I'm sure."

"With drug men filling up the country, it's not going to get better. You're taking a big chance living on this old wood pile with me."

"I'm not afraid, if that's what you're thinking."

"You should be. That's what I'm trying to tell you. It could get bad. And I won't roll over for these guys."

"It isn't in you, I know."

"If I had any quit in me, maybe somebody would give me a plaque I could hang on my wall, a good citizen plaque. For not fighting, for looking away from all this badness and acting like it's normal, like it doesn't matter. Nobody's giving me any plaques."

"Stop it," Merry said. "You're a good man, the finest I've ever met. You're just what this sick old world needs."

"Just so I'm sure, that means you're staying, right?"

"You can be so dense sometimes. Really, just a complete brick."

"I want to hear you say it."

"I'm here to stay, Will Zachary."

She threw her arms around him and kissed him. Harley leaned on his horn. Lovesome let out a long, high-pitched holler that got the horses in the corral whinnying.

Merry kissed him again. "There's something I need to tell you. About how I decided to come back. Something incredible happened to me in California."

But it was impossible to continue. Harley wouldn't stop blasting his horn. He stepped out of his truck carrying a twelve-pack of Schlitz and a half-eaten bag of Cheetos. Lovesome clapped and pumped her arms like a cheerleader.

Bob Ashmont was there, too. He stood alongside Harley and Lovesome, the three of them smiling and gawking at Will and Merry.

Lucy stepped onto the porch and delivered a piercing two-fingered whistle. "Get in here, you lousy peepers," she barked.

When everyone went inside, Will said, "What did you want to tell me?"

"It's a truly amazing story," Merry said. "But not now. I'll tell you later. We'd better go inside before our friends lose their minds."

CHAPTER TWENTY-NINE

Levi returned and got to cooking. He had a new chili recipe that he couldn't wait to try. The party crowd grew.

Cuco Muñoz walked in with a bottle of *bacanora*, a Sonoran mescal made by roasting agave stalks underground. Right after him came three young hands from Caballo Blanco and an old friend of Buck's, a silver-haired cowpuncher named Riley. In retirement he raised racing pigeons.

Sweetie Taylor threw open the kitchen door, thudding it against the wall. She made a startling sight, a large, apple-cheeked woman with too much blue eye shadow and that pile of short white hair.

"Happy birthday, Will!" she bellowed. "Great to see you, too, Merry. Too bad you missed Christmas. I was looking forward to seeing this place decorated up."

"Well, what's stopping us? A late Christmas is still Christmas."

"That's a great idea," Sweetie said. "We'll make it look like the old country. My cousin runs a craft shop in Tucson and can send down what we need."

"Can't wait. Let's do it."

"I'll call you when the stuff comes in." Sweetie rubbed her hands together. "I'm ready to eat whatever dish you got here, Levi, and come back for seconds!" Noise became Sweetie. She couldn't read a book without scaring the birds.

Simultaneous to Sweetie's grand entrance, the cowboys at the table jumped up and abandoned their seats. They knew Sweetie would enforce the rule against spurs at the table and didn't dare risk her disdain.

Bob Ashmont came wearing an appalling and previously unseen piece of finery—a black snap-button Western shirt with white smile pockets and embroidered red bucking horses on the shoulders. It sparked a discussion during which Ashmont fingered his wife, Eleanor, as the purchaser.

She had cropped gray hair and a pleasing manner and denied any knowledge of the offending item. In the end, there was general agreement that the shirt was so wrong that Ashmont had gained a certain admiration for having the gumption to wear it.

Levi served his chili to each newcomer and stood over their chairs as they ate. No one escaped the moment of judgment. Was it good? Too spicy? A pinch more sugar? Levi hovered until he got a full report.

He had an instant admirer in Eleanor Ashmont. She found Levi's cooking exploits endlessly fascinating. She helped him keep the table set and cleared of dirty dishes, and just when they thought the work was done, new guests would arrive, forcing them to set more places.

Doc Gonzáles came, too, the only visitor who knocked, five gentlemanly taps on the door. They came during a lull in the jumble of conversation, followed quickly by three voices at the table simultaneously saying, "That's Doc."

He shook hands all around, welcomed Merry back with a hug, and settled into a chair.

For all of Will's days, Doc had been the one with the answers, the one to go to in times of trouble. But he'd changed since Buck's death. His face looked hollow, as if exhausted by life and by death. Merry sat beside him holding his hand as the kitchen brimmed with happy, colliding conversations.

Without prompting, Lovesome rolled out her George Strait playlist. Bob Ashmont, in total sincerity, said, "I've heard that name several times. May I ask who this Strait fellow is?"

The question proved so incomprehensible to all in the room that they looked at each other in awed silence. Lovesome leaned close to Harley and between tightly squeezed lips, said, "Okay, what's happening here? Did he really just say that?"

Lucy, firmly in the anti–King George camp, enjoyed Ashmont's confusion and jumped in with her oft-repeated argument: "If you don't like Conway Twitty and Pabst Blue Ribbon beer, there's something wrong with you."

Then Lovesome fired back and she and Lucy launched into an argument that became general. The stakes were high. A George Strait–Conway Twitty fight had the potential to blow the house down, until Doc intervened, in the quietest way possible. He simply raised his hand, as if in benediction, and the two of them promptly quieted.

The night was cold. After supper, Will built a piñon fire and looked at Merry and smiled, and she looked at him and smiled back, and Cuco poured three fingers of *bacanora* all the way around. He knew to skip Levi, who dived into his private Dr Pepper stash.

Cuco raised his glass. "*Salud para todos.*" For him, a stemwinder.

They all raised their glasses and drank.

Sweetie gave another toast to good health, to tall grass, to the Flying Z, and to Merry and Will. Their eyes met again and neither wanted to endure the heart-pounding wait to be alone, but they couldn't cut the party short. "Take care of each other and things will work out fine," Sweetie said.

Seconds later, after the powerful alcohol had traveled all the way to the bottom of their feet, the room erupted in a series of high-pitched wheezes and thigh slaps. Lucy offered a toast to Merry's Mustang.

"That reminds me," Merry said. "I need to get it out of your yard."

"Too late," Lucy said, raising her glass again. "I sold it for parts."

Merry turned her face to the ceiling, said, "Of course you did," and joined in the toast.

They say *bacanora* changes the night, and it did. With glasses refilled, Will got out a deck of cards and the late-staying partiers all gathered around the table to play go fish.

They talked, laughed, and hooted and for one night didn't think about Buck's murder and the hunt for Abrazo as they drank more toasts to the best things they knew of in life or could think of.

Past 3 a.m. and Will had scarcely said goodbye to the last of his departing guests when Merry threw her arms around his neck and pinned him against the door. "That was wonderful and I love those people, but I thought they'd never leave."

"Me, too."

"A kiss would go beautifully right about now."

"I can do better than that." Will picked her up, one arm across her shoulders and the other under her knees. Screeching as she went airborne, Merry said, "You've got to be kidding. Are you seriously doing this?"

"I can put you down if you want."

"Don't you dare."

Will swept her shoulder against the kitchen light switch to turn it off. He stumbled in the sudden darkness but held on tight. He laughed and Merry laughed, and he felt her breath against his neck, and her lips against his.

It made him dizzy and he stumbled again.

Getting himself upright, he found his way down the hall to the bed and laid her gently down and pressed his lips to hers, Merry with her arms around his neck.

"Fresno," she whispered.

"Fresno?"

"That's where I was when I decided to come back here. Fresno. On a freezing-cold Christmas Day."

"Stopped there a bunch of times when I was driving truck."

"We'll have to go there someday. In ten years, the whole family."

She looked at him and smiled. He didn't blink, didn't doubt the future they'd have together. It was the completion of everything. It was what he wanted, all that he wanted. And at that moment it was settled.

"I'll mark it on my calendar," he said.

"Please do. Now, my boots, if you don't mind. Just like the first time. Do you remember the first time?"

She lay back with her arms over her head as he pulled off her Ramírez boots. It took longer than the rest of her clothes, and his, and after that his skin felt hot in her hands, and her mouth opened to his and her breathing became coarse and she shivered and moved her hips and he moved his until there was nothing else and finally, perfectly, they were together again.

Afterward, Will put more logs on the fire in the living room. On the way back, he flipped on the hall light and the spillover hit Merry, outlining her naked body lying on the bed, a dark form against the white sheets. Will got in beside her and pulled the covers over both of them.

Lying on his back, he said, "Fresno, huh? I never knew Fresno could have that effect on people."

"Where have you been? Everybody knows it's the most romantic place in the West."

"That's how I've always thought of it."

"I have to tell you my story. I didn't want to tell you in front of everyone."

"That's right, you have a story."

"It happened in a restaurant in Fresno called Jack's. It's a truck-stop-diner, plastic-menu-type place. Whatever."

"Been there, yeah. It's a good feed."

"You won't believe this, but it's absolutely true."

With great excitement, Merry told the story of her Christmas conversion.

She was sitting at Jack's eating something called chicken-fried steak at a shiny table in a stiff red boothand feeling miserably alone. She couldn't stop thinking about the Flying Z, and how it might look if she'd been able to decorate it, as Sweetie had suggested.

At just that vulnerable time, she received a text from Peter, the stableman at Ballyfeard, her father's estate in Ireland. The message included a photo of the big house and the barn and the outbuildings, all shining behind strings of red and green lights and displays of Santas and reindeer and the manger scene.

Peter told her all about their traditional Christmas Eve celebration. Merry, her father, Michael, and the household staff dressed in nineteenth-century costumes, the men in knee breeches, the women in red petticoats, and they rode horseback across the countryside to neighboring farms and homes. They led a horse-drawn carriage loaded with gifts for the kids, and everyone sang carols in the snow. Peter had a beautiful singing voice.

In the morning, the party continued with the estate staff gathering to open presents, and at night they all sat down to a feast of corned beef smothered in beer and brown sugar.

Merry missed all of it on that cold Christmas Day in Fresno. In her loneliness, she could think of nothing else, and to give herself a boost, to feel some of the same magic, she reached into her bag for her tattered copy of *One Hundred Years of Solitude*.

She was reading along, lost in it as usual, when an unwashed man, without introduction or hesitation, slid onto the opposite seat and began discussing the book.

"My first impression was he needed either an exorcism or a bath," Merry said. "I was about to tell him to buzz off when I noticed his hands. Sparrow hands. That's how Gabriel García Márquez described Melquíades, the character I love so much. I thought, 'Okay, this is deeply weird,' so I listened to him."

She described a man wildly alive in his passion and knowledge. He pulled from his pocket his own copy of *Solitude* and opened it to pages bent from use and marred by yellow highlighter, and the two of them, strangers in Fresno, opposites in Fresno, began discussing the Buendía family and their lives in the isolated town of Macondo, and the encroachment of a ravenous outside world sure to destroy it.

They talked about flying carpets, about the character who builds a memory machine and the ghost who tries to stop up the spear hole in his throat with grass. They talked about the infant born with a pig's tail and the rain of flowers so heavy it smothered the animals and blanketed the streets.

The man, a truck driver as Will had been, helped Merry realize something important. Over those hundred years, the Buendías fought to hold on to their way of life in a place where magic happened around them all the time, and didn't that sound a lot like the Zacharys?

Was the story of Domingo Opata's search for Kazoh any further beyond the physical world than Macondo's giant ants?

That scruffy stranger had asked Merry why, if she'd fallen under the spell of *Solitude* and believed its every word, she didn't believe the story of El Jinete of the Flying Z. "I was right on the edge of coming back," Merry said. "All I needed was a push and suddenly there's this man across from me."

"At Jack's."

"At Jack's, and he was awful. His grammar was atrocious and he smelled like a dumpster. But I listened because he was brilliant. He understood that García Márquez wanted to take us beyond ourselves, to understand that reality isn't only in the mirror. And he appeared at that perfect moment."

"You're saying he was a sign, that somebody sent him?"

"Yes! The immortal gypsy Melquíades sent him. What am I supposed to think? I'm sure of it. He changed my whole way of thinking."

"I have to read this book."

"Yes, yes, you must. After all, I read *Shane*. It's only fair."

"What was this fellow's name?"

"He left before I could ask." Merry made a puzzled face. "Come to think of it, he left his check for me to pay."

"Never trust a wall-eyed wizard you meet at Jack's in Fresno."

"But he wasn't a wizard. He was an ordinary man. That's the whole point. All the wild things that happened in Macondo were daily occurrences. Normal as the sunshine, normal as the wind. Just like Opata is here."

Only yesterday, Will had thought it would never happen this way again, that he would never hold Merry in his arms, in his bed, his heart beating with hers. Every hour she'd been gone, he'd felt all the misery and emptiness that life could throw at him, and now she was back with him and everything was right again.

"You had to leave this place to finally understand it," he said.

"I'll never leave again."

"If you do, I'll track you down. I'll be like a Pinkerton guy."

"You know what's so cool? I keep thinking of this. You came looking for me just like Opata looks for Kazoh."

"I couldn't find you. That's like Opata, too."

"Do you think he'll ever find Kazoh?"

"Yes. He has to."

"You're right, he has to. That's the only way the story can end, with them together. It's decided, it's already written. Because when you love somebody that's the way it has to be."

They lay together in happy reunion. Before falling asleep, Will explained that in the morning, he and Lucy were going out on the trails again searching for Abrazo.

In the afternoon, Lucy would go back out alone, while Will went to meet Boone Macklin in town. This was the meeting Macklin had requested. Will and Levi had worked up a surprise for him.

"I'm going with you to look for Abrazo," Merry said.

Will believed it his job to keep her safe but said nothing.

Sensing his reluctance, she said, "I'm not staying at the house waiting and wondering. I should've insisted the last time and I'm not doing that again. I'll go with you in the morning, and while you're in town meeting Macklin, I'll go out again with Lucy in the afternoon."

"You can handle riding alone with her?"

"Can she handle me?"

Will laughed. "I'd say you've got the hang of this place."

"This is the way it's going to be from now on, Will. I'm all in with you and the Flying Z, so you and Levi and everybody else better get used to it.'

CHAPTER THIRTY

Next morning. No wind, bright sunshine, belly down on an outcropping, Will glassed the Canyon Trail as far south as his vision would allow and saw them coming.

At first, they were nothing but dark spots in the wiggling air, until the spots became larger and took the shape of men walking. They looked like a centipede dressed in camouflage.

No way of telling how many were lined up behind the leader. No way yet of identifying the leader or whether he carried a weapon. Lucy lay on one side of Will and Merry the other.

"We're in business," Will said and handed Lucy the binoculars. "Focus on the lead dog. Recognize him?"

She looked. "Yeah, yeah. Guess who? It's Jazzy again. We need to be careful with this dude. He ain't no cupcake."

"Armed as usual?"

"Yup. Never seen him without his AR-15 and I don't expect he'll give it up without persuasion." Lucy turned to Merry. "Looks like you're gonna have some excitement your first day out. We been doing these stop-and-talks a while now and it can get tricky. Are you ready, Miss Mustang?"

"Just tell me what to do."

"Me and you, we ride straight up on Jazzy talking nice, acting nice, like we got no problem in this big wide world. He knows me and that'll put him at ease. All we do then is wait for Will to come up from behind and relieve him of his weapon."

"What if he spooks?"

"Up to us to see that he don't."

"We can do that, and don't you doubt I'm ready."

Lucy gave Merry a long, measuring look. "I do believe you are, girl."

Will watched as Jazzy came closer, stopping his group of thirteen in the shade of the mesquites below the outcropping. The mules dropped their loads and drank from their water jugs. They joshed and tossed twigs at one another.

Sitting alone on a rock at the head of the pack, Jazzy glared back at them and at once they stopped their fooling. He grabbed a water bottle at his feet, drank, poured some into his palm, and rubbed the back of his neck. He stretched his back, looking ahead along the trail and back the way they'd just come.

Not worried, not suspicious, just looking.

"Okay, time to go," Will whispered. "Slow and easy. I'll be along."

Lucy and Merry scrambled down to their horses, ground tied at the bottom of the ridge. They rode in the shelter of the outcropping to get ahead of the group and doubled back. Jazzy stood quickly when he heard them coming along the trail.

He went to unstrap the AR-15 from his shoulder, saw Lucy, and relaxed. He fixated on Merry, leering. He tilted his head toward Lucy to silently ask about her.

"Boss's woman," Lucy said.

Jazzy stared some more. "Pretty girl, eh?"

He was short, had fat cheeks and several days' growth of beard. He wore a ratty black coat and blue jeans and expensive Timberland hiking shoes. Merry sat her horse beside Lucy, who talked pleasantly to Jazzy until Will walked up behind him with his Winchester.

He pointed it at Jazzy. "I'll take that rifle."

Realizing his position, Jazzy gave Lucy a hard look. He knew he'd been had. Slowly, he shook it off his shoulder, held it by the buttstock, barrel down, and handed it to Will. In Spanish, Will ordered the mules to line up. They hesitated, looking at Jazzy for help.

"*¡Yo manda ya!*" Will said. "*¡Haga lo que digo!*"—I'm in charge now! Do what I say!

They obeyed and lined up. Will walked past the bedraggled men holding up a sketch of the Abrazo hoofprint and asking if they'd seen it. He pressed it against their faces, and one by one they shook their heads.

Only one of them made eye contact. He had bruises on his face and his lips were fat and cut as if by blows. With Will holding the sketch close to his face, the beaten man nodded slightly and licked his lips.

Will pulled him out of line, sat him on a rock, and asked what had happened to his face. The man's eyes shifted quickly to Jazzy and back. He lowered his head and refused to speak.

To Jazzy, Will said, "You don't treat your people right."

"He works for me, Señor Zachary. He's mine."

"Not anymore. He's coming with me."

"And his bundle? What happens to that? I have a job to do."

"Pick it up later. I'll leave it on the trail. Your satellite phone, hand it over."

Jazzy didn't budge. He scowled at Will. Without the phone, he couldn't communicate with his scouts and couldn't call for help to get his mule back or collect his product.

"Do it," Will ordered.

Slowly, Jazzy pulled the phone from his pocket and tossed it to Will, who dropped it on the ground and used the butt of the AR-15 to smash it.

Jazzy mumbled, "*Pinche hijo de la puta Yaqui.*"

Will straightened. He felt the muscles in his neck knot up. He stepped close to Jazzy. "I'd like you to repeat that, my friend. With all this excitement, I didn't quite hear you."

"He called you the no-good son of a Yaqui whore," Lucy said. "And I don't believe he meant it in a nice way."

Will had nothing of his mother, no memory of her touch or her voice, no scent, none of her essence, only that wrinkled old photograph. But the remark bruised his honor. He pushed his face close to Jazzy's.

"What's your problem with my blood? I want you to tell me."

Jazzy didn't speak. His eyes stayed fixed on Will's.

"Right now. Go on, tell me. I've got the time."

Jazzy was breathing hard and his mouth was crooked with hate. But with the Winchester on him and Lucy nearby and armed, there was nothing he could do.

"If I find out you cut my fences," Will said, "I'll put a crease in your head shaped exactly like this AR." He pulled the magazine out and threw the rifle at Jazzy's chest. He caught it with two hands.

Immediately, Will said, "You know what? I changed my mind. I'm keeping all these bundles with me. They'll make a nice fire. That's because of your big mouth. Now, you and your men get the hell out of here as fast as you can go."

When Jazzy and his group had left, Will sat on a rock next to the bruised man. He was filthy and shivering from the cold. His tattered clothes barely clung to his body. His left shoulder was bare where his shirt had been ripped away, and the skin was raw from the strap on the bundle he'd carried.

Will leaned forward in an intimate posture and spoke softly. "I'm good at reading faces, and I can tell you know something about Abrazo. I can forget about you smuggling across my property."

He paused and stroked his jaw as if thinking things over. "Yeah, I believe I can let that go. But you have to tell me what I want to know."

Frightened, the man just stared at the ground.

"Don't cooperate and I leave you here for Jazzy."

"No, no, no," the man said, extending his hands in a plea. "You can't. No, *favor*."

"Agree to talk and I'll take you to my ranch and give you water and clean socks and a change of clothes. You can eat until you're full and when you're done you can walk away in any direction you choose, a free man."

"No *chili verde*."

"Sure, no *chili verde*."

"*¿Recompense, también?*"

"You're not shy, are you?" Will said. "A man in your predicament ought to at least be shy. The reward comes after you talk."

"My family in Chicago. I need to get to my family. I need money."

"There's something we have in common."

"*Por favor, mi familia*."

"Quit begging. The sound of it makes me sick. What's your name?"

"José."

"Wish I had a dollar for all the Josés I've run into over the years." Will regarded him with his sharp black eyes. "I like a man with bark on him, José, but not today."

"*Por favor*." His face became animated as he delivered his plea. "My family is in Chicago, my wife, my sons. They hold them until I pay. That is why I carry drugs for Jazzy. I don't like drugs. I don't use drugs. I owe these men and I work to pay my debt."

"You lived in Chicago before all this?"

"*Sí, sí.* At the hotel." He put on his work voice. "'Hello and good morning. Welcome to the Drake Hotel. How can I help you?' I work there until they deport me. That was my job. 'Hello, hello, hello.'"

"How much do you owe?"

"Nine thousand. I walk the trails to pay my debt. They take my family prisoner until I pay them. Now I have no way to pay. I have to get to Chicago to see these men, to explain. Before Jazzy talks to them and they hurt my family. I have to go now. *Por favor,* Señor Zachary."

"I can help you get to Chicago, but you need to tell me how to find Abrazo."

José didn't answer right away. He looked around as if the answer were written on the mountains. Finally, he pooched his lips to point south, and said, "Bandera."

"Abrazo's at Rancho La Bandera?"

He nodded. "Chicago, Señor."

"I hear you. You can't get there without money, so it's business first. We're going to the Flying Z to talk."

Before leaving, Will gathered Jazzy's bundles together and set them on fire. Lucy gave him an admiring smile from the saddle. "I gotta say, Will, you got no backup in you. Not a bad way to be, long as it don't kill you."

She pulled José onto the horse behind her. They rode back to the ranch and sat him down at the kitchen table. Merry gave him a water bottle that he drained in a swallow. She gave him another with the same result.

Will went to the dresser in his bedroom and got $400 in $20 bills out of a drawer. Back in the kitchen, he slapped the money down on the red-and-white-checked tablecloth, spun a chair around, and hung his arms over the back.

"Abrazo," he said.

José looked at Lucy leaning against the kitchen counter with her arms folded, and at Merry, who was getting out the fixings to cook breakfast. His eyes angled down to study the bills. "This man you want, he rides out of Bandera," José said. "They move a dozen shipments a week through Bandera."

"You're sure about that?"

"I know this, I see it. Many times, I see it." He pointed to his eyes.

"I talked to Francisco Perez myself," Will said. "That's not what he told me."

José shook his head and grinned. His two front teeth were gold. "Francisco lies. Bandera is Marcelino's property. Francisco works for him. He makes sure Marcelino's loads get through. Francisco runs all of it."

"I need Abrazo's name."

"I don't know. No one does. He works through Marcelino's top men. Talks only to them, no one else."

Merry put a plate of scrambled eggs and bacon in front of José. He wiped the plate clean and she gave him a second helping. Lucy pulled out the sketch of Abrazo's hoofprint and showed it to José.

"Perez told us Abrazo rides the Carranza Hills." Lucy stabbed her finger down on the hoofprint. "Have you seen this track out there?"

José held the fork in his closed fist as he shoveled in the food. He shifted his eyes to the sketch and shook his head. "Never," he said and went back to his breakfast.

"That was a little quick, don't you think?" Lucy grabbed the back of José's shirt and pushed his face down until it was almost in the food. "Perez told us he's working the Carranza right now. Look again."

"He lies. I walk Carranza every day. I know this." Jose used his fingers to mimic someone walking. "If he was in Carranza, I would see his tracks. I would see him."

"Where's Abrazo riding now?" Lucy twisted the shirt tighter.

"I don't know, I swear. But Francisco Perez knows."

Lucy let him go and stuffed the sketch in her pocket. "If this *pollo*'s telling the truth, we been played, Will. Your dear friend decoyed us, got us chasing our butts."

When José couldn't eat any more, Merry gave him clean clothes and Will gave him the $400 and told him to take off. But José wanted Will to drive him to town.

"That wasn't part of the deal," Will said.

"Jazzy and his men are looking for me," José said. "They look right now."

"He's got no phone. It'll take them a while to catch up with you."

"They have scouts all over and they have phones. I won't make it to town alive. You burned Jazzy's whole load. He kill me for sure in revenge. Señor Zachary, *por favor*."

From the sink, Merry gave Will a pleading look.

He threw up his hands in frustration. "What?"

"You did burn the load," she said. "Besides, you're going into town to meet Macklin anyway."

"That's what I do around here, isn't it," Will said. "Give money to drug smugglers and drive them wherever they want to go."

"You can't just send him away," Merry said. "They'll kill him."

Will swallowed his disgust and said to José, "Looks like it's you and me. Go on outside and lie down in the bed of the Silverado and stay down. No matter what happens, I don't want to see your head popping up."

"*Muchas gracias*, Señor Zachary."

Will threw a tarp over José and started out. A short distance from the house, a Border Patrol truck going in the opposite direction pulled alongside him. Before it got there, Will stuck his head out the window and said to José, "*Chile verde.* Keep your mouth shut and don't move or you'll be arrested."

Will and the female agent exchanged pleasant greetings, and she said, "We've been busy the past few days. You seen anything?"

"Been quiet all day."

"Something different, right?"

"I could get used to it."

"I don't know how you live with it, Mr. Zachary. Stay safe." She smiled, wished him a pleasant day, and drove deeper into the mountains.

In Patagonia, Will rolled slowly along Naugle Avenue. At the south end of town, he pulled over beside a gully near State Route 82. "This is it," he said, and threw off the tarp. "Down a few miles you'll find Solero Road. Take the left fork and keep going and you'll reach Rio Rico and I-19. Half a day's walk."

Will had more bills in his pocket. He had no idea the amount. He fished them out and handed them over. José was too surprised to take them at first.

"Go on," Will said. "Go and rescue your people in Chicago."

José held the bills with two hands in front of his face like he couldn't believe his good fortune. "Señor Zachary, Señor Zachary." José's voice cracked.

"Get lost. If I find you around here again, I'll bury you myself."

José ran down the gully.

Will pulled a U-turn and was starting back to town when he spotted Bud Tisdale's Dodge truck coming toward him. He rolled down his window. Tisdale did the same and hung his arm along the side panel. They talked lane to lane.

"I thought you were working at the Double R," Will said.

"Going back tonight. Came up to buy groceries."

"You don't look so bad, Bud. Macklin's bruises healed up good."

"I'm a tough old boy, Will. You know that."

"He would've killed you if I didn't pull him off. Pick somebody shorter next time."

Tisdale bellowed his *har-har-har* laugh. "I'll have to go to the grade school for that."

Somebody behind Tisdale blasted their horn, and he gunned it and took off, waving goodbye out the window.

CHAPTER THIRTY-ONE

Early in the afternoon, Will met Boone Macklin behind Sweetie's Feed, a boxy cinder block on the north side of Naugle Avenue. Broken furniture was stacked up by the rear door, beside a dumpster and a storage shed.

Macklin sat next to the shed on an upturned crate, elbows resting on his dwarf legs. He wore a military-green field jacket, no hat, his hair spiky and unwashed, his eyes glistening.

"I don't see why we needed to do this here," he said. "The Remuda would've been fine. Got my own table over there."

"I wanted a private place," Will said. "Your meeting, so talk."

"Miss Queen asked me to deliver a message. Word is, you been bushwhacking Marcelino's men on the trails." Macklin clucked his tongue. "Not a smart move if you wanna stay alive. No, sir, I wouldn't recommend it."

That confirmed that Queen and Marcelino were working together.

"And you want me to stay alive," Will said.

"Was up to me, I'd go ahead and let Marcelino do what he does best. But Miss Queen likes it quiet. No gunplay, none of that nasty business."

"She's a good citizen is what you're saying."

"You bet. Has cats and a garden, too." He grinned. There was whiskey on his breath. "Miss Queen's message is simple. Sell to her and your Marcelino problem goes away."

Will stared, and Macklin stared back.

"I've thought about this and decided to take her offer," Will said.

Surprised, Macklin said, "I didn't think you had it in you, Zachary. The brains, I'm talking about."

"But before that can happen, you need to do something for me."

The back door of the store opened and Sweetie Taylor stepped out. She was dressed in her customary baggy blue jeans and blue work shirt. She carried a bucket of water.

"Thought I heard voices," she said. "Looks like we got some kind of meeting going on."

"Who the hell are you?" Macklin said.

Sweetie drew the bucket back and heaved, spilling the water onto the ground. Macklin scrambled to lift his boots to avoid the wave rushing through the dirt.

"Sweetie Taylor," she said, and raised her chin with pride. "Of the Fort Crittenden Taylors."

"This don't concern you, lady."

"At my store it concerns me."

"You smell like wet hay." He waved his hand back and forth in front of his face.

"Why, thank you." Sweetie set the bucket down and leaned her arm on top of the storage shed. She clasped her hands together and gave Macklin a cockeyed smile around the wad of tobacco swelling her cheek.

"Tell you what, Macklin, I'll stand here and keep an eye on things," she said. "You think you got what it takes to move me, go ahead and try. I'm down to my last lung, but I can handle the likes of you."

Macklin frowned. "What kind of freak-show town is this?"

"The only way I leave is if Will Zachary wants me to. Will, what'll it be?"

"Got a pot of coffee inside, Sweetie?" Will said.

"Always. A fresh pot of Baja Joe's finest."

"Bring a cup for him, too."

"Are you serious?" She gestured at Macklin. "This galoot ain't deservin' of one drop of that coffee."

"Today he is, Sweetie," Will insisted. "And hurry it up."

She came back carrying two steaming cups and handed them out. Will said, "Go on inside now," and haltingly, unhappily, she did.

Macklin pulled a pint bottle of Southern Comfort from his coat pocket and poured a taste into his coffee. He stirred the concoction with his finger, sucked on the finger, and sipped his drink with satisfaction.

"Okay, Zachary, what is it you want?"

"I need to find the man who killed my uncle. He works for Marcelino and rides a horse with specific shoes, abrazo shoes."

"Can't say I know him."

"Did you hear me right? I'm selling to Stacy Queen. I'm doing what she wants. Or I could change my mind and walk away."

"Can't give you what I don't have. Marcelino bosses the trails and you best not worry too much about him. Man's a badass, okay?"

"Jimmy Benson," Will said. Benson was the rancher who'd been murdered two years before on the Double R. "Rumor says Marcelino did it himself."

Macklin sipped his drink. "You heard that?"

"I heard it."

He held the steaming cup with two hands, arms on his thighs. He had fat fingers for a bantamweight. "Well, it's a fact." He gave a loose wave. "Sometimes I hang my ear out, pick up bits and pieces along the way."

Will could see that Macklin wanted to talk. He waited to let the booze do its work. Macklin took another sip and out it came.

"Benson lost a couple shipments. Serious product. Can't have that. They call that a death sentence. He was missing a week before they found him floating in a stock tank."

Macklin wiped the corners of his mouth with his fingertips. "Marcelino insisted on looking Benson in the face before doing him. Took his time, too. Freaked Miss Queen out that he'd come up here and kill somebody on this side. Don't go spreading that around. Marcelino will put your head on a stick."

"You work for interesting people."

"Miss Queen ain't that way," he said. "That's why I'm here. Fact, she takes certain steps to protect herself from Marcelino. Lady's smart." He tapped his temple. "Got stuff locked in her safe on the Benson hit, eyewitness statements from old clients. She can pull them out any time if Marcelino's mind wanders."

"Leverage."

"Life is leverage and leverage leads to the good life." Macklin stood and drained the remainder of his drink and dropped the cup in the dumpster. "I'll tell Miss Queen to draw up the papers. Don't make this hard, Zachary." He started walking away in short, cocky steps.

"Eli James Fontaine," Will said.

Macklin stopped on a dime with a nickel in change.

"Yeah," Will said. "Seems there's a warrant out of Nevada for a pawnshop robbery. Man had a tattoo just like yours."

Levi had heard from Ralph Reyes at the Washoe County Sheriff's Office. Not only did the pistol tattoo on Macklin's arm match the robber's, but the body type did, too.

Macklin turned on his heels. Speaking quickly: "I didn't do no pawnshop job. You don't know what you're talking about, Zachary. You got the wrong guy." He was trying hard to look unworried. But his face had filled with shadows.

"If I was holding a birth certificate, it wouldn't be better proof than the way you look right now," Will said. "You're Eli James Fontaine."

Macklin stood fifteen feet away, his arms rigid at his sides. For a moment he looked to be thinking, then, finding that hopeless, reverted to what he did best. With his eyes bulging, he made his neck disappear under drawn-up shoulders, twisted his face into a scowl, lowered his head, and charged.

The distance gave Will the space to time his punch, and he did so perfectly, a short, powerful right to the nose. It stood Macklin up but he didn't go down. He found his balance and caught Will with a rainbow right that glanced off his ear. A stabbing pain shot down Will's neck.

Macklin came again, this time with a left that Will blocked with his right forearm, leaving Macklin open for a left uppercut. Will used his thighs and back and punched as hard as he could, the blow reverberating back up his arm to his shoulder.

But Macklin was strong. He caught his breath and tried again. Will was ready. His third punch landed right where it was aimed, underneath Macklin's chin. He went down and when he tried to scramble back up, Will straddled him, grabbed his shirt, and hit him again. Macklin's head snapped back. His body went limp and his eyes rolled.

"I've been waiting a long time to do that," Will said and shook Macklin until his eyes focused. "'Buck Zachary had it coming.' Isn't that what you said?"

"That didn't mean nothing. It was just words, okay?" Macklin reached into his back pocket for a red bandanna. He held it over his nose and squeezed. "It's bust." He moved his nose slowly back and forth and heard the crack of loose bones and cartilage. "You busted it."

Levi walked out of the store's back door followed by one of his deputies. Sweetie came, too. The deputy fished Macklin's cup out of the trash and dropped it into a plastic evidence bag.

"You didn't leave prints at the holdup, and your disguise hid your face from the cameras." Levi said. "So far so good. But DNA is tricky these days. All it takes is a single hair. Don't even need the root anymore."

He pointed to the plastic bag. "Pretty soon we'll be comparing DNA from that cup to what they got in Reno. Want to bet it's a match?"

Macklin sat up with his arm straight back, balancing himself on one palm. "What do you want from me?"

Will leaned close to Macklin with his hands on his knees. Their faces were inches apart. "Abrazo. Give me something."

"Told you, I don't know nothing."

"You know Francisco Perez? Down at Rancho La Bandera?"

"No, I don't. Who is he?"

Will told him.

"If he runs Marcelino's operation in Mexico, I don't want to know him. Even if I did, I wouldn't talk. Nobody talks about Marcelino. That's a rule."

"Are you forgetting, Macklin? You just told us he was a murderer."

"Never happened. I don't know what you heard, Zachary. Go ahead and hook me up, Sheriff. I'd rather do time in Nevada than have Marcelino after me."

Sweetie went to the storage shed and grabbed a small tape recorder off the top. She'd placed it there when she'd first stepped outside. She tossed it to Will and he pressed play. The voices were clear. He let it run for several seconds.

"The math here should be easy even for you," Will said. "Tell me what I need to know and the tape stays with Sheriff Johnson.

Otherwise it goes to Marcelino, and there's no way to describe how dead you'll be."

His confidence gone, Macklin said, "Hold on now, hold on."

"Leverage," Will said. "The only thing better is apple pie."

"Look, Miss Queen don't tell me about the Mexicans, what they do down there. I don't know Francisco Perez and I ain't never met this Abrazo."

"Somebody's got to hook up with him on this side."

"That ain't me. They change people all the time and it's never the same location twice. They're real careful about that. Even the load drivers don't know the location 'til the last minute. They don't want no leaks." Macklin leaned over and spat a silver-dollar-sized plug of blood.

"You have to do better than that," Will said. He hit rewind on the tape and pressed play. The sound of his voice talking about Marcelino put panic in Macklin's eyes.

"Stop, stop it. Okay, okay, I'll tell you this much." He breathed deeply and blew it out hard. "I know when the next load moves."

"I'm listening."

"I heard Miss Queen on the phone. It's coming up in three days and it's a big one. That's all I know. If there was anything else, I'd tell you."

Will pressed him for details on the route and the drop site, and so did Levi. But Macklin swore he knew nothing more. The deputy cuffed him.

"Come on, I helped you out," Macklin said. "How about letting me go and I leave here and never come back?"

"Can't do that," Levi said. "You assaulted Will Zachary."

"I didn't assault him, I punched him is all. What about the tape?"

"It stays with me," Levi said. "After Nevada is done with you, if you land back in Arizona, I send it to Marcelino." He turned to Sweetie. "Is she out there?"

"She's waiting in front."

"Thanks for the help," Levi said.

Sweetie stiffened like a soldier at attention, struggled to suppress a grin, saluted, and went into the store. Levi said he needed a couple of hours to handle business at the jail and asked Will to meet him at 4 p.m. at the Hurdy House Restaurant.

"There's something we need to talk about," Levi said and walked around to the front parking lot.

Stacy Queen's black GMC Yukon Denali was there. When she saw Levi, she stepped out from behind the wheel dressed in a nondescript gray business suit, her hair pinned up.

"You had me drive all this way to meet at a feed store? What's so urgent, Sheriff?"

"There's something I want you to see."

"I'm in court in two hours. Make it fast."

The deputy came around the building escorting Macklin. Looking shocked, Queen said, "Take those handcuffs off. That man is my client. What is this about? I demand to know what this is about."

When Levi didn't respond, she followed Macklin as the deputy shoved him into the backseat of the squad car. "Don't say anything, Boone. Not a word. Sheriff, I demand to know what's going on here. Mr. Macklin has rights."

"Yes, he does. He has the right to remain silent, but he couldn't help himself. It's all here." He held up the tape recorder. Pleasantly, Levi added, "Pardon my boldness, ma'am, but your client's a real donkey."

Too shocked to speak, she stared at Levi with her mouth hanging open.

"Follow me to the station, Miss Queen," he said. "I'll pour you a cup of coffee and fill you in."

CHAPTER THIRTY-TWO

The Hurdy House was empty ahead of the supper crowd. The tables had glass tops with cattle brands burned into the wood underneath. Levi got there at exactly 4 p.m. The rickety board floor creaked as he walked to Will's table.

The waiter hurried over with a cup of Earl Grey, Levi's regular. His name was Paco and his fingers were black. He did charcoal sketches of well-known local characters and sold them at the register. He drew Levi in his uniform, badge, sidearm, and hat. But even with those accessories sharply presented, the most prominent feature was his soft face.

They each ordered a muffin. Levi had called Ralph Reyes. Washoe County was eager to take custody of Fontaine. Levi had talked with Stacy Queen at the station, and to keep the tape recording from reaching Marcelino, she'd agreed to sell her holdings in the county.

"I don't think we'll be seeing her around here again," Levi said.

Will told him about José the mule. Levi frowned across the table. "If Border Patrol catches you driving smugglers around, they might just charge you. They don't care for that."

"How's Border Patrol going to find out?"

"Can't imagine. You believe his Chicago story?"

"Let's just say I'm having one of those rare days when I have faith in human nature. I'm sure it'll pass."

"These drug pushers all have family in Chicago, Will. And they all have fake names, multiple DOBs, and heartbreaking stories. Don't tell me you gave him money, too."

"If Jazzy catches up with him, he's a dead man."

Levi shook his head in resignation and sipped. "Dang, that's good tea."

"I'm tired of finding bodies. Had my fill of seeing human bones bleaching on my land. It does something to a man."

"Well, it'll stay between us."

Western movie posters decorated the walls. Lee Marvin, Robert Duvall, and Kevin Costner were there. McQueen and Eastwood were there. Paul Newman and Robert Redford, too. Will had seen all the movies, and some he enjoyed. With others, he couldn't understand how they could get it so wrong.

All Will knew for sure, about the movies and everything else, the only thing that mattered to him, was that when it came to working horseback, he could outride and out-rope all those famous men looking down at him, as he could their stunt doubles, and anyone else he'd ever known, except Buck when he was younger.

Paco brought the muffins. He was stooped at the shoulders and had black spike earrings. He practically bowed at Levi as he departed the table.

The restaurant door opened and four tourists walked in. They wore North Face jackets and floppy canvas sun hats. Their faces were blotched red by the sun, except for raccoon circles from their $150 Oakley sunglasses. They carried cameras and binoculars. There was a popular guest ranch close by.

"I'm going to tell you something, and I'm serious," Will said.

"What's that?"

"If it ever comes down to me having to squire a bunch of rich dudes around horseback to make money, you have permission to shoot me."

"You'd look fancy in a turquoise scarf."

The two of them ate. Will eyed the tourists over Levi's shoulder.

"They're staring at you, Levi. It's the Thompson brothers again."

Four years before, two men on the run from the law showed up in Patagonia, robbed a store, and ran into Levi as they were fleeing. He hollered at them to stop. One of them fired two shots and missed. Levi fired back and missed as well, at which point the bad guys thought better of continuing to fight and gave up.

The episode lasted all of ten seconds.

But someone had captured it on camera and it hit the Internet. Levi, standing in a perfect pose, tall, Stetson sitting high and majestic on his head, his gun barking, became a sensation known for his daring, the man who captured the Thompson boys.

He was the subject of newspaper and TV stories claiming the Wild West still lived in the person of Sheriff Levi Johnson. The publicity inspired Paco in his artwork. His rendering of Levi had become his bestseller.

"Want to bet they come over for a picture?" Will said. "Show the folks back home they met a real Western sheriff."

"Do they know I missed, for Pete's sake?"

"Pathetic. The man with no name never missed."

Levi rolled his eyes in excitement. "The spaghetti westerns? Are you kidding me? They're the best. I watch them over and over."

"You need to let it go."

"Butch and Sundance? Come on. I can't get enough of them either. That song, 'Raindrops'? Did you know I shave to that in the morning?"

"That's just sad."

Will laughed with great pleasure and Levi laughed along with him. They went back to their muffins. The tourists kept whispering and sneaking looks at Levi.

"Ever feel like a relic, a museum piece behind glass?" Will said.

"Matter of fact I do, time to time."

Will had forgotten about his muffin. He had a serious face now. "Sometimes it feels like it's all coming to an end, living the way I do, and there's not a thing I can do about it."

"I believe you got time yet."

Will pointed to the movie posters on the wall. "That's what all these pictures are about, men trying to keep on being cowboys, living their lives the way they want. But it's dying, Levi. I can't drive Morales Road without thinking this might be the last time."

"Hey, you don't have it so bad. When you're out riding, I'm at a meeting with the board of supervisors fighting for an extra dollar or two."

"Feels like it's happening fast, Levi."

"They've been saying that since barbed wire."

Paco freshened Will's coffee. Levi waved him off. When Paco was gone, Will said, "I'm going to take a trip tomorrow."

Levi glanced over his shoulder to make sure Paco wasn't close enough to hear. "Bandera?"

"Francisco Perez is going to tell me what trail that load is traveling on Friday. I don't like being lied to. I'll break him if I have to, but come Friday, I'm going to be waiting for it."

"Way things are going, you need to have somebody watch the ranch. I'll be working."

"I just called Cuco and can't reach him. He's probably off on one of his Mexico deals. Can't find Harley either. He's missed work three days now and I don't know what's up."

"Ain't like him."

"Sweetie said she'd get help at the store and come out."

Levi cut one of the muffins in half and buttered it. Deliberately, he scraped the excess off the knife using the edge of the plate. "Merry going?"

"There's no telling her she can't, not now."

Levi took a bite. Chewing, thinking, he said, "You sure about this? Marcelino wants you dead and you're going across to Bandera based on what one of his drug pushers told you?"

"José was talking straight. He has no use for Perez."

Levi sat back hard as if shoved. "Nobody shoots straight, Will. This is the drug business. You know that better than anybody. You're going to Mexico to find somebody that could be right under your nose. Abrazo himself could walk in this restaurant right now. Look what happened with Hector."

"I don't need to hear that name ever again. He's lion scat to me."

"Don't forget, you found tracks, not a body."

"Can't forget anything about that man. I see his face in my sleep. I see that border hat of his wherever I go."

"There's more angles here you need to consider." Levi finished his muffin and pointed to Will's. "If you're not gonna eat that—" Will granted permission with a nod. Levi snatched it up and went through the same cutting and buttering ritual.

He said, "All the ranches around here not run by a corporation, or by Robert Reginald Ashmont III, are hanging on any way they can, and plenty of town folks, too. Man comes along waving dollar bills and what do you know—" Levi grimaced, showing his bottom teeth. "All I'm saying is when it comes to Abrazo, I got a long list of suspects."

"You've got a helluva job, Levi. Getting up in the morning thinking the whole world's crooked."

"You fall for people, Will. That's your problem."

"Is that why you asked me here? To tell me I'm a damn fool?"

"That and one other thing." Levi looked over his shoulder again. He lowered his voice. "When the time comes with Abrazo,

I know there's only one way it can go between you two to make this right. I'll give you the room you need."

Will nodded. Nothing more had to be said to seal their understanding.

Levi pointed to the movie posters. "It'll be good for you to do it for real. I just hope I don't get a stiff neck looking the other way."

He finished the second muffin. He wiped his face with a napkin and went back to talking in his normal voice. "While you're gone, I'll give myself a treat, head over to Paul Bond's."

"You don't need another pair of cowboy boots, do you?"

"I got a pair for every day of the week. Two for Sundays."

"How do you work that?"

"I rotate my Sunday boots. One week on, one off."

"They say when you've got boots for all seven days, you've made it."

"They line up nice in my closet."

"I'm surprised you can afford another pair of Bond's. That's real money."

"Oh, I can't buy. I like to browse. Walk around and smell the leather."

Peering over the rim of his cup, Will said, "What'd I tell you? Here they come."

The four tourists surrounded Levi's chair. A man in tortoise-shell glasses leaned down. "I hate to trouble you, Sheriff Johnson. But we recognized you and would love to get a picture. Would you be so kind?"

In a perfect drawl that Levi rolled out on special occasions, he said, "Don't reckon I can say no to that." He stood in front of the movie posters, positioning himself so the actors were visible. He threw his thumb over his shoulder.

"Be sure to get my friends in the shot."

They all scrunched together, Levi in the center. He wrapped his big arms around the two standing at his sides and hung his head forward. He towered over them all. With his photo session done, he said goodbye and started for the door.

Paco ran over to hold it open for him. Levi touched the brim of his hat to each of his admirers in turn and walked out.

CHAPTER THIRTY-THREE

The three riders departed the Flying Z in the predawn dark. They rode east with the air smelling powerfully of rain but none falling, and the low clouds giving a strange twilight color to the breaking morning with the sun pushing through.

At the northern extension of Bandera Road, they turned southwest to Cinco Lanas Mountain. They fought through the wait-a-minute brush and climbed single file to its peak and down into Sierra Gap and started south.

They rode side by side, Will in the middle in a black denim jacket and a sweat-stained slouch hat. Lucy wore her black beanie and brown trench coat, the tails billowing back in the wind. Merry had on a tan canvas jacket with white fur along the collar. Her black hat had taco brims and conchos dotting the band.

They kept in formation all the way through the gap and across the international border to the same cottonwood enclosure. The problem now was getting to Francisco Perez. On their previous trip, he'd lied about Abrazo working the Carranza.

Will Zachary would be the last man he'd want to see back at Bandera.

But luck was with them. Beyond the cottonwoods, they saw a girl racing a paint pony across the meadow. Will recognized her from the picture Perez had shown him. It was his daughter, Juana. If they could get her to the enclosure, they could use her as leverage to get Perez there.

After a brief discussion, Merry volunteered to talk to Juana. Will agreed that that was the best approach and she jumped onto her horse and rode across the meadow.

As she came alongside Juana, both riders reined to a stop.

"Hello, Juana," Merry said. "You don't know me, but some people have come a long way to talk to you. It's important."

"What people? Who are you?"

"My name is Merry. This will be easy, I promise you. How about coming with me to the cottonwoods?"

Juana studied Merry and then glanced toward the trees at the edge of the meadow. "I guess so. What's going on?"

"An old friend wants to talk to you. Will Zachary. He taught you checkers on your porch when you were little. Do you remember?"

"Checkers? I guess, I don't know."

"He's waiting for you. Come on."

Merry reached down and took Juana's reins and turned her horse. Juana didn't resist. Merry spurred her horse forward, pulling Juana's along, and the two of them rode that way across the meadow. Juana jumped down, tied her horse, and walked in under the trees.

"Hello, Juana," Will said.

Hesitant, confused: "Hello."

"You don't remember me?"

She studied his face. "Sorry, I don't." Juana was short and thickly built through the hips. She had a wide face, mildly scarred by acne, long raven hair with picket-fence bangs. She wore earrings shaped like the *B* of the Bandera brand.

"I'm Will Zachary. I used to work here." Will nodded toward the hacienda.

"You worked at Bandera?"

"Broke horses for your dad. Was younger than you are now."

They stared, sizing each other up.

"I'm home for Christmas break," Juana said. "I go to school in Austin." She wrinkled her brow and gave a half smile. "What's this about?"

"We need to talk to your father," Lucy said.

The wheezy sound of Lucy's voice startled Juana. When she turned and saw Lucy's face, it unnerved her even more. "What do you want with my papa?"

"It's business," Lucy said.

"If it's honest business, why are you hiding here? Come to the house."

"This is going to happen our way, Juana," Lucy said. "I need you to call him and tell him to come here and do it now."

She stiffened. "I don't think I like this. This isn't right. I'm not calling Papa. Anyway, I can't. My cell phone, I—I lost it."

Lucy pulled the phone out of Juana's back pocket. "Whoops, found it. How's that for luck?" Lucy held the phone up to Juana and in a commanding voice said, "Call right now, girl."

Juana's face twisted in defiance. "What if I don't?"

"I go to the house and grab him up." Lucy swung her buckskin coat back and put her hand over the holstered pistol. "No telling how that's gonna go."

"There's no need for that." Merry stepped forward, holding her hands up in a calming gesture. To Juana, she said, "Nobody's going to hurt your father. This is just a conversation. That's all. But it is urgent."

Juana took a moment to consider, then took the phone from Lucy and punched in the numbers. "Papa, there's some people here by the cottonwoods. They want you to come and talk to them—but don't come, Papa!" She began talking rapidly: "Don't come here, Papa. I'm fine. I'm all right. Don't come here! I'm fine!"

Lucy grabbed the phone out of her hand. "We need to see you, Francisco."

"Who is this?" he demanded.

"There's an important meeting going on here and we don't have a lot of time," Lucy said. "I suggest you get here." Before Lucy punched off on the call, Juana yelled, "I'm fine, Papa! Don't come!"

She lunged for the phone. Lucy stiff-armed her. Merry stepped between them, took Juana by the arm, and led her away from Lucy.

Speaking softly, Merry said, "Just let this play out, Juana. Nothing bad will happen to you or your father. This is just a conversation."

Within moments, Francisco Perez's truck came speeding across the meadow. He left the driver's door open and the engine running and burst into the enclosure like a man on fire. The first person he saw was Lucy, and he started for her.

She grabbed a fallen branch and held it like a baseball bat ready to swing. "I wouldn't, Francisco. I'll knock you clear out of the park."

Perez thought better of fighting and turned to Juana. "Are you all right? What is happening here?"

"You're going to tell me about Abrazo," Will said.

Perez spun angrily on Will. "You kidnap my daughter for this? To waste my time? We already had this conversation."

"Not the one we're about to have."

"What're you talking about?"

"You handle Abrazo. I need to find him."

"Papa, what is this about?" Juana said.

Before Perez could answer, Will said, "It's about the cartel your father works for. He runs the smuggler operations out of Bandera and one of them killed my uncle."

Juana looked stricken. "Papa, is this true?"

"Of course not," Perez said. Then weakly, without confidence: "No, not—not exactly."

"Not exactly?" Juana said. "What does that mean?"

"It's complicated, Juana. You don't understand and don't need to."

She put her hands to her face in shock. "You work for them, don't you? It's true, isn't it? You take their money."

"I run a ranch, Juana. How do you think I pay for your school? Do you think Tejas Academy is cheap? Do you think cattle pay your tuition?"

"Oh, Papa, no."

"Life is simple when you're young, *mija*."

"You promised Mama you wouldn't get involved with those men."

"Your mom is gone," Perez said. "You can't know how much I miss her, but she's gone. There are no compromises in the next world, only this one."

"You're wrong," Juana said. "She's here now. She's with me and with you and always will be. She hears all the words we say. You promised. And I need to know."

Perez wanted no part of the truth, but he had no choice.

"Okay, Juana, if that's what you want, I'll tell you." He paused to gather himself. A bird sang somewhere beyond the cottonwoods. "They store their shipments in the old barn and I tell them what trails to take, that's all. I sell information. I don't move a thing for them. That I won't do. I need you to understand that."

"This is how you pay for my tuition, for my apartment?"

"I've tried so hard to keep this away from you, Juana."

"Well, you've failed. Here I am. I want to know what you do to help these killers."

Perez was a strong man, but it did him no good against his daughter's withering stare. He sat down hard on a deadfall log. It had rained in that country not long before. The air in the enclosure smelled of it and the rocks under the trees still gleamed from where the water had washed over them. But soon the rocks would be dry, too.

Looking down, turning his straw hat in his hands, Perez said slowly, "A man calls to ask what trails are clear. I keep my men away from the loads to avoid any problem. I take a phone call and I talk to a man. I don't know his name. It's just a voice. And when the shipment goes through, I get—I get an envelope."

"An envelope. Cash." Juana looked up through the trees at the sky. "Do you hear that, Mama? Are you listening?"

Will broke in. "Tell me about Abrazo."

"He moves Marcelino's biggest shipments," Perez said. "If a delivery has to reach Phoenix at a certain time, he uses Abrazo. But I don't know this man. I've never seen him."

"His loads are stashed in your barn and you've never seen him?"

"It's the old barn above the house. We don't use it anymore. Abrazo picks up the loads at night. That's how he wants it done. I have no contact with him. I'm telling you the truth. I do not know him, I swear."

"But you know the route he'll take?" Will said.

"Yes, yes, I told you. I choose the route."

"There's a load moving in two days. That's Friday. I need to know which trail he's going to be on."

Perez looked up at Will, surprised at what he knew. "I'm responsible for these loads getting through to the drop. There's no such thing as failure. Do you know what that means? Do you have any idea?"

Juana stood before her father. "What does this man carry, Papa?"

"Pills of some kind. Wrapped up in plastic bricks. I don't know what it is. Isn't my business to know."

"No more lies," Will said. "Tell your daughter what he carries."

"On Olivia's soul, I don't know."

Will turned to Juana and said, "If it's pills, it's fentanyl and it's deadly. Customs has tightened up at the ports, so Marcelino's using the backcountry. I'll bet Abrazo can carry $2 million worth on the back of a pack mule. Isn't that right, Francisco?"

Perez dismissed the question with a gesture, as if he had no idea.

"I'm asking again," Will said, "where's Abrazo riding on Friday?"

"If I talk, my time at Bandera is over."

"Listen to me, Francisco," Will said. "You're going to talk and I'm going to find Abrazo. If he's alive when I'm done with him, I'll tie his hands together, put him in the saddle and take him in. If not, I'll say a prayer over his no-good murdering bones and take him in facedown. Same way I brought Buck home."

"What happens to me?" Perez said. "What happens when I lose $2 million of Marcelino's product?"

"Nothing happens to you," Will said, and looked at Juana.

Perez moaned, a desperate cry. "No. No. I can't have that. I can't. Not my daughter, too."

The silence under the cottonwoods had become heavy. Perez realized he'd reached his last moments at Bandera and brooded over all he'd lost. The wonderful mornings, the birds singing, the creek that meandered past the hacienda where Juana had been born, where he and Olivia had been married, and all the magical places on the land he knew of that no one else in the world could even imagine.

When he'd cataloged all his misery and decided there was no more to be found, he said in a small voice, "He'll be crossing the Tres Vacas."

Will and Lucy traded looks. Bumpy Rodriguez ran the Tres Vacas for Stacy Queen, and Harley Jones had worked there. It was the one ranch Harley hadn't mentioned when he listed all the places he'd worked. The Tres Vacas abutted the border east of Bob Ashmont's in what was known as Musk Hog country.

Perez continued: "There's a trail below the west slope of Musk Hog Mountain. Abrazo will be riding late in the day. That's how he likes it, in the shadows. There are some cliffs that connect to the mountain peak. From there you can see a good portion of the trail."

"That's where the scout will be, on those cliffs?" Will said.

"Yes. You'll have to deal with him first. A limestone bridge connects Musk Hog Mountain to the cliffs. That's the quickest way to reach the scout, but it won't be easy without being seen."

Perez gave his daughter a pleading look. "I've tried to protect you, Juana. I wanted you to have a good life that has nothing to do with this ugly business. You understand what this means?"

Juana sat beside her father. "Yes, I know."

"School, your friends, your life in Austin, it's all over. You can never go back. My cousin owns a farm in Nebraska. We can start there. We'll have to build our lives all over again."

"I don't care about any of that." Juana wrapped her arm around her father and put her head on his shoulder. "I care about you and Mama. I want us to be together again. If you keep your word, we will be."

"My God, you're exactly like her." Perez stroked his daughter's cheek. She buried her face against his shoulder. "For all the world, Juana."

⚜   ⚜   ⚜

Perez returned to the hacienda and packed a few precious items into a small bag. He told his top hand he'd return soon, and drove away to catch the highway north to the Nogales border crossing. In a matter of one hour, his life at Bandera had ended.

Not wanting to abandon her horse, Juana rode with Will, Lucy, and Merry to the Flying Z and corralled the animal there. After supper that night, Will and Merry drove Juana to Nogales, Arizona, to meet her father.

In the parking lot of the McDonald's near the port of entry, Perez talked of his relief at being out of Mexico, of what lay ahead for him and Juana. His talk made Will sick. He made it sound as if the past had been erased, as if no blood had been spilled and no lives destroyed.

When Perez extended his hand, Will refused to shake it.

"You won't say goodbye to me?" Perez said.

"All the misery in your life right now, and in mine, you caused it."

"You have to understand, Marcelino gave me no choice. It was *plomo o plata*"—take the lead or the silver, the bullet or the money. "I didn't want to die and I didn't want to lose the life we'd built. I'd already lost Olivia. You can understand that."

To keep his temper in check, Will turned his back. "Let's go, Merry."

"I wish our reunion had been different," Perez said.

That was more than Will could take. He wheeled around to face Perez. They were nose to nose and Will was angry. "Reunion? I find out you worked with the man who murdered my uncle and you call this a reunion?"

Merry squeezed between them. Their voices got loud. Passersby stopped to watch. Merry grabbed Will by the arms to pull him away. He fought her, shaking his arms loose from her grip. She said his name over and over while using all her strength to keep him back.

When she finally got his attention and the spell broke, they left the parking lot and drove back to the Flying Z in silence.

CHAPTER THIRTY-FOUR

On Thursday night, Will, Merry, Levi, and Lucy gathered in the kitchen of the Flying Z. Will spread a map out on the table. Musk Hog Mountain sat just north of the border at five thousand feet. Will and Lucy knew that terrain only by its rough reputation. It had sent many riderless horses back to headquarters.

Harley Jones knew it better than anyone, and Will wanted to talk to him. But he was still missing. Multiple calls to locate him or Lovesome had yielded nothing. Even a request for information on Sweetie Taylor's chat network had produced no word on their whereabouts.

Will dragged his finger along the twisting path of the Musk Hog Trail, below the mountain's west-facing slope. It ran north for three miles to Chavez Dam, where two four-wheel-drive roads converged.

"Abrazo's drop is going to be along one of these two roads," he said. "Either one will get that load to the highway quick." He moved his finger back to the mountain. "But I want to intercept him here, before he reaches the dam."

They were all crowded together, leaning over the map. Lucy dragged her finger from the base of Musk Hog Mountain up the eastern slope to the peak and down the west slope to Musk Hog Trail.

"If this map's telling the truth, it's pretty steep going, and there'll be lots of brush to get through," she said.

"Perez said he rides late in the day," Will said. "I want to get there by two at the latest. Get ourselves set up."

"I believe we can do that," Lucy said. "Once we're on top, we'll be able to see him coming along that trail and can take him easy."

Levi took out his Ben Franklin glasses and put them on. "Need my cheaters more and more these days." He leaned on his elbows and traced the limestone bridge leading to the connecting cliffs. "The scout will be here, correct?"

"According to Perez," Will said. "And he'll see us coming."

"Maybe not," Levi said. "Bad weather's forecast and it might work out good for us. If the clouds are low enough, that scout could have three riders on him before he knows what time it is."

"Four," Merry said.

Levi slowly folded his glasses and put them in his shirt pocket. He pulled out a chair and sat. He looked at Will and scratched the back of his neck. The conversation he knew was coming had arrived.

Merry read their faces. "I'm thinking you two talked about this already, am I right?"

"Kicked it around over a cup of Hurdy House tea," Levi said.

"It'd be nice to be involved in discussions that are, you know, about me."

Merry poured herself a shot of Seagram's and sat opposite Levi. She gave him a challenging stare across the table. "I came back to the Flying Z to be part of this, Levi. That means all of it. I explained that to Will and he agrees. No way I'm staying back."

"As long as you understand," Levi said.

She sipped her whiskey. "Understand what?"

"With bad weather and a bad man, a lot can go wrong."

"Whatever it is, I'm going to be there for it."

"You ride with me and only me and don't leave my side. That's my condition."

Merry went around the table and wrapped her arms around Levi's shoulders from behind and kissed his cheek. "It's a long ride, so try to stay with me."

Lucy wheezed and slapped her thigh. "Ha! Whaddya think of that, lawman!?"

Ignoring Lucy's outburst, Levi turned in his chair and put his hand on Merry's arm. "Before we go anywhere, I need you to make that a firm promise."

Matching his resolve, Merry said, "You have my word, Levi. I promise I won't leave your side."

That night Levi slept in Buck's reading chair by the fireplace. Will and Merry went to bed early, but Will couldn't sleep. When he heard the refrigerator door open and close, he knew Lucy was out. He threw on a coat and found her on the porch rocking chair with two cans of Pabst Blue Ribbon, her customary nightcap.

Will sat beside her, the propane heater working hard between them.

"I wish we could ride right now," he said. "I hate waiting."

Lucy had one foot up against a mesquite post, a cigarette burning in her hand. "I like it when things are happening. When there's action, something we gotta do to set things right."

"It's time."

"Riding together's what we do, ain't it, Will?"

"It is."

"I love it, truly I do. It feels righter than anything else. Like we was put here all those years ago just to ride tomorrow."

"I believe that's true."

"We're going to find us a killer, and the devil better look away."

Nothing moved in Cabezas Canyon and there were no sounds, but for the snuffles and snores of JB and Bond. After a while Lucy finished her beers, squashed her cigarette out, and stood up.

"Well, by God," she said, and stretched.

"You all done?"

"Worked over. Gonna walk the canyon."

"It's early. Sit with me."

"Not tonight. Got the jumps."

"Guess I'll see you in the morning."

"Nighty-night, darlin'," Lucy said and walked away.

Will sat staring out at the night. JB sat up quickly as if he'd heard something that startled him. He raised his muzzle and sniffed, and Bond did the same, letting out a deep, rumbling growl that went on for several seconds.

Then came the unmistakable clank of metal on metal, the exact sound Buck had described. Domingo Opata was there, a presence beyond the porch.

Apart from the dogs, there was nothing to announce him, no change in the air, no whirling wind. There was no sense of lost time or great sound to bring him forth or vivid dream to give him life.

Opata was there without any of that, as he'd been for all of Will's life in the stories that Buck told. Will had grown up with them. As a boy, they filled his dreams, and each morning he took them to school with him, and he carried them through the years more faithfully than anything he'd learned in a book.

They were what Will and Buck had together, that and the land and the work they did and what Buck had taught him after his father had disappeared.

"I've waited a long time," Will said. "I'm glad you're here."

"Your uncle sent me," Opata said. "There's work to do."

The voice was strong and clear and didn't come from any particular place. It was just there. It came from the canyon, from the darkness, from all directions at once. It dropped rootless from the sky. But in his mind, Will saw the Horseman as plainly as a mirror reflected.

He wore a sleeveless jacket-vest spotted like the skin of a Jaguar and decorated with ornamental shells and colored glass beads. His shirt underneath it was dark blue, of layered cotton, and his strong arms bulged against it.

His hands were thickly veined with ornate silver rings on all the fingers and both thumbs. The flesh on his hands was dark and scaled like a lizard's except where it was split bloody from the cold. His face was the same texture, rough and carved like a rock. The eyes were dark, the whites a startling white, and rimmed with starbursts of fine wrinkles.

Opata's horse was a magnificent stallion, stocky with heavy muscling through its chest and lean and powerful legs. Light gray over most of its body with striking patches of white, it had a forelock of the darkest black, and the long mane, also black, hung in thick curls.

"I'm afraid something's coming that will change everything," Will said.

"Keep your nerve," Opata said. "I'll be with you."

"Never been short of nerve. I'm full up with nerve. Always have been."

"Then what is it?"

"This killing I was born with. I feel it now, the truth of what Buck always said. It's hunting me down and tomorrow's the day it finds me and there's nothing I can do to escape it."

"If that's so, let it come, Señor. You have reason to kill this man."

Opata's horse swished its tail and snorted, excited from its exertions on a winter night. The smell of the animal was powerful.

The hounds slinked behind Will's chair and peered out on either side of him, alternately growling and whining, their long ears hanging to the floorboards.

"Whenever I close my eyes to sleep, I see Abrazo dead on the ground, and I put him there," Will said.

"Is that what you want?"

"If I know anything, I know it doesn't matter what I want."

"Evil found you when this man killed your uncle."

"Yes. But because of what I have to do tomorrow, I could lose Merry, too. I can't lose her, Don Opata."

"You didn't seek this out, but it has come to you just the same."

The dogs grew more agitated. Will reached down and petted them. They quieted, but their eyes stayed fixed on the pulsing emptiness beyond the porch.

"You didn't choose the blood that runs in your veins," Opata said. "You didn't choose to be born on this land, or for your uncle to take you in as a boy, or for your woman to drive down your road. And you didn't choose what you must do tomorrow. But it is here and so am I."

"How will I find you?"

"Memorize the tracks my horse makes here tonight. When you're halfway up the mountain, follow them and I'll be there."

"I will, Don Opata. And when Merry and I come home tomorrow night, I'll hold her as tight as I can, because that's when I'll find out what she can live with and what she can't."

The door behind Will opened and Merry appeared wearing her white robe. "What's going on? I heard voices."

"Me and the dogs. Are you all right?"

"I'm too excited to sleep."

"You don't have to worry."

"No, it's a good excitement. This is going to work out fine. I just know it." The certainty in her voice told Will she had doubts and was trying to convince herself as much as him. "Levi will arrest Abrazo and bring him in, just the way it's supposed to happen."

"Yes, everything the way it's supposed to happen."

She squeezed the robe tight against her throat and gazed out at the canyon. "It's such a weird night. The air is so still."

"The wind will be up soon. We should go inside."

They snuggled close under the blankets. Merry buried her face against Will's neck and wrapped her arms around him. She loved the warmth of his flesh against hers, the steady rhythm of his breathing, the ridges of muscle at his shoulders, the feeling of safety.

She felt a rush, a sensation of pure happiness, and in the clarity of it she could see all the way to the end of her life, in that place with this man.

"Do you know how much I love you?" Merry said.

"I love you, too."

They kissed and said good night. When Merry fell asleep, Will got up on one elbow and studied her beautiful face and kissed her gently on the lips. She stirred but didn't awaken. He pushed a strand of hair off her face and kissed her again.

He thought if this was to be their last night together, he wanted to remember every angle of her face, every roll of her lips, every breath they'd taken together.

He tried to sleep but JB and Bond were scratching frantically at the kitchen door. He got up quietly and went out, and when he opened it, they bumped into one another in a frantic rush to get inside.

Will walked outside and down the porch steps. He found Opata's hoofprints in the dirt and traced their outline with his hand, memorizing them.

He stood and looked around. A thick cloud cover had moved in, making the night black, and the wind had started to blow. The mares in the corral were running wildly around the enclosure, bumping into the rails, throwing their heads, and neighing the way they do when a stallion is near.

"Find a place to shelter up, Don Opata," Will said to the darkness. "There's a storm rolling in."

CHAPTER THIRTY-FIVE

In the morning, the four of them gathered at the corral to ready their horses, and there wasn't much talk. They rode out like soldiers, erect in the saddle. They could see rain sheeting down to the southwest, and they were heading right into it.

To avoid having to stop, they put on their slickers and kept a steady pace over grass lowlands and jackrabbit draws, all the land alive and wintery under the roiling sky.

The rain came hard and drenching, but the cell passed quickly as they rode along a narrow dirt road bordered by sycamores that came right to the edge of it, their horses' hooves thumping in rhythm on the wet ground.

They crossed Bob Ashmont's land onto the Tres Vacas and pushed through the rocks and brush at the base of Musk Hog Mountain and started up the steep slope, Will in the lead.

Snow had started to fall. Halfway up the mountain, he came to a plateau and reined up to wait for the others. Studying the ground he found Domingo Opata's tracks leading to a ledge trail that dropped sharply off the plateau's northern end.

He kicked his horse to the trailhead and followed the Horseman's tracks around the mountain for a short distance. He saw nothing, only snow and called out, "I'll come back alone, Don Opata. Wait for me."

When the other riders caught up, the four of them continued on the main trail to the top of the Musk Hog. They tucked themselves in under the clouds, their hats there and gone in the swirling snow. The flat mountaintop formed a bowl around a wide gorge. To their left, the limestone bridge led out onto the scout cliffs.

Will used his binoculars to examine the mountain's west-facing slope. "No way we can get down to the trail along these drainages," he said.

"Not alive," Lucy said. "They're running with water."

Will glassed the slope on the opposite side. A low-flying hawk screamed and soared. "Might be we can make it down over there," he said. "But I won't know until I check it out."

"Okay, change in plans," Levi said. "The three of us will take care of the scout. Will, you check the drainages on the other side."

Merry objected. "I'm going with Will."

"No," Levi said quickly.

"He shouldn't be riding alone," Merry said.

"Okay then, Lucy can stay with him. You made a promise as I recall."

Merry started to object again, but Levi interrupted. "You're staying at my side. There's no debate." That rare forcefulness made Levi's command all the more powerful and Merry pulled back.

To Will, Levi said, "If you and Lucy find a way down, wait for us. We won't be long. Are we clear? Wait until we get back."

"I heard you," Will said.

"Nobody's going home across a saddle today," Levi said. "Do we all understand that?" He looked at Merry. When she didn't object, he said, "Good. Now, let's go." He and Merry rode onto the limestone bridge and out of sight.

Lucy took the binoculars and looked across the gorge. "I don't know what you're talking about, Will. From what I can see that side's no better." She wore her black beanie and a black bandanna covering her face below the eyes. She lowered it, blew out both nostrils and tugged the bandanna back in place.

"I'm guessing you got something else in mind," she said.

"Follow me."

"Follow you where? In this snow? Hey, where're you going?"

Will didn't wait. He spurred Lobo back down the mountain trail with Lucy close behind. He stopped on the plateau and told her to continue on to the bottom, and head north from there to Chavez Dam.

"Pick up the Musk Hog Trail at Chavez and double back this way," he said.

"Chavez? You think Abrazo's gone that far north already? We ain't even late. It's right at two o'clock."

"Perez said Abrazo liked having cover and this weather gives it to him. I'm thinking he might've set out early and gotten ahead of us." Will motioned toward the plateau's northern end. "I'll follow this ledge trail around to the bottom."

"That skinny old trail might take your life." She looked at the stormy sky. "Snow's picking up, Will."

"He's not getting away. If we split up, we're sure to catch him."

"You ain't making sense. You don't know where that wrap-around trail grounds out. Could land you in a box canyon and you gotta come back up and there ain't no way, not if this weather gets worse. I need to ride with you."

"Are we going to stand here talking or are we going to catch a killer?"

Lucy hesitated. Her horse kicked at the ground and snorted. Lucy knew something was up but wasn't sure what until she looked in Will's face and saw what she needed to see.

"I get it now," she said. "My brain don't work so good in this cold."

"Do what I tell you. Get on outta here."

"Don't worry about me. My feelings ain't hurt."

"You know it's not personal."

"Everything's personal, Will."

"If it makes you feel better, you're the best cowboy I ever saw." If Will had one last thing to say to her, that's what he wanted it to be. He waited for her to go, but she stayed put. "If it gets you moving, I'll say something else nice, but I can't think of anything right now."

"You ponder it and tell me tonight when we get back home," Lucy said.

"Deal."

"Just so you know, the first shot I hear, I'm coming back on the jump. And if I find you on the ground, by God, Will Zachary, I ain't gonna be happy." Lucy spurred her horse and went.

Now Will had what he wanted. He was alone and ready to meet Abrazo.

He led Lobo down the trail and there was Domingo Opata sitting upright on his stallion, face taut, eyes clear, his hands stacked on the saddle pommel.

"Follow me," he said.

They rode into a veil of sideways-falling snow. The trail was like a coiled snake, and it narrowed so much that Will's shoulder nearly bumped the side of the mountain. He feared a deep breath might rob him of the space to stay upon it, and he'd sail off the open side, into the black gloom.

He took shallow breaths. He lowered his chin and kept his eyes between Lobo's ears. With each switchback, the air grew colder until his hands turned to concrete. He bottomed out in a wide gorge rimmed by rock spires, tall, smooth, narrowing to sharp points at the top, and artfully weathered as if by craftsmen.

Will had lost all bearings. He didn't know how many times he'd gone around the mountain. Twice? Three times? He didn't know if he was on the Musk Hog Trail or how to find the scout cliffs.

It was a new experience for him. He'd never been lost on the Flying Z. The mountain peaks had always guided him. But in that rock world he had only storm clouds just above, snow-covered ground under his feet, no wind, all a hush, and no idea where to go from there.

"I need you now, Don Opata," Will said. "What is this strange canyon?"

"It was important to Kazoh's people," Opata said. "They were safe from their enemies here. All their ceremonies were here, all their councils."

"I can see why. Right now I need to find the Musk Hog Trail."

"I'll show you," Opata said.

Will tried to stay close but soon lost sight of Opata's gray-white stallion in the snow. He had only the sound and smell of the animal to guide him. He felt something solid brush against his left leg and shifting in the saddle felt the same brushing on his right. They were riding through a narrow split bordered by sheer rock walls on both sides.

Clear of the passage, they emerged onto a wide, sandy flat cut by a rushing creek. Thin shafts of sunlight had broken through the clouds. Using that meager light reflecting on the water, Will followed the creek until finally striking the cliffs to the east.

Only then did he know for sure that he was on the Musk Hog Trail.

He pulled up behind a fallen cedar tree, dismounted, and led Lobo into the brush under the cliffs and tied him. Pulling his Winchester out of the scabbard, he returned to the tree and got down on the ground behind it. He laid his rifle over one of the branches and spied down the trail.

His vision didn't extend far. He worked his fingers open and shut to get the blood moving and listened to the creek burbling beside him and thought how long he'd waited to hear that sound, the most beautiful sound he knew.

He had less confidence of ever hearing it again than in seeing Opata. He'd never doubted Opata. His trust in him was complete because his trust in Buck was complete, and Buck had told him he would come.

And he had come when Will had needed him the most.

"Be alert," Opata said. "Abrazo is near."

"I can't see," Will said. "He'll be on top of me before I see him."

"The sun will chase away the storm," he said. "Now do what you must."

Will heard the metallic clanking of Opata's sword against his saddle riggings as El Jinete turned his horse. Then he was gone. He left in the same way a wind dies.

Alone now, Will squinted through the thinning snow and watched. The sun shone down, and far off he saw a black mass that gradually took the shape of a horse and rider. The first detail he could make out was a hat, a black, wide-brimmed, flat-crowned border hat.

Will's throat tightened as if being strangled. "Eight years," he said.

His finger slipped inside the trigger guard. Every muscle in his body told him to shoot. But he held back. He watched until he saw the horse and a trailing mule, the heavy packs on its back causing it to sway with each step.

Closer in, the rider took shape. He wore a rain slicker. His chin hung against his chest, concealing his face.

"Come on, Abrazo, look up," Will whispered. "Let me see your face. Look at me."

LEO W. BANKS

With the rider nearly on him, Will leaned his shoulder against a side branch and aimed at a point next to Abrazo's right ear. The boom of the shot sounded like the end of the world, and it went on and on as the sound echoed off the cliffs.

Abrazo's horse reared and he lost his grip on the reins. He became like a doll in the saddle, hanging on against each violent lurch, and when he couldn't hold on any longer, he went airborne, arms flailing, hat flying.

He landed hard on the ground and rolled to his knees.

With his face pressed into the snow, he screamed a curse and struggled to his feet. "Don't shoot me!" He held out two beseeching hands to the mortal threat he couldn't see. "Don't shoot! Who are you!? Who *are* you!?"

Will waited, silent. *Let him feel the terror in his gut. Let it hollow him out and leave him empty and sick.*

"You nearly killed me," Abrazo shouted. "Who's out there?" He saw a glint of sunlight on the gunman's rifle. "Whoever you are behind that tree, you missed. You missed! Don't shoot no more! Declare yourself!"

"I could've shot you dead," Will said.

Abrazo relaxed now, for he recognized the voice, knew the identity of the man behind the gun. He blew out a cold breath and glanced at the sky. "Good day for a killing, ain't it?"

"Nobody'd ever find you out here," Will said.

"Don't suppose so. You gonna shoot me, Will Zachary, or can we talk?"

"The hell of it is, I can't pull the trigger on someone I know as well as you. Even the man who murdered my uncle."

CHAPTER THIRTY-SIX

Will stepped out from behind the tree. Face-to-face with Abrazo, he stood unmoving and ready, steeled by a moment he'd long awaited.

"You're right about one thing," Bud Tisdale said. "We've known each other a long time."

"Too long. You're hauling for the cartel."

"That's right. But I didn't kill your uncle."

"You sat in my kitchen, Bud. You put your elbows on my table and asked how Buck was getting on. You fought Macklin because he said Buck had it coming."

"Hold on, Will."

"But that was a lie. Macklin was trying to get you to hold off killing Buck. Stacy Queen didn't want any killing, isn't that right, Bud?"

"I didn't kill nobody. I can explain." Calmly, Tisdale grabbed the reins of his horse and stepped toward Will. "Killing ain't my side of things, Will."

"How come you're wearing Hector's hat?"

"It's my hat. Bought it three days ago. These flat-topped border hats are in style again. You can buy one for cheap down south." He picked up the hat, brushed off the snow, and put it on. He pointed over his shoulder to the pack mule.

"This other business is a situation that got crazy on me," he said. "I agreed to haul supplies to Marcelino's scouts, but he pulled me in deeper and deeper until he got me moving these bricks, and now I can't quit. Threw me into quicksand is what he done."

Tisdale coughed a wet cough. "I gotta ride when I get the call, sick or not. Got me a flu that's kicking my butt and these pills I'm taking make my head all swampy. And I got you threatening to shoot me, an unarmed man."

A lie and Will knew it. But where was the gun?

"That slicker," Will said. "Cross your arms and pull it off over your head, Bud. Two hands and slow."

"You don't need to do this, Will. I'm telling you straight out, I ain't carrying. It's too bulky to ride with a gun."

"Do it now. Empty your front pockets and throw the coat my way."

Tisdale pulled the slicker over his head and dropped it on the ground. He wore a black wool coat with four big buttons up the front. He got the buttons undone, let the coat slip off his shoulders and heaved it to Will.

He wore a fleece vest underneath. He unzipped it and pulled the sides wide to show he was unarmed. Will picked up the coat and felt through the pockets for a gun. Nothing. Tisdale pulled out his front pockets. No gun there either.

Tisdale never went anywhere without his Ruger .22.

"See, I ride light when I'm on a job. Don't like no obstructions."

Will ordered him to lift the horse's front hoof to inspect the shoe. Tisdale complied. Will stepped closer and saw the Abrazo shoe. "What I figured, you're Abrazo," Will said.

"Like I told you, killing ain't my side of things."

"You're wearing a dead man's hat and riding a killer's horse."

"It's the horse Francisco Perez gave me. The man you call Abrazo's dead and I never knew who he was."

Tisdale's tone had changed to a mix of confidence and frustration. "Marcelino used him to kill Buck and Hector then disappeared him. I don't wanna join him so I'm delivering these bricks. I got no choice or he goes after me and my family, rips my whole life to pieces."

"You're lying. How much did he pay you to kill Buck?"

"Believe me or not, that's up to you. Fact is, I thought Buck Zachary was a helluva man. But all I want now is to get to my drop and go on home to bed." Tisdale zipped the fleece vest and picked up his coat.

"Catch a death out here." He shouldered it on, buttoned it, and wrestled the rain slicker over his head. He moved easily, as if dressing in his bedroom. "If you wouldn't mind not shooting me, Will, I'll pass on by."

"I'm going to burn that load, Bud. Cut it loose."

"Burn it?" Tisdale couldn't believe what he was hearing. "Isn't that how all this business started, your temper?"

"You're not going another step with that poison."

"This is where you wanna make a stand? I ain't even on Flying Z land."

"You've used my ranch plenty and will again. It stops now, Bud."

"You're not thinking too good today, Will. This load goes up in smoke, what then? You think Marcelino's going away? If it ain't me moving this stuff, they'll find someone else."

"But they didn't find anyone else. They found you."

"I'm glad they did." Tisdale squared his shoulders in defiance. "Got me a new truck. Don't have to worry about prices when I go to the store."

He coughed and growled something thick and yellow out of his throat. "The money's ridiculous. You might think about it. You and that pretty girl of yours, that Merry O'Hara, you two could live high at the Flying Z."

"I don't want to hear that name coming out of your mouth."

"She wouldn't have to work like your people have been doing all these years. Knocking theirselves out and for what?"

"I'm warning you, Bud."

Tisdale's eyes rounded in anger. "Good old Will, the knight in shining armor that's gonna show us the way out of this. You're a sanctimonious sonofabitch, you know that?" Contempt twisted his face. "What're you fighting for? You think anybody cares whether you live or die trying to be a good man?" He said "good man" with scorn, stretching out the words.

He continued without shame or hesitation: "That's all over with in this country and everybody knows it. You take what you can get. I lost my business, are you forgetting that? If you're happy working for camp biscuits until you die, that ain't my lookout."

He coughed some more. "I feel like crap." He pulled a pocket watch out of the vest, flipped open the lid, and checked the time. "I got people waiting on me and I'm running late."

Will felt rage blow through his body. His legs and face burned with it. He thought about Buck and how Tisdale had shot him off his horse, and about Merry, and what pulling the trigger might mean for the two of them.

He had a choice to make. He didn't ponder it long. He knew what he was going to do, and his heart was glad.

Tisdale slipped the watch back into the vest pocket. "I'm gonna get back on my horse and ride on outta here. If it's all the same to you."

Will tucked the rifle tight against his shoulder, bent his head over the sight, and took aim. He heard the faint neighing of a horse coming up behind him.

Tisdale spread his arms. "What does shooting me accomplish, exactly?"

"Sweetens my dreams, for one."

"It's going to be a cold-blooded assassination of an innocent man, and I don't think you have what it takes." Tisdale turned and started for his horse.

"Hey, Bud. What time you got?"

Tisdale stopped with his back to Will. He recognized immediately the mistake he'd made. Silently, he cussed himself and Will and the weather and the flu and the medicine he'd taken that had turned his head to stew.

"Did you think I wouldn't come for you?" Will said. "That I'd let it go? Like Buck's life meant nothing to me?"

"Easy does it, Will. Come on, now."

"If you did, you don't know me."

"Let's think about this. Can we do that for just a minute?" Tisdale's voice had become shaky and fearful. He knew he'd come to the moment of death and needed to find a way out. He put his arms in the air and turned to face Will.

"That money I'm making? You can take it all. All I got with me. Every dollar. How about that? There's a purse in my saddlebag."

That told Will where Tisdale's gun was.

"I'm gonna get you that money. Right away. Easy now, easy." With his hands raised, Tisdale walked backward one step at a time.

"You were right about one thing, Bud."

He took a slow step back, then another. "Yeah, what's that, Will?"

"That I won't shoot an unarmed man. And I won't shoot a man with his hands in the air. Or a man that isn't ready to go where I'm about to send you if you keep on with this." Face unyielding, bright with purpose, Will held the rifle steady on Tisdale's chest. "So that's the question I have for you, Bud. Are you ready?"

"No, no, no, Will. I know you. I know you too good. All these years." Tisdale kept his arms in the air in surrender, but his eyes were quick.

"Don't think I won't shoot, Bud. No man would judge me wrong for it."

"No, you won't, Will. You're just thinking wrong. The money will help. I got a pile of it in my bag."

"Your call, Bud. You got one play left, so speed it up."

Beside his horse now, Tisdale tilted his head toward the saddlebag. "It's in the bag. Cash. It's a bundle, too."

"There's no money, Bud."

"No, it's all right here, I swear, Will."

"You can end this right now or die right now."

"It's a lotta money, Will. It'll get you out of the hole. You and your girl, right? You can start again?"

Tisdale lifted the flap on the saddlebag and plunged his hand inside. He knew he had to be quick, and he was quick. Will saw the hand and the pistol and the desperate look on Tisdale's face as he whirled around, teeth bared, eyes wild, swinging his arm to fire.

The pistol was small. It made a sharp cracking sound. Will felt a tug on his arm as if from a punch.

The second shot belonged to Will. He'd fallen to the ground, rolled to his knees, jumped up, and fired. The Winchester made its point emphatically. The blast sounded like a building falling down, then a series of buildings with the chasing echoes off the cliffs.

Tisdale staggered back and his torso twisted around, but his legs held. He righted himself, and now his mind caught up with the moment.

Death had come. It stood before him, staring at him, grinning, showing its rotting teeth.

Not much time now. Must respond. Must even things up before the end comes. Can't just die. Can't be put down this way. They do this to crippled old dogs. Can't let that happen to me.

But as hard as he struggled, as much as his brain shouted at him to do it, his arm holding the pistol was too weak, and he fired three times at the sky. Will fired again and the charge knocked Tisdale to the ground.

Will stepped forward. Tisdale's eyes were open and he was breathing, but it didn't look easy.

"You did me decent, Will. Gave me a chance. I appreciate it. One thing, though." The sky was all blue now, and the late-day light hitting the cliffs turned them a magnificent lavender.

Tisdale smiled. "It's like I'm seeing all this for the first time. Seeing this country for the first time. Beautiful, ain't it, Will? Aw, hell, I don't mind dying out here."

"How much did Marcelino pay you to kill my uncle?"

"There's one thing I need you to promise me."

Will smacked him hard across the face. "That's for Girl Dog. I don't know how a man who wears Wranglers can shoot down a dog."

The blow sent Tisdale soaring through the air, wingless, free, away from the known world and its sorrows. He could see it far below, all the troubles, the ruin of his life, and all of it moving farther and farther away.

When he opened his eyes again, he was back in the Musk Hog, fighting to breathe, feeling the oxygen being sucked out of his body through the hole in his chest.

"Don't die on me." Will grabbed Tisdale and shook him. "Don't you die on me. I need to know how much."

"P-p-promise me." Tisdale could barely hiss out the words.

"Promise you what?"

"Don't drag me across the line. I don't want to die on that side."

" I need to know how much Buck Zachary's life was worth to you."

"Did I tell you I got a grandkid comin'? A boy."

Will shook him and shouted, "How much!?"

Bending his finger for Will to lean closer, Tisdale whispered, "A lot." At that, his eyes became glass and off he went, gone a second and final time from that wintry place.

CHAPTER THIRTY-SEVEN

Will reached into Tisdale's vest pocket and removed Buck's heirloom watch, handed down from Silas Pearl Zachary. He squeezed it in his palm, printing it against his skin, feeling its history, feeling all that it meant to Buck, the century and a half of devotion to his family, to his home and to his place on the land.

He touched the tear in his coat that Tisdale's bullet had made, and his fingers came back bloody. That was the first he knew that he'd been hit. Only after the idea had penetrated did he feel the warmth of the blood under his coat.

Running footsteps came up behind him. It was Merry, the rider he'd heard earlier. She threw her arms around his middle from behind. Her body flush against his, her face pressed to his back.

"I saw everything. He was trying to kill you. Are you all right?"

Will turned. She linked her arms around his neck and hung on to him. He could feel her shaking. "Why didn't you wait?" she said. "You told Levi you'd wait."

"What about you? You were supposed to stay with Levi."

"Halfway there I thought, 'What am I doing?' There's no way I could leave you alone."

"You came down that jackass trail yourself?"

"Followed Lobo's hoofprints in the snow."

"You got leather in you, girl. I know bowlegged cowboys wouldn't risk that trail."

"They're not in love with you."

For all her time at the Flying Z, she hadn't cried. Now she choked up. Her breathing became ragged. He put his left arm around her. The right one wouldn't move. It felt like a block of concrete hanging off his shoulder.

"I can't hold you like I want to," Will said.

"I'll hold on tight enough for both of us."

"Wish you didn't see that."

"He was going to shoot you. Oh, Will."

Her voice was muffled against his clothes. She cried a little more. She looked up into his face and smiled. With the tips of her fingers she traced the creases around his eyes and the whiskers on his crooked jaw.

She straightened his hair and kissed him. "Tell me it's over, Will. Tell me we can go home and spend the rest of our lives together. Tell me that's what you want. Isn't that what you want?"

"Since that first day on Morales Road."

With those words, his adrenaline dumped, the pain surged and his legs buckled. Merry tried to hold him up, but he was too heavy and slid down her front.

"Will—Will—you're hurt!" She saw the blood on his jacket, and blood on her hand from touching the jacket. She peeled it off and tore at his shirt to inspect the wound. "You've been shot."

The shaking had left her voice and she stopped crying. That was a way she had. When things got bad, she toughened up. He'd always admired that about her.

"It's not bad," she said. "The bullet just grazed you."

Lucy rode up behind them and saw Will sitting on the ground. She folded her hands over the saddle horn, a satisfied grin on her face.

"Well, well," she said.

"You, too?" Will said. "You were supposed to go to the dam."

"Come on, now. You really thought I was gonna leave you alone?" Lucy leaned over and spat in Tisdale's direction. "Didn't figure on this peckerwood."

"Me either," Will said.

"You want me to haul him across, let the Mexicans worry about it?"

"He wanted to be here."

"Who cares what he wanted. The man murdered Buck, shot him down cold. Was me, I'd drag him across."

"He wanted to die here and that's how it's going to be."

"Never will understand you," Lucy said. "One of these days maybe I'll quit trying." She studied Tisdale's corpse in the snow. "I guarantee you'll remember this, Will. You'll remember what comes after, too."

"If you're fixing to tell me a story about your mysterious past, don't."

The pain screamed down Will's arm. He lowered his head and grimaced and thought about Buck's prophecy. He'd often wondered how he'd react if it came true. Now, in that remote country of snow and blood, he knew he'd live with it well, without doubt or remorse.

He tried to stand up and nearly toppled over. Merry grabbed his shoulders.

"Don't. You're too weak."

"No. Tisdale's on the ground and that's where he belongs. Not me." Full of pride and using all his strength, Will fought through the pain and wobbled to his feet.

Levi got there. He'd captured the scout and tied him to a tree and followed the tracks down the ledge trail. He dismounted and looked at Tisdale's body. He saw Will's Winchester on the ground, and Tisdale's pistol still in his grip.

Thinking of the Thompson boys, Will said, "I didn't miss, Levi."

Nodding at the blood on Will's shoulder: "You okay there?"

"I'm okay."

"Tell me."

"I waited for him to pull. I'm proud of that."

"You're lucky he didn't kill you."

"Yup."

"You do things the hard way, Will. Did I ever tell you that?"

"Believe so."

Levi studied the scene like a cop, his eyes stopping on each part of it and moving to the next. He was writing his report in his head. "Heard the shots. Pistol first, the Winchester after, then three more pistol shots. That should keep the county attorney on his leash."

"That's how it was," Merry said. "I saw everything."

The sound of her voice reminded Levi that she was there. He stared at her under the brim of his white Stetson. His eyes were clear and intense, but there was no anger in them.

"I'm not sorry, Levi," Merry said. "I'd do it again."

"Oh, I'm sure of that."

"You can't protect me from all this."

"You made your choice," he said. "Guess you're one of us now."

Levi got down on his haunches beside Tisdale. He stared at the body for a long time. "I don't enjoy seeing you like this, Bud. I'm just as sorry as I can be, but we all make our choices."

CHAPTER THIRTY-EIGHT

It turned out that Tisdale's chance meeting with Will on the highway outside town hadn't been chance at all. He'd said he was picking up groceries before returning to the Double R, but in fact, he'd been alerted by Jazzy's scouts to track José down and kill him.

Levi's deputies located the body in the brush along Solero Road. The coroner found a .22-caliber bullet in his head, fired from Tisdale's gun.

The work at the Horseshoe continued. Having returned from his trip to Mexico, Cuco came to help, and Harley Jones, too, the mystery of his disappearance solved.

He and Lovesome Magdalena Bravo had run away to Tucson, and on the morning of her seventeenth birthday were married under the turquoise dome of the Pima County Courthouse in downtown Tucson.

The bride's mother signed the permission paper, making it legal. Standing by were two witnesses, yawning strangers from the clerk's office pressed into emergency service.

The newlyweds honeymooned at a Holiday Inn Express along the I-10 freeway. They had cable TV for the first time in their lives and Harley couldn't stop talking about the food at the IHOP next door.

Merry worked harder than ever those first days back. She kept moving, never allowing a still moment, for when she stopped her mind would spin. Will worked alongside her, doing the best he could with his arm in a sling.

Twice they talked about the Musk Hog, the first time being the night it happened. Merry wanted to know if Domingo Opata had been there and had led Will down the ledge trail to Abrazo. He told her, yes, it was Opata.

"I saw him riding away," she said. "On a beautiful gray-white horse."

"The sky was clear by then."

"Opata called on the sun to clear away the clouds, didn't he?"

"Yes."

Nothing in the way she spoke left room for doubt. She said nothing more. She'd come to believe in El Jinete after all.

The second time came five days later. They were in bed together on a blustery night. The living room fireplace roared against the cold, and they could hear the piñon logs breaking and falling as they settled under the flames.

Merry said, "I keep seeing things in my head, Will. Pictures, one after another. They don't stop."

"You can't be in two places and trying to do this work. I need you all in at the Horseshoe."

"Levi knew you weren't going to wait for him, didn't he?"

"The work will heal you if you let it. Go to sleep and forget about this."

"I can't." She sat up. The room was dark but for a blinking light at the window made by clouds racing across the moon.

"I know what happened," Merry said. "You didn't think I'd figure it out? When Levi got there, he never even asked why you didn't wait. He knew you weren't going to wait. You two had it planned all along."

Before Will could speak, she kept going: "Levi was following the plan. So was Lucy. They were giving you what you wanted, the chance to take down Abrazo yourself. That's the way it had to be, the way your people have always done it, the way the people in your books do it, the way Shane did it. The code had to be upheld."

"It happened the way it happened, Merry, and now it's over."

"He wanted to kill you. I saw everything. You were defending yourself."

"So what's keeping you awake?"

"You planned it out, step by step. You walked intentionally into a killing. You wanted it to happen."

"I did what I had to do the right way."

"What if next time it's you on the ground dying? Because the next time is coming. Marcelino is still out there and there'll be another Bud Tisdale. And you'll go after him, too."

"I don't go hunting men."

"You tell yourself that. But remember when I said you were a dangerous man? I was right. And I love you more than ever. How is that even possible?" She laughed in disbelief. "The border is such an unfair, terrible place, the way it changes you."

"Don't you see, Merry, the things we do to survive make the border a beautiful place. Not many have what it takes to struggle on, and that sets us apart. It marks us as special and that makes this a beautiful place. My place, our place."

Merry lay in the dark and thought about the photo she'd gotten from the stableman at Ballyfeard and Christmas at the estate, and it came over her again, that great aching for home.

She fought it off, reached across the bed, and took Will's hand and squeezed.

"You know what, Will? You're right. And Levi was right. I'm one of you now and I'm here to stay."

"You have to be sure. There's no halfway in this place."

"I'm sure, and do you know how I know? I haven't given a thought to Bud Tisdale since it happened. I can't work up a single tear, not even for a dead man."

Three days later, they were back working the Horseshoe. Cuco, Harley, and Lovesome were there. In case Marcelino made a move, Lucy had stayed back at the ranch on guard duty. Merry wasn't herself. When Will asked if she was all right, she gazed around, eyes empty, not seeing anything but the pictures in her head.

She snapped out of it and said, "Yeah, just thinking. Anyway, there's something I need to do at the house. You can finish up here."

Merry left, and Will couldn't stop thinking about how she'd been acting. Uncertain, distracted, talking on about Ballyfeard. He pushed the worry aside, but it kept building until he shut down work for the day and went down to the house to check on her.

He found Merry gone and his heart fell into his boots.

"She went up the hill to make a call," Lucy said. "When she come back, I asked her what was going on and she ignored me. Jumped in my truck and gunned it outta here."

"You shouldn't have given her the keys."

"They were already in the ignition. Anyway, she didn't take time to ask."

"Did she say where she was going?"

"Not a word. She was breakin' jail, Will."

He hurried up the hill behind the barn with his cell phone.

"Here we go again!" Lucy yelled. "You're gonna chase her, ain't you?"

At the top he got a signal and called Merry's cell. Straight to voice. He tried again with the same result. He called Levi and told him to be on the lookout for her on the highway out of

Patagonia. Levi said he'd have his deputies stop Lucy's truck if they spotted it.

Will ran into the house to get his keys and jumped into the Silverado. The truck wouldn't start. He tried again. The engine choked and groaned and threw out oily smoke but wouldn't turn over. He pounded the steering wheel.

As they sat in their truck about to leave for the day, Harley and Lovesome watched what was happening. Harley waved out the window to offer Will a ride. Lovesome joined in. She whistled and shouted, "We'll find Merry O'Hara. She ain't getting away from us! Come on, Will!"

He jumped into the backseat. "Let's go! Let's go!"

Lucy said, "I can't miss this parade," and climbed in beside Will.

Watching the proceedings, Cuco shook his head and said, "*A que Americano loco.*"

Harley had just bumped over the cattle guard when Lucy's truck appeared at the top of the canyon and began inching down the spur. Merry was behind the wheel. She pulled up next to the corral and stood by the open door.

Innocently, puzzled by the commotion, she said, "What's going on?"

Will walked to her side. "You came back."

"Of course I came back. I went to town to pick up decorations."

"Decorations." Will was out of breath. "You left in such a hurry."

"I couldn't wait to get my hands on them. There's a whole bunch back there." She pointed to boxes in the backseat. "We've got ivy, pinecones, candles. There's strings of lights and a holly wreath that we can hang on the front door. It's artificial, but it's really pretty."

"Decorations," Will repeated, befuddled.

"Sweetie's cousin sent them down from Tucson. We didn't have Christmas this year and that won't do. Even if it's late, we're having Christmas at the Flying Z. I'm going to make this house light up like Ballyfeard."

"You could've said something," Will said. "I near had a heart attack."

"I had a text from Sweetie. I wanted to surprise you." She wrinkled her forehead in confusion. "What'd you think I was doing?"

Lucy broke in. "He thought you was pulling another big old skidoo."

Surprised and hurt, she turned to Will, her green eyes bright and alive and fixed on his. "Is that what you thought? Really?"

He shrugged. "Coming back here and finding you gone, I didn't know what to think."

"I'm going to tell you something important, Will Zachary, and I need you to listen. I know I'll never get my first homes out of my blood, but I have another one now and it's right here at the Flying Z. I want our kids to grow up here. I want to teach them how to care for the animals and the land and I want them to know about Don Opata and Kazoh.

"I want to get old here, Will. I want to stay here with you until all the time I have left in this world can fit in the palm of my hand. I want to look at these canyons and mountains until my eyes stop seeing and I want to listen to the coyotes at night until my ears stop hearing.

"I love you and you love me and that's the best and truest thing this world can give us. It's a gift few people get and we'd be fools to walk away from it. It's going to be hard and dangerous, knowing there are bad men wanting us gone. But we can't hide from them.

"Living not to die isn't living. You taught me that, Will, so we'll just have to see who wins. I'm getting a shiver saying those words. But I keep thinking of that night at Padre Pedro's Saloon when I first said it to you. I meant it then and I mean it now—if you find it, fight for it."

Merry had her hands on her hips staring, clear-eyed and undaunted. Every woman who'd ever lived on the Flying Z had that same look.

"So what I want now, Will, is to get to living. With you, in this little house, in this little canyon. If that's something you want, too, we should quit talking about it and get on with it, don't you think?"

"You're the one doing all the talking."

She grinned sheepishly. "That was my dissertation, the one I never wrote. What do you think?"

"I think if we start now, we can get these lights strung up before dark."

Lovesome pulled herself out the passenger window of the pickup and sent her best wolf whistle out over the cab roof. Harley grinned and pumped his fist out the driver's window and drove off.

Lucy said, "I need to get outta here, too. Can't bear to watch you two turn this place into Coney Island, Arizona division." She threw her hands in the air and stomped up the canyon.

Merry put her arm through Will's and leaned her head on his shoulder, and the two of them stood staring at the house. "I can't believe I'm going to live in a hundred-and-fifty-year-old adobe with bullet holes in it."

"Perfect, isn't it?" Will said.

"Exactly how I planned my life."

4 9 9
3 49
1 5 0

Made in the USA
Coppell, TX
20 September 2023

21792491R00163